Praise for the novels of P

VILLA MIRABEL

"The feel-good storyline is well thought out and well written, and warrants a spot in this summer's beach-read bag."
—*Publishers Weekly*

ITALIAN LESSONS

"Pezzelli makes readers want to believe in love at first sight, and his earnest storytelling should win over its share of readers."
—*Publishers Weekly*

"Poignant and emotionally revealing, Pezzelli's latest will have you laughing, crying and simply enjoying a first-rate novel."
—*Romantic Times*

"Pezzelli tells an engaging story that is as leisurely paced and satisfying as a fine Italian meal."
—*Library Journal*

FRANCESCA'S KITCHEN

"Pezzelli will bring a smile to anyone's heart with *Francesca's Kitchen.*"
—*The Albuquerque Journal*

"Home cooking, good pasta and traditional family values conquer all in this amusing and touching story."
—*Publishers Weekly*

EVERY SUNDAY

"A sweet, brave, and funny novel—with a heart as big as the entire state of Rhode Island."
—Claire Cook, author of *Must Love Dogs*

HOME TO ITALY
A BookSense Pick!

"A delightful story of second chances."
—*Desert Morning News*

"A warmhearted novel, perfect for an autumn evening in front of the fire."
—*Litchfield Enquirer*

Books by Peter Pezzelli

HOME TO ITALY

EVERY SUNDAY

FRANCESCA'S KITCHEN

ITALIAN LESSONS

VILLA MIRABELLA

Published by Kensington Publishing Corporation

Home to Italy

Peter Pezzelli

KENSINGTON BOOKS
www.kensingtonbooks.com

KENSINGTON BOOKS are published by

Kensington Publishing Corp.
119 West 40th Street
New York, NY 10018

Copyright © 2004 Peter Pezzelli

All rights reserved. No part of this book may be reproduced in any form or by any means without the prior written consent of the publisher, excepting brief quotes used in reviews.

All Kensington titles, imprints, and distributed lines are available at special quantity discounts for bulk purchases for sales promotions, premiums, fund-raising, educational or institutional use.

Special book excerpts or customized printings can be created to fit specific needs. For details, write or phone the office of the Kensington Special Sales Manager: Kensington Publishing Corp., 119 West 40th Street, New York, NY 10018. Attn: Special Sales Department. Phone: 1-800-221-2647.

Kensington and the K logo are Reg. U.S. Pat. & TM Off.

ISBN-13: 978-0-7582-8762-5
ISBN-10: 0-7582-8762-3

First printing: September 2004
20 19 18 17 16 15 14

Printed in the United States of America

For Corinne,
with love, always

Home to Italy

CHAPTER ONE

After the funeral they all went back to the house. It was a cold, bleak day with a raw north wind that drove a slow procession of dark, heavy clouds through the early November sky. Everyone headed straight for the coffee as soon as they stepped inside. Before long the house was filled with people, some who had gone to the cemetery and others who had come straight from the church. They settled in, chatting in quiet, somber tones while they milled about in the kitchen and living room. Little by little, though, life returned to their conversations. The food was put out in the dining room and soon everyone was talking and eating.

Peppi walked in. He had been out back by himself for a time, strolling slowly about, looking over the yard and gardens. The Peppinos' manicured lawns had always been the envy of the neighborhood. Most years, every leaf in the yard would be raked and bagged by this late date. The lawns would be trimmed to perfection and the gardens cleaned and covered with a layer of thatch for the winter. But this autumn the gardens lay untended and overgrown, and the leaves covered the long grass on the lawn like a red and yellow quilt.

Silence fell over the kitchen when Peppi came in through the back door. Everyone stopped and looked sadly at him.

"Eat, eat," Peppi told them, embarrassed that he had made

them feel uncomfortable. "Go on." He gave a stoic smile and moved past them into the living room where he was greeted by the same awkward silence. He gestured for them to continue on as if he weren't there, then he sat on the couch. His cousin Angie slid in beside him and put her arm around his shoulder.

"Come stai?" she asked him.

"Eh," sighed Peppi. He gave a shrug and gazed down at the floor. "The yard's a mess, Angie . . . everything's a mess."

"I know," she said, squeezing him close. "I know. But you'll put everything back in order and by next spring the yard will be as glorious as ever, the way Anna loved it. You'll see. The tomatoes, the grape vines, the flowers. It will all come back to life again. It has to."

"Sure," he said, still looking down. "Maybe."

"Hey," said Angie, giving him a shake, "almost forty-five years you had her. Think about all of them. You two had a good long time together, more than most of us get."

Peppi looked up at her. "It *was* a good long time," he told her, forcing a smile that faded quickly, "but it wasn't enough, Angie. It went by too fast."

Thinking back, it was all like a blur to Peppi now. In his mind he saw the years he had spent with his wife racing away from him. Snippets of memories, the day they had met, the year they bought the house, happy and sad times alike, all sped by like pages of an album flipping inexorably to its end. He looked across the room to the window. Outside the cold wind buffeted the house and swayed the trees, shaking from them the last few leaves that clung desperately to their branches. On the street, the dust swirled by with scraps of litter and dry leaves tumbling alongside. Everything outside looked dead to Peppi.

Angie squeezed his shoulder once more and got up. "Stay here," she said. "I'll bring you something to eat."

While she was gone Delores, one of Peppi's sisters-in-law, sat down beside him and took his hand. That's the way it went for much of the afternoon. The women took turns, sitting beside him, telling him everything was going to be all right, while the men kept to themselves, giving Peppi a nod every now and then to let him know that they understood.

Later, the sun was hanging low in the sky when everyone started to leave. There were hugs and kisses and everyone fretted about whether Peppi should spend the night all alone in the house. He just nodded and assured them that he would be fine. Some time alone would be good for him now.

Darkness had come by the time the last of Anna's family went home. Peppi closed the door and watched from the window as they drove away. With a weary sigh he turned and walked back to the living room, turning the lights off as he went along. He stopped at the archway to the living room and stood there for a time, letting his gaze drift about the room. Everywhere it alighted, everything it touched evoked a memory of his wife. Her knitting basket by the chair. The fashion magazines on the coffee table. The mantel above the fireplace where stood the miniature bronze of Saint Francis, the one they had found years ago in an antique shop on the Cape. The bookshelves lined with the collection of first editions, some quite rare, that she had acquired over the years. He gazed longest at her beloved piano in the corner, convinced he could still hear the echoes from the innumerable hours she had sat there playing for friends and family, or sometimes just for Peppi and herself. Anna played beautifully; she did everything beautifully.

Wonderful as they might have been, the memories now pressed down on Peppi like an immense weight, grinding out of him the energy to remain on his feet. His mind and body aching with fatigue, he stepped into the room, slumped onto the couch, and fell fast asleep.

Peppi slept for hours, dreaming all the while of nothing but the warm feeling of Anna resting in his arms. It was near midnight when the rattling of the wind against the window woke him. Instinctively, he reached for his wife, but all he found was a pillow. He let out a groan for his arm and shoulder were cramped from the awkward position in which he had been reclining. He sat up and rubbed them.

Peppi's stomach growled, for he had barely eaten a bite all that day. For a moment he considered going to the kitchen, but it hardly seemed worth the effort. He wanted only to close his eyes now and find his wife once more. He started to pick himself up, intent on going upstairs to bed, but the thought of Anna not being there with him, the cold absence of her touch, was more than he could bear. He sat there alone in the shadows, his mind suddenly whirling in a dizzying spin of indecision, helplessly wondering where he should go or what he should do. Mercifully, exhaustion finally overcame him. Surrendering to the darkness, Peppi stretched back onto the couch and fell promptly back to sleep.

CHAPTER TWO

Angie came by the next day to check on Peppi. She brought with her a little bag with two cups of coffee from Dunkin' Donuts. It was late in the morning and she was sure that no matter how tired he might be, Peppi would be up by now. When she rang the doorbell, though, Peppi didn't come to the door. Angie waited a few moments and tried again. She strained to listen for the sound of any movement in the house, but there was none. The bell had rung inside, of that she was sure, so she tried knocking, but still Peppi didn't come.

Her breath quickening a little, Angie put the coffees down on the step and squeezed in behind the azalea bushes below the front window. Pressing her face against the window pane, she peered inside.

"Peppi?" she called anxiously.

Still no answer.

Angie pulled herself out of the bushes and headed toward the house next door, intent on asking the neighbor to call for help right away. It was just then that she heard the scratching of a rake in the backyard. She stopped and listened harder. Yes, there it was, no question about it. Angie hurried to the back of Peppi's house and poked her head around the corner. Sure enough, there was Peppi, busy at work raking the yard. From the looks of it, he had already managed to bag most of the leaves. At the moment, his back was to her as he vigorously raked along the back fence to get the last few.

"*Cosa fai!*" Angie exclaimed at seeing him. "What are you *doing?*"

The sound of her voice so startled Peppi that he dropped the rake. He whirled around, instinctively throwing his hands up in a defensive gesture when he first saw Angie stomping across the yard toward him.

"What's the matter?" said Peppi when he realized that it was just his cousin and not some crazed assailant.

"What's the *matter?*" cried Angie. "You scared me half to death, that's what's the matter. *Mannagia,* I was just about ready to call nine-one-one and have them break down the door!"

"For what?" said Peppi.

Angie scowled at him and shook her head. "Oh, never mind," she grumbled, turning away. "I'll be right back . . . and don't go anywhere!"

"Who's going anywhere?" shrugged Peppi as she walked back around to the front of the house. "And where would I go?"

Angie soon returned with the two cups of coffee in hand.

"Here," she said, handing him one. "I would have brought donuts, but I knew you had plenty of pastry left over from yesterday."

"Thanks," said Peppi. He pulled the lid off the cup and took a sip. It was another chilly day, so the warm brew was a welcome surprise. "Come on," he said, nodding toward the little stone table in the garden, "let's go sit."

The table was tucked in the back corner of the garden where the fence met the row of arborvitae trees Peppi had planted years ago when he and Anna first bought the house. High above the table, grapevines, now brown and dry, coiled around the arbor. The spot was sheltered from the wind by the trees and fence, and the sun warmed the curved stone benches that flanked the table. No matter what time of year, it had always been the most pleasant part of the whole yard.

"You gave me a scare, *cugino mio,*" said Angie, sitting down. "For a minute I thought . . ."

"What?" said Peppi.

"Nothing," said Angie. She took a sip of coffee and looked about at the yard. With the leaves all raked and bagged, the yard was already beginning to take on a semblance of order once more. "I can't believe you cleaned the yard so fast," she said, shaking her head.

"Eh," grunted Peppi, waving his hand, "the grass still needs to be mowed and the gardens . . . the gardens . . ." Peppi sighed wearily as he looked about at the weeds and the withered tomato plants.

"Leave it for another day," said Angie. "What's the hurry? You should be resting."

"Who can rest?" said Peppi. He looked up and let the sun shine on his face. Closing his eyes for a moment, he soaked in its warmth. With a yawn, he rubbed his eyes and ran his hand across the gray stubble on his face. He looked at Angie and smiled.

"Anna used to like sitting right where you are," he said. "She loved having lunch out here."

"I don't blame her," said Angie. "It's beautiful out here."

"I don't know," said Peppi. "I never did as much back here as I'd planned to. I meant to put more grapevines in, maybe a pear tree. Of course, back when we first moved here I always

meant to build a little play area if we ever had children, but . . ."
Peppi looked wistfully about the yard. "Anna would have been
a good mother," he said.

"She would have been a wonderful mother," agreed Angie.
"She was so good with kids."

Peppi nodded and looked out across the yard to the kitchen
window. His thoughts drifted back to a day many years ago,
not long after they had first purchased their house. On that
day, Anna had hosted a baby shower for one of her faculty
friends from the elementary school where she taught music.
Everything—from the invitations she had hand-written and
the food she herself prepared to the flowers decorating the
house—was done to perfection and the party had been a great
success. The women all had a lovely time and the mother-to-be
was thrilled with all the beautiful gifts. When the party was
over her friend had thanked Anna profusely, her eyes wet with
gratitude.

For his part, Peppi had made himself scarce during the festivities, and only showed his face near the end of the day when
it was time to help carry the baby presents out to the car. Anna,
he had noted with a smile, was beaming. There was nothing
she enjoyed more than a successful party. Afterwards, though,
when everyone had gone and Peppi was helping to straighten
things up, Anna suddenly became very quiet. Without a word
she went upstairs to the bathroom and closed the door. Peppi
went to the bottom of the stairs, intending to go up to see what
was wrong. But then, above the sound of the water running in
the sink, he could hear Anna sobbing and he understood that
it would be better if he simply left her alone and let the moment pass. Things like that happened from time to time.

Peppi shrugged away the memory. "Who knows what *Dio* has in mind, eh?" he said to Angie.

Angie took a sip of coffee and looked thoughtfully at him. "Nobody knows," she told him, "so you can't waste time trying to figure it out by yourself. You'll just give yourself *agita* for the rest of your life."

"I know," sighed Peppi, "I know. But now and then you can't help yourself."

After they had finished their coffees, Peppi walked Angie back to her car. Peppi was glad to have had the company, but now he was anxious to finish his work in the backyard. Angie admonished him once again to take it easy. Peppi promised to try, but as soon as she drove away he returned to the backyard and resumed raking.

Forgetting about lunch, Peppi worked outdoors until well into the afternoon. After finishing in the back, he raked the front and side lawns. When he was done he bagged the leaves and dragged them to the side of the garage. He would leave them there for a few days before putting them out with the trash. Satisfied that he had done enough for the day, Peppi brushed himself off and looked up into the sky. The sun had already arced far toward the horizon and the trees were casting shadows like long, dark fingers across the lawn. While he was busy raking, Peppi had worked up a considerable sweat. Now, standing still in the dwindling sunlight, he felt the cold gathering around him and the dull ache of hunger in the pit of his stomach. He picked up his rake and headed back indoors.

Peppi hesitated when he came to the threshold of the back door. How many times had Anna given him an earful for traipsing into her nice clean kitchen wearing his dirty work boots? Somehow or other, almost without fail, Peppi managed to forget to take them off. It had always been one of her pet peeves with him, but he never did it on purpose. It was just one of those things. So, while he would sit at the table nibbling on a snack, or as he stood at the sink guzzling down a glass of water, he was always taken by surprise when his wife burst into the room and let him have it. Sometimes, when he was truly filthy, Anna would order him to remove his clothes right there at the door and throw them into the laundry before letting him set foot in the house. At those times, Peppi would inevitably try to assuage her ire by playfully reaching for her with his naked arms. More often than not, Anna would give him a healthy shove and send him on his way to the shower. Sometimes, though, when she was feeling playful herself, Anna would smile knowingly, coil her arms about his neck, and let him take her in his embrace.

Now, as Peppi stared into the kitchen, he was struck by how quiet and dark and lonely things were inside. There were no dishes set out on the table for dinner, no warm aroma of food wafting from the oven to greet him. There was no jingling of silverware being placed or the clamor of pots being stirred. The radio Anna would listen to while she cooked stood silent on the counter and the apron she wore still hung from the peg on the wall. It seemed to Peppi that the departure of one life had drained all life from his home. There was no one left but himself to bring life back into it. It settled in on him that he was now on his own. What was left of his life was his to do with as he chose, to come and go as he pleased. Just the same, heeding a voice he heard whispering in the back of his mind, Peppi reached down and began to unlace his boots.

CHAPTER THREE

Over the next few days, people came and went. Relatives, friends, fellow parishioners. They'd stop by, talk for a little while, see if Peppi needed anything, and then be on their way. It was nice of them. As the days went by, Peppi continued his work in the yard. He mowed the lawns, trimmed the hedges, and raked out the gardens. He weeded all the flower beds and wrapped burlap around the more delicate bushes to protect them from the cold weather to come. It was a lot of work, but soon everything, at least on the exterior, had appeared to return to normal. Just as soon, the flow of daily visitors slowed to a trickle until one day no one came.

That day, Peppi chose to relax by spending the afternoon in the garage working on his bicycle. Peppi's garage was a bicycle lover's dream. From the rafters hung racing wheels of every description. On the wall Peppi displayed an old Italian-made bicycle frame, the one he had used as a boy growing up in the Abruzzo foothills. It was his favorite, a bright red Bianchi frame, the same type used by his boyhood hero, Fausto Coppi, *Il Campionissimo,* the champion of champions. A picture of Coppi, as well as one of Gino Bartali and dozens of others of all the great European cycling champions, adorned the wall above the work bench in the corner. There Peppi kept the collection of bicycle tools he had acquired over the years.

Peppi's latest bicycle, a beautiful blue Colnago, was suspended from a hook in the rafter. He took the bike down and mounted it onto his work stand. The shifting had not been working quite the way he liked it back at the end of summer when he last rode the bike. He turned the pedals over and pressed the shift lever on the handlebar; the rear derailleur snapped inward, moving the chain across the cogs of the wheel with each successive shift.

Peppi kept turning over the pedals, spinning the wheel while he made delicate adjustments to the derailleur. The whirring of the drivetrain and the distinctive ticking of the wheel as it spun gladdened him. It was a happy sound for Peppi that recalled to his mind the endless miles he had ridden over the years, the thrill of racing in his younger days, and the many friends he had made along the way. Save for an occasional spill onto the pavement, rarely resulting in more than a few scrapes and some torn bike shorts, nothing could diminish the pleasure he took in riding a bicycle.

Peppi paused and looked over to the door that opened to the back hall. As always, Anna stood there in the doorway, quietly watching him. In her hand she held a cup of coffee she had just poured for him.

"How long do you plan to stay out here ignoring me?" she chided him playfully. "I swear you love that bike of yours more than you love me."

"I'm just adjusting the derailleur," answered Peppi, smiling from ear to ear.

"Ayyy, that's how it always starts," said Anna. "First the derailleur needs adjusting, then you have to true up your wheels—whatever that means—and then you have to fix something on the bike of one of the kids from the neighborhood, and then before you know it you've spent the whole night out here, leaving me all alone. I'm beginning to think maybe you've got a girlfriend out here someplace."

"I do," Peppi chuckled. "She's hiding in the rafters right now."

"Well, you'd better watch out because one night you might come in and find out that I've got a boyfriend of my own."

Peppi pretended to frown before breaking out in a mischievous smile. "Well, I could live with that if he knew how to replace a bottom bracket. I think the one on this bike is shot."

Shaking her head, Anna came closer and handed him the cup of coffee. "Here," she told him, "drink this to stay warm. And don't be out here too late, I've got a cake in the oven, you know."

"I can smell it," said Peppi, dreamily. "I love that smell." He closed his eyes and breathed deep. As he did so, he felt Anna's warm hands caressing his face.

"Who needs children, eh, *carissimo*," she told him gently, "when I already have a little boy to take care of . . ."

The wheel of the bike had long stopped spinning by the time Peppi realized that he was alone, still staring at the empty doorway to the house. He bowed his head for a moment and took a deep breath before looking back at the bike. Ignoring the tears rolling down his cheeks, he turned the pedals over again. Round and round they went, turning the chainring that pulled the chain, turning the cogs that kept the wheel spinning. Over and over Peppi turned them, cycle after cycle, always spinning in the same direction, for that was the way things worked.

CHAPTER FOUR

One December morning, Peppi awoke very early. The sun was just creeping over the horizon when he parted the curtain to look outside. Everything in the yard was bathed in the dawn's soft glow. Looking up, he saw that, save for a few patches of gray drifting off toward the east, the sky was cloudless. It was going to be a beautiful day.

Peppi sat up and yawned. He stayed there for a time, looking at the empty space beside him on the bed. He turned back to the bedside table and gazed at the picture of Anna. It was an old photograph, a closeup he had taken of her years ago during one of their many trips to Vermont. Peppi loved the highlands of Northern New England. The few hours of driving it took to reach them from Rhode Island were more than worth the effort to him, for the mountains there reminded him of his native land.

The picture of his wife had always been Peppi's favorite. He loved the way Anna's dark, luscious hair framed her face, the mountains behind her a *sfumato* blaze of red and orange and yellow. It had been a sparkling fall day, Peppi remembered, the kind that made you feel that everything in life was at its best. They had been strolling along a road overlooking the valley, soaking in the beauty of the trees aflame in all their autumn splendor, when they stopped and sat for a few moments on a stone wall. When Anna had turned and smiled at him, Peppi couldn't help but snap a picture of her. The beauty of the moment was much too precious to let slip away.

In some ways, as he sat there in bed, it all seemed so long ago to him now; but at the same time it was like yesterday, almost as if it were part of a very pleasant dream from which he had just awakened. Slowly, Peppi pulled his legs out from beneath the covers and set his feet on the floor. With another yawn he arose and walked into the bathroom.

When he was done Peppi came out and stood for a moment at the dresser, wondering what clothes to put on. The yard work was completed, so he wouldn't be working outside. Except for Thanksgiving dinner at Angie's, he hadn't left the house since the funeral. He wasn't planning to pay anyone a visit nor did he expect anyone to visit him that day. He had no errands of any import to run, so Peppi glanced once more out the window at the brightening sky before opening the bottom drawer where he kept his cycling clothes.

When Peppi rolled up to the barber shop he could see through the window that Tony was already working on his first customer of the day. Despite the early hour, Gino, Sal, and Ralph had already installed themselves on the benches in the little waiting area off to the side. There the three sat, as always, hidden behind the pages of the morning newspapers, voicing their opinions on whatever issues of the day happened to interest them.

Peppi leaned his bike against the wall of the shop and opened the door. The cleats on the bottoms of his cycling shoes made a familiar clack clack sound as he stepped inside. Upon hearing it, everyone in the shop looked over at him.

Ralph squinted at Peppi through his Coke bottle eyeglasses.

"Peppi!" he cried. He tried to stand, but the arthritis in his hip was acting up that day, so he collapsed back down and gave him a wave with his cane.

"Hey, Peppi!" called Tony. "Good to see you!"

Before Peppi knew it, Gino and Sal were beside him, patting him on the back as they guided him to the bench.

"Peppi, Peppi, come and sit," said Gino. "Right here, your old spot."

"We've been saving it for you every day," said Sal. "We were beginning to get worried that maybe you weren't planning on coming back."

"I wasn't," said Peppi with a shrug, "but I had nothing better to do today." They all laughed because that was what Peppi said every day when he stopped by the shop to kibitz with his cronies.

"How far are you riding your bike today?" asked Ralph.

"Not far," answered Peppi. "Twenty or thirty miles maybe. It's cold out there today. We'll see how it goes."

"Twenty or thirty miles," cried Sal. "I'd croak if I rode a bike twenty or thirty feet!"

"You're due to croak any day now anyways," Gino needled him, "so what difference would it make?"

"Ayyy, I got a good twenty years in me," said Sal, patting his well-rounded midsection with his pudgy hands. "Don't worry about me, boys. I'll be coming to the funerals for all you guys." As always, Sal was wearing his jogging outfit and sneakers even though it was obvious he had not run a step in years. He tugged up the elastic waist of his pants and sat back down.

Peppi settled in on the bench next to him and reached for a section of the newspaper. "So what's in the news these days?" he said. "I've been out of touch lately."

"Ayyy, just the usual," said Sal.

"You haven't missed much," Gino agreed. "Trust me."

"All bad news," added Ralph, shaking his head. "The whole country's going down the drain, if you ask me."

"So who's asking you?" Tony chimed in. He had just finished with his customer and sent him on his way. He grabbed a broom and started sweeping up the hair around the barber's chair. Tony looked over to Peppi and gave him a nod. "What's the news with *you*?" he asked. "That's the important question. How are you doin' these days?"

For a moment they all fell silent and listened intently to what Peppi had to say. Peppi squirmed a little bit and looked down at the floor.

"I don't know, Tony," he finally replied with a sigh. "It's hard to explain. It's like every day is dark, you know? Even when the sun is out it doesn't feel warm to me. I bathe myself, put on clean clothes every day, but I really don't care how I look. I eat, but I don't taste the food. People talk to me, but I don't really hear them. It's like I'm walking around half asleep. Nothing gives me any pleasure anymore, or any pain for that matter. It's like I can't feel anything."

Peppi stopped and looked about at his friends. They were all looking down now too. Sal was the first to look up.

"Well, thanks for brightening our day, Peppi," he said, rolling his eyes. "I think maybe now I'll go out and throw myself off a bridge someplace."

At that they all cracked up, even Peppi. It was the first time he had truly laughed in many days. When they finally quieted down again, Tony came and sat down to take a look at the newspaper.

"Best thing for you to do," he said, flipping through the

pages of the sports section, "is to find yourself another wo-man."

"He's right," said Gino. "You can't go through life all alone. It's no good. You need somebody."

"What are you talking about, Gino?" said Sal. "Your wife's been dead twenty years and you haven't remarried."

Gino smiled and ran a hand across his slicked back silver hair. "What can I say?" he joked, admiring himself in the mirror for the benefit of the others. "I like to play the field now."

"What field is that," said Tony, "the cow pasture?"

Gino laughed. "Hey, don't kid yourself. It's a rare night that I sleep alone."

"That's because your cat sleeps on the bed," said Ralph. "But he's right, Peppi. Give yourself some time, then go out and find somebody."

"No," said Peppi, shaking his head. "Not to darken your day any more, Salvatore, but I don't think I could ever love another woman. Never."

"Why not?"

"Eh," Peppi said with a shrug. "What can I say? It's like my heart is dead inside of me, you know?"

Peppi couldn't begin to put it all into words. He had loved his wife with every ounce of his being, but even he was aston-ished at how desolate the world had become for him without her. It was as if Anna had filled up everything inside of him, even the air in his lungs and the blood in his veins. Now, with her gone, it had all been drained out of him, leaving nothing but emptiness behind. How could he expect someone else to just come along and fill that terrible void?

Peppi paused and rubbed the back of his neck. "Besides," he went on, "it's way too late for me now anyway."

"What are you talkin' about?" cried Ralph. "It's never too late. You're still a youngster, believe me. Wait till you get to be my age. Besides, the way you ride that bicycle of yours all the time, you're in better shape now than most of the guys half your age, and a lot of guys half *their* age. Believe me when I tell you, you got a lot of life ahead of you."

"Nah," said Peppi, shaking his head. "It'll never happen."

"So what are you gonna do with yourself," said Gino, "just mope around for the rest of your life?"

Peppi turned to the window and gazed out into the distance. "I've been thinking a lot about that, actually," he replied.

"And?" said Tony.

"I've been thinking that maybe I'll go back to Italy," said Peppi.

"Italy?" they all cried.

"Che bozz', what do you want to go to Italy for?" said Gino.

"Eh," said Peppi, "I was born there. I might as well go back and die there."

"But where are you gonna go?" exclaimed Tony. "Where are you gonna live?"

"Il mulino," Peppi replied, a faraway look in his eyes.

"The *what*?" said Tony.

"That's right!" said Ralph. "The family *mulino.* The little mill attached to the house you grew up in. I remember you talking about it a long time ago."

"That's the one," said Peppi. "It hasn't been used in years and years, but it probably still works."

"But what the hell are you gonna do living next to an old mill all by yourself?" said Tony.

"Grind some corn, maybe?" suggested Sal.

"That's right," Gino said, laughing. "Then you can invite us all to come over and stay and you can cook us some homemade polenta."

"Ooh, I love polenta," said Sal, "with some *sausicc'* and some nice rabes. *Dio mio,* why did you have to say it? *Mannagia,* you got my mouth watering now!"

"Seriously," said Tony, "can you still live in that place? And is there anybody around there who'll even remember you if you show up someday?"

"I don't know," Peppi admitted. "But Luca will be there."

"Who?"

"His best friend," said Ralph, "the one from Villa San Giuseppe. The one he used to race his bicycle with."

"What is this, you know his life story?" said Gino.

"What do you want?" said Ralph. "I remember when people talk about things. It's about all I remember these days."

Gino turned back to Peppi. "So what do you think?" he said. "Is this Luca still around? I mean, how do you know he's not dead or something? Remember, you've been gone a long time."

"He's not dead," Peppi chuckled. "I'd know."

"But how can you be sure?" said Tony. "When was the last time you talked to him?"

"I haven't talked to him since I left Italy."

"Then how will you find him!"

"Easy," said Peppi. "I'll just show up at the piazza one Sunday morning on my bicycle and he'll be there with the others, all ready to ride just like every Sunday morning. He's a cyclist. That's what cyclists do."

"What a surprise that'll be for him!" said Ralph.

Peppi shook his head. "No," he said, "he won't be surprised. Luca's been expecting me for a long time."

"And I think all those miles riding your bike have finally gone to your head," said Tony, ducking once more behind the sports page.

Later, Ralph left for an appointment with his orthopedist and Sal went to shop for groceries with his wife. Tony was busy with another customer and Gino was getting ready to go to the pharmacy. Peppi decided it was time for him to go too. He walked out the door with Gino and stood by his bike for a few moments.

"Where are you going now?" asked Gino.

"I don't know," said Peppi. "It doesn't really matter. I'll just let the wheels roll wherever they want to go. I've been off the bike for quite a while now."

"Well, it's good to see you back on it," said Gino.

Peppi smiled and mounted the bike. He gave Gino a wave and pedalled off down the road, thinking all the while about Italy and Villa San Giuseppe and Luca and the mulino. Little by little, as he gathered speed, turning the pedals over faster and faster, he began to notice the glare of the sun, the contours of the road, and the feel of the brisk wind in his face.

CHAPTER FIVE

Peppi waited until well after the New Year before announcing to the rest of his friends and relatives that he intended to return to Italy. The news was greeted by almost unanimous dismay and anguished attempts to dissuade him. By then, however, Peppi had already booked his flight for Rome. His mind was made up to go in early February.

The day before he was to leave, Angie and Delores came to help him pack. Peppi could have managed the job well enough on his own for he didn't plan to take much, but the two women had insisted. They were worried sick about him. In truth, Peppi finally relented and agreed to let them help him partly because he knew it would make them feel a little bit better, but mostly because it would keep them from pestering him about the whole thing.

"I still don't understand why he wants to go back and live next to some filthy old mill when he has this beautiful home right here," said Delores.

"I don't understand either," Angie agreed. "It doesn't make sense. I tried my best to talk him out of it, but he won't listen."

They were folding Peppi's shirts and trousers, placing them in neat stacks on the bed. On the floor two suitcases lay open, awaiting the final decision on which articles of clothing would be chosen for the journey and which would be left behind.

Peppi was in the closet, sifting through his old suits and looking over his shoes. Before long he emerged with two sports jackets, one pair of dress shoes, and a pair of work boots.

"That's it?" cried Angie.

"How can you go to Italy with just those two pairs of shoes?" added Delores.

"I'll have the walking shoes I'll wear on the plane," offered Peppi. "Plus I'll have my cycling shoes."

The two women glared at him and shook their heads.

"Your cycling shoes?" said Delores. "Why are you packing those?"

"How else will I ride my bike?" said Peppi.

"What bike?" said Angie.

"My bike," said Peppi. "I can't leave it here."

"You have a lifetime's worth of things in this house and all you're worried about taking is your bike? And how do you plan on carrying it onto the plane?"

"Don't worry, I'll manage," Peppi replied. With that he left the room and headed downstairs.

"How did Anna ever put up with him all those years?" he heard Angie saying as he descended the staircase.

"They're all the same," echoed Delores.

Once downstairs, Peppi went into the garage. Wasting no time, he took the stepladder, opened it, and climbed up to the rafters. Peppi kept in the rafters many of the things he and Anna had collected over the years. Souvenirs from their trips together. Boxes of old clothes he'd been meaning to give away to the poor. Books and magazines. Some broken chairs Peppi had planned to repair one day when he found the time. The bicycle traveling case he wanted was kept stored against the back wall along with some old bicycle rims and an odd assortment of cycling equipment for which there was no storage space down below. Nearby was a cardboard box atop which rested a photo album that caught Peppi's eye.

Peppi knelt beside the box and opened the album. Inside were pictures from a trip Anna and he had taken to Saint Thomas some twenty years earlier. Until that very moment he had long ago forgotten the trip. Seeing the pictures from it brought back a flood of wonderful memories. Peppi flipped through the pages, pausing now and then to marvel at how tanned and beautiful his wife had been, how happy they were together. He gazed at every picture, trying to relive every moment. One in particular made him pause. It was of Anna. She was standing on the balcony, her face and hair bathed in the warm, soft light of the sun setting over the bay behind her. He gazed at the picture for a long time before he heard Angie calling for him. With one last look he kissed the picture, closed the album, and tucked it safely into the box. With a heavy sigh he grabbed the bicycle case and climbed back down into the garage to dismantle his bike.

The next day, Angie and her husband, Carmine, came to drive Peppi to the airport. Peppi's flight wouldn't depart Boston until after eight o'clock, but it was midafternoon and a few snowflakes were drifting down from the slate gray sky. It would be dark before long and Angie was anxious for them to leave before the weather turned bad. She hurried inside to get Peppi while Carmine kept the car running.

Peppi was sitting at the kitchen table, looking over a checklist he had written up of things that needed to be done in the house at different times throughout the year. Angie came in and looked over his shoulder.

"Boiler to be serviced every first week of September," she

read. "Change batteries for smoke alarms every six months when clocks are set forward or back. What's this for, Peppi?"

"It's for Stacy," he told her. "When she gets married and moves in here next year, I want her to know what to do."

"I'm sure my daughter and her husband will be able to figure out all that on their own, Peppi."

"Eh, you think so," he replied, "but it's hard to know all these things the first time you move into a house."

Angie looked at her cousin and smiled. "Don't worry, Peppi," she told him. "They'll take good care of the house. Besides, they won't be here very long."

"Why do you say that?" said Peppi.

"Ayy, because you're going to be moving back here before long, that's why."

"No, Angie," he said. "My mind's made up. When I go, the house will be theirs."

"But why!" cried Angie.

"Because this house has always been a happy house," he tried to explain to her. "Anna and I worked hard to make it that way and that's the way I always want it to stay, happy, with happy people in it. I don't belong here anymore."

Peppi paused and looked about the room for a few moments. It truly had been a happy house. He and Anna had always loved entertaining family and friends in their home. Whether it was hosting a surprise birthday party or serving a holiday dinner to a houseful of guests, or maybe letting some of their nieces and nephews enjoy a sleepover at Uncle Peppi and Auntie Anna's, it seemed that the two of them were rarely alone. One of Peppi's favorite events was the party they held each year the first weekend after Christmas. Peppi loved the dreamy, relaxed days after Christmas Day when all the hustle and bustle had passed and people finally slowed down enough to let themselves catch their breath. It seemed to Peppi that it wasn't until then, when the frantic rush was over and all the stress had evaporated, that the true spirt of the season settled onto everyone.

The party was a day-long affair with people coming and going all afternoon and well into the evening. Everybody would come, friends and family alike. Anna's brothers and sisters with their wives and husbands and children always came early and stayed late, as did Angie and Carmine and their kids. Peppi's cousin Erio would make the drive down from New Hampshire with his family. Even Vincenzo, another of his cousins from his mother's side of the family, would fly in every few years from California to visit. Anna would always lay out for them a feast worthy of King Wenceslaus. For starters she would put out some appetizers for them to pick on, a variety of dried sausages and cheese, olives, roasted red peppers, and fresh baked breads. These she would follow with a big platter of the real antipasti: clams casino, fried squid, broiled scallops wrapped in bacon, snail salad, smelts, and other seafood delights. Later she would bring out the lasagna or the penne or whatever type of pasta she decided to cook that day. As if that weren't enough, there was always a sirloin roast on hand with rabes and roasted potatoes and other vegetables on the side. Anna never bothered to prepare a dessert because the other women inevitably brought more pies and cakes and cookies than they could possibly fit on the dessert table. The eating and drinking and laughing and talking would go on all day, but the festivities were never quite complete until Anna sat down at the piano and the children gathered around to sing their favorite carols. That was always Peppi's favorite part of the day, for he loved the magical sound of their angelic voices.

Inevitably, Anna would be too exhausted the day after the party to even lift a finger, so Peppi would light a fire in the fireplace and the two would recuperate by spending the day snuggled together on the couch. The blissful glow from those wonderful times would stay with Peppi and Anna for days afterward and always carry them into the New Year on a high note.

Now, sitting at the kitchen table, Peppi let out a sigh. Even though he would not be there to see them, he hoped that, one day, happy times such as those would return once again to the house.

"But all your things . . ." said Angie.

"I'll send for what I want once I get settled," he told her. "The rest stays with the house."

Angie pressed him no further on the subject. Instead she let out a long irritated sigh before giving him a slap across the shoulder that knocked the pencil from his hand.

When it was time to leave, Angie held the front door while Peppi carried his two suitcases out to the car. Carmine had opened the trunk. He waited there with Angie while Peppi went back inside to get his bicycle case.

It was dark and quiet in the house now. Peppi stood for a few moments in the front hall, looking about, wondering if there was anything he had forgotten to do. When he was satisfied that he had not, he picked up the bicycle case and walked out onto the front step. He turned to close the door, but something made him stop. He paused, opened the door wider, and peeked back inside.

"Anna?" he called softly.

Peppi waited, half-expecting to see his wife come to the door to make sure that he was wearing his hat or to fuss with the scarf around his neck or to make him promise to call if he was going to be late coming home. Slowly, Peppi pulled the door shut and turned the key to lock it.

"*Ciao, bella,*" he whispered. Then he turned from the door and walked away.

CHAPTER SIX

"You'll be back one day, Peppi," Luca had assured him that morning long ago when Peppi left Villa San Giuseppe for the last time.

They had been standing on the piazza by the fountain, waiting for the bus to come that would take Peppi to Naples where the ship for America awaited him. Luca nodded to the mountains on whose roads they had trained together so often. "And when you do, I'll make you suffer, *amico mio,*" he added for good measure. "Of that you can be sure."

"Well, at least I'll always have something to look forward to," Peppi told his friend.

There was a long silence.

"I'd stay and wait for the bus," said Luca, his voice quavering, "but I have a hundred kilometers to ride today."

"I know," replied Peppi.

With a nod of his head, Luca turned quickly, mounted his bike, and began to pedal off out of the village.

"Ciao, Peppi!" he called over his shoulder.

"Ciao, Luca!" Peppi called after him.

Peppi stood there watching and waving until his friend had disappeared down the road. It wasn't until that moment that he realized all that he would be leaving behind. He looked about the village at the houses and the familiar faces. The tears had just begun to well in his eyes and Peppi was sure he was about to cry, but then from behind him he heard the sound of the bus rumbling into the village.

Peppi awoke with a start, the roar of a bus still ringing in his ears. He felt sad and alone, the dream and the memories still fresh in his mind. He opened his eyes and looked about at the unfamiliar surroundings of the sparsely furnished room. Sitting up, he peered through the dim light to the window. The shutters were closed, but they did little to muffle the incessant clamor of the traffic crawling up and down the street below. Peppi might just as well have been sleeping out on the sidewalk for all the difference they made. With a yawn, he set his feet on the floor, stood, and walked to the window. He opened the shutter a crack and looked out at Rome.

His was not a particularly inspiring view of the Eternal City. The street below was snarled with traffic and people hurried to and fro along the crowded sidewalks. It was a colorless section of town, but Peppi didn't mind; he hadn't come to sightsee. He had chosen the hotel in which he was staying because Termini, Rome's central train station, was just a few blocks away. His plan was to spend a day in Rome to get adjusted to the time change before taking the train to Abruzzo the following day.

This was only the second time Peppi had ever visited Rome. The first was as a teenager when he came to compete in a bicycle race on the outskirts of the city. The race, he well remembered, had ended badly when he was unable to avoid a spectacular crash just meters from the finish. Peppi was one of the first riders to go down in the pileup. Afterwards, scraped and bruised and vowing never to ride in Rome again, he quickly cleaned his wounds and headed straight back home to Villa San Giuseppe on the next available train.

Looking down the drab, congested street, Peppi was just as eager to get out of town as he had been that day after the race. But first he needed to rest. The trip over the Atlantic had tired him more than he had expected and he had slept almost all of the seven hours since he first checked into the hotel.

It was late afternoon now and the sun had already dipped behind the buildings across the street. Near the corner, the neon sign of a little trattoria glowed amidst the gathering gloom. It had been many hours since Peppi last ate and he felt the first few pangs of hunger gnawing at his stomach. He turned from the window and went into the bathroom to throw some water on his face. When he came out he sat on the edge of the bed for a few moments. Feeling as much revived as he could reasonably expect that first day, he slipped on his shoes and reached for his jacket.

The air was cool and dry when Peppi stepped outside and began to make his way down the sidewalk. It felt good to get out and walk after being cramped up like a canned anchovy for so many hours on the plane. Now, with all the shop lights glittering in the growing darkness, the street seemed far livelier to him than it had when he first rode in from the airport that morning. He strolled along, glancing into the windows as he passed. Soon he came to the trattoria he had spotted from the window of his room. He gave the menu taped to the window a cursory examination before stepping inside. It was still early for dinner by Roman standards and the tables were all empty.

"Buona sera, Signore," the owner greeted him. He smiled at Peppi and made a sweeping gesture to the rest of the room. "The restaurant is all yours," he said in English.

"Un tavolino vicino la finestra," responded Peppi, nodding toward a table by the window.

"Ma lei parla bene italiano!" exclaimed the delighted owner. "You speak Italian very well for an American."

"How do you know that I'm an American?" said Peppi, still speaking in Italian.

"Le scarpe," sighed the owner, looking down at Peppi's well-worn shoes. He shook his head and clicked his tongue. "Only an American would wear such shoes to dinner."

Peppi looked down at his feet and chuckled. "I've been away from Italy for too long," he admitted. "Not that I had much of a sense of style when I left."

"Stay here in Rome a little while, my friend," said the man, "I can tell you where to get some nice shoes."

"Maybe," laughed Peppi, "but for now I need to eat."

"D'accordo," the owner agreed. "Go sit and I'll bring you a nice bowl of minestrone while you look over the menu."

Little by little, the restaurant began to fill while Peppi ate his dinner. Most of the patrons seemed to be tourists or students. They arrived two or three at a time and talked excitedly amongst themselves in French and Spanish and German. The trattoria's owner, who later introduced himself to Peppi as Marcello, waited on all the tables with practiced efficiency. He was always busy, always in motion, but he still managed to find time to exchange a few words of lively banter with the other patrons in whatever language they happened to be speaking. As Peppi was the only one dining by himself, Marcello paid extra attention to him so that he wouldn't feel alone amidst the hubbub.

Later, when Peppi was finishing and there was a quiet moment in the restaurant, Marcello brought out two cups of espresso and sat down at the table with him. He slid one cup over to Peppi and kept the other for himself.

"I need a little break," he told Peppi, taking a teaspoon of sugar and dumping it into his cup. Then he added another spoonful, and then another.

"You've earned it," said Peppi with a smile. "You work hard."

"Everybody works hard," sighed Marcello. "We all take our turns. That's just the way of things."

"It's a good way," said Peppi.

Marcello took a sip of espresso. "So tell me, Signor Peppino, how is it that you speak our language so well, and what brings you all the way across the ocean from America to my little trattoria?"

"I was hungry," said Peppi with a shrug.

Marcello burst out in laughter. "Well, I hope it was worth the trip!" he exclaimed. "Tell everybody else to do the same when you go back to America."

"I'm not going back to America," said Peppi. "I'm going back to live in Abruzzo where I grew up."

"*Che pazzo!*" cried Marcello. "You give up living in America to come back here? What are you, crazy?"

Peppi smiled and took a sip of his espresso. "That's the same question everyone back home kept asking me. Now that I've come back to Italy, people are still asking."

"That's because it's a good question, my friend," said

Marcello, wagging his finger at him. Then he broke out in another great smile. "Of course, if you're going to be staying, that's a good reason to go get some new shoes." He was just about to tell Peppi where to find the best shoes in Rome, but then one of the other patrons called to him to order a second bottle of wine.

CHAPTER SEVEN

The train for Sulmona pulled out of Termini a few minutes past noon. Peppi had spent the few extra dollars needed to sit in a first class compartment. It would be a long trip and he wanted to be comfortable. Besides, it would be easier to keep an eye on his luggage, particularly the case containing his bicycle, which was far more valuable to him than the combined contents of the other two suitcases. For the time being, Peppi had the compartment all to himself, so he settled into his seat and passed the time by staring out the window at the flat, uninteresting landscape. Before long his eyes grew heavy and he dozed off.

When he awoke, Peppi discovered that he had been joined by two other passengers. One was an attractive young woman. Sitting one seat over on Peppi's side of the compartment, she flipped through the pages of a fashion magazine. Across from her sat a young, smartly dressed businessman. The young man, Peppi noted with amusement, was pretending to scan the headlines of the financial news while periodically looking up in the hope of catching the young woman's eye. For her part, the young woman never so much as glanced his way, completely ignoring the young man in that maddening and devastating way that only Italian women know how to do.

Peppi sat up straight and gave a little yawn. To the consternation of the young man, the young woman turned and smiled at the older gentleman.

"I'm sorry, Signore," she said, pulling her belongings closer to her to make more space for Peppi. "I hope I didn't disturb you."

"Not at all, Signorina," answered Peppi. "Far worse things can happen to an old man than to wake up and find a beautiful young lady sitting beside him."

The young woman beamed. The young man fumed.

Peppi smiled and turned to look out the window as the train clattered along. The landscape had changed dramatically, the flatlands now replaced by rolling hills that would soon give way to the mountains. It wouldn't be long before they reached the Abruzzo region.

"I hope I didn't miss my stop," said Peppi, stretching his arms and legs.

"Where are you traveling to, Signore?" the young woman asked.

Peppi turned back from the window. "Sulmona," he answered. "And from there to Villa San Giuseppe."

"Villa San Giuseppe," she repeated. "I don't think I've ever heard of it."

"It's a little *paese,* outside the city."

"*I've* heard of it," the young man offered, hoping to join the conversation. He might just as well have been talking to himself for all the heed the young woman paid him.

"Forgive me," she said to Peppi, "you look like an American, but your Italian is very good."

"I am an American," Peppi replied. "But I was born in Villa San Giuseppe."

"Ah, going there to visit family?" she said brightly.

"No, I'm going there to live."

"To live, how nice!" said the young woman. She paused and glanced at the ring on Peppi's finger. "Is your wife already there?" she asked.

Peppi shook his head. He glanced over at the young man, who immediately understood the look in Peppi's eyes. The young man gave a little cough, hoping the young woman would get the hint.

"Oh, then she's waiting for you back in America," she continued, oblivious to him.

"No, Signorina," said Peppi gently. Then he explained to her that Anna had recently passed away.

"*O, Dio!*" the young woman cried, throwing her hands up. "You poor thing, I'm so sorry for having asked."

"Don't worry," Peppi assured her. "I'm sorry for having told you."

Upset with herself at having made what she obviously considered a terrible blunder, the young woman sat there fretting for a time about how to make up for it. The fashion magazine on her lap no longer held any interest for her. She tossed it aside and looked at Peppi with sympathetic eyes.

"I know it's none of my business, Signore," she said at last, "but I can't help asking. Why are you going back there to live all alone? Where will you go?"

Peppi shrugged and looked out the window. Just then the train entered a tunnel. All went dark for a few moments and the only sound he could hear was the muffled roar of the wind caught between the train and tunnel walls. Just as quickly, the train burst back into the sunlight, the mountains now rising all around them. Peppi turned away from the window and saw the sincere look of concern in the young woman's eyes. Even the young man had set aside the newspaper to pay attention. Peppi looked at them both and smiled.

"What is your name, Signorina?" he asked.

"Loredana."

"Mine's Claudio," the young man added.

"And yours?" said Loredana, giving Claudio only the vaguest hint of acknowledgment that they were on the same train together.

"My friends call me Peppi," he replied.

"Tell us about it, Signor Peppi," said Loredana. "Please, tell us where you are going."

"It's a long story," Peppi said.

"And it's still a long way to Sulmona," she replied.

Peppi gazed at her for a time. He smiled again, for there was something pure and irresistible in her youthful eyes. Peppi had never been one to wear his heart on his sleeve, particularly in the company of complete strangers. All the same, he could see no harm in talking about his life and the simple plans he had made for what was left of it. If nothing else, it would help pass the time. Peppi sat there for a moment, rubbing his chin.

"Where do I begin?" he wondered aloud.

Loredana smiled. "Begin at the beginning," she suggested.

"Hmm, the beginning," said Peppi thoughtfully. "I was born in the mountains. I guess that's a good place to start."

As the train clacked along the tracks and the compartment gently swayed back and forth, Peppi told them about growing up in Villa San Giuseppe and how his family had made its living from the little mulino next to the house. Before long he was talking about cycling and how much he had loved to race his bicycle when he was young.

"I used to race too," said Claudio brightly.

Peppi assessed the young man's slight build. "A climber," he guessed.

"Like a feather on the wind!" Claudio boasted. "I could pedal uphill with the best of them." Then he shook his head and shrugged. "Of course I wasn't much good going down the hills, or in the sprint for that matter."

"Cycling is an unforgiving sport," said Peppi.

"But it's the best sport," Claudio enthused.

Loredana give a little cough to let them know that they had discussed cycling long enough. Peppi nodded to show that he understood.

"Did you come from a big family?" she asked.

"No," said Peppi. "Actually, I was an only child. Now and then, when I was small, I used to ask my parents why I didn't have any brothers or sisters."

"What did they say?"

"They always told me that the house was too small," he chuckled. "If another baby came along I would have to sleep outside."

At that Loredana and Claudio laughed.

Peppi laughed as well. He could still remember riding off to bed at night on the broad shoulders of his father, Allesandro. Peppi loved to reach back and give his father's dark mustache an impish yank. His father would always pretend it hurt and let out a howl like a wolf. Without fail, Peppi's mother, Angelina, would playfully scold him for being so mean to his father. "Mario," she would say, for that was Peppi's real name, *"basta!* Enough! Be nice, don't hurt your poor papa, he has to work for us in the morning."

The memory brought a grin to Peppi's face.

"But I had lots of cousins," he went on, "so there were always lots of people in our home. I never felt lonely, at least not until the war came and suddenly everyone began to disappear. Some of my parents' relatives went off to live in America before things got bad. Others just ran away to God knows where. Many of the men of course were taken away to become soldiers. Lots of them, like my father, never returned. It was as if he and the rest of them just vanished from our lives."

"How awful," said Loredana.

Peppi paused and shook his head. "It was a terrible war, like all wars," he said. "It seemed like everything was destroyed. After it was over and the Germans were all gone and the Allies finally went home, it was to time to rebuild our lives, but there wasn't much left for us to build on. My father was gone and then my mother became ill a few years later. After she died, my uncle arranged for me to come to America. I had relatives in Rhode Island and some out in San Francisco. My plan was to stay in Rhode Island for a while to get used to things, then move out west to California where one of my cousins had a job as a construction worker waiting for me."

"What was it like living in California?" Loredana asked. "Beautiful, I would imagine."

"Yes, I've heard it's wonderful there," Claudio agreed.

"Actually," Peppi chuckled, "I never lived in California."

"What happened?"

"Eh," shrugged Peppi, "I met my wife."

Peppi told them the story. After arriving in America, he had gone to work at his uncle's music store in Providence, intending to wait until he had earned some money before heading out to California. One day he was carrying a box full of sheet music and lesson books across the store. It was a sizable box and Peppi had to keep leaning to one side to watch where he was going. Just as he was passing the front door a young woman walked in. She was a piano teacher and had come in to inquire about giving lessons at the store. Somehow or other the two collided and the box went toppling to the floor.

Embarrassed that he had caused such a commotion in his uncle's store, Peppi dropped to his knees and quickly began to pick everything up. He was so upset with himself that he barely noticed the piano teacher who had knelt down beside him to give him a hand. It wasn't until he had finally collected everything and restored it to the box that he stood up and turned to her so that he might thank her for her help and apologize for running into her.

Peppi took one look at her and went speechless. Though dressed plainly, the young woman had dark, silky hair and the most serenely beautiful face he had ever seen. As she gazed at him with her soft, warm eyes, Peppi felt certain that he had encountered an angel.

A long, awkward silence ensued as the two regarded one another.

"Hi, my name is Anna," the young woman had finally said, extending her hand to him.

Peppi was a strong young man, but when their hands touched for the first time he had the odd sensation that he had lost all the strength in his well-muscled limbs, almost as if he were suddenly melting.

"I am Mario," he had answered in faltering English. "But everybody calls me Peppi," he added hastily.

"Why?" she said, giving him an inquisitive look. "Is there something wrong with the name Mario?"

"Why, no," said Peppi, by now completed flustered.

"In that case, *I'll* call you Mario," Anna told him with a mischievous sparkle in her eye, as if she had understood right away that this would be a great annoyance to him.

Peppi stopped talking for a moment and let himself enjoy the memory.

"So what happened next?" said Loredana eagerly.

"Well," he shrugged, "I took one look at her and forgot all about California."

"You got hit by the thunderbolt," laughed Claudio. Then he looked at Loredana and added, "I know how that is."

Loredana responded by rolling her eyes and looking the other way.

Peppi went on to tell them about how he and Anna were married a little over a year later. He told them about Anna's parents and brothers and sisters, and how they had all welcomed him into the family as one of their own. He told them about how Anna eventually took a job teaching music at an elementary school while he started his own landscaping business. He told them about how they scrimped and saved every nickel until they were able to buy their first and only home in Providence, a move that had caused everyone in the family great consternation even though they all lived in Cranston, just a few miles away. Peppi spoke of the many happy times he and his wife had enjoyed there, the memories flowing from him like water over the falls. Now and then he glanced at Loredana and Claudio, certain that he must have been boring them to tears, but he saw that the two were listening attentively, their faces all smiles.

"Do you have children, Signor Peppi?" Loredana asked.

"No, Signorina," Peppi said wistfully.

"Well, that just gives a husband and wife more time for each other, right?" said Claudio at seeing the sad look in Peppi's eyes.

"Yes, that is true," Peppi replied. "Still, we always wanted them, but it just never happened for us. Back then of course things weren't like they are today, with all the different tests they have. In those days the doctors couldn't tell you why someone couldn't have children. It was just one of those things and you learned to live with it. People used to tell us that we should have adopted a child, but to tell you the truth, we had so many nieces and nephews around us all the time that we just never gave the idea much thought. Besides, it's better to just accept things the way God gives you them and then get on with your life."

Loredana and Claudio nodded in agreement as Peppi continued to recount some favorite memories of his marriage, but their smiles soon faded away and their eyes started to well up when Peppi eventually told them about the day Anna became sick. Without warning, she collapsed at home one afternoon. It wasn't until later at the hospital that Peppi learned that she had suffered some sort of stroke. For a week, while she was recuperating in the hospital, Anna had been unable to speak. It was an agonizing time for both of them. Gradually, though, as the days passed, she regained her voice and the movement she had lost on her right side showed signs of returning. Peppi had been sick with worry for her the whole time, but he was encouraged by the progress she was making. It seemed as though everything was going to be all right.

One night at the hospital when visiting hours were nearly over, Peppi tucked the blankets in around his wife to make sure that she would be comfortable. When he finished, Anna reached out to him.

"You're a good husband," she told him, kissing his hand. "I'll owe you a nice dinner when I get home."

"I can't wait," Peppi said, caressing her face. He gave her a kiss and began to head toward the door. He turned and waved.

"I'll see you tomorrow," he told her.

Anna smiled. *"Ciao,* Peppi," she said. Then she blew him a kiss.

That night, after Peppi had gone home, Anna passed away.

Now, sitting on the train with the mountains looming all about them, Peppi still wondered about that final night. "I don't know why she called me Peppi," he said. "She never did that. But whatever the reason, God decided to take her that night." He paused and looked down at his hands. "After that, the light went out of the world for me and I knew it was time for me to finally come back home to Italy."

He looked back up at the two young people and shrugged. "So that's all there is to tell, I guess," he said. "I left for America all alone and now I'm coming home all alone."

By this time, Loredana and Claudio were both in tears.

"Dio mio," sniffled Loredana, "how sad—but how beautiful too."

"What a life you've had," Claudio added, wiping his eyes on the cuff of his sleeve.

"Eh, not so different from anyone else's life," said Peppi, "not so different at all." He gazed out the window and spoke no more for a very long time.

When the train finally pulled into Sulmona, Loredana and Claudio hurried to help Peppi with his luggage. It was late afternoon and a chilly wind greeted them when they all stepped out onto the station platform. Peppi had pulled on a heavy sweater and jacket just before they arrived, but Loredana and

Claudio had left theirs on the train. They stood there shivering, unsure of how to say farewell.

"There's no one here to meet you," observed Loredana.

"No one knows I'm coming," Peppi replied.

"Are you sure you'll be all right?" said Claudio. "Do you need help finding a place to stay for the night?"

"I could come with you and help you find a hotel," offered Loredana. "There's another train for Pescara later on."

"*I'm* going to Pescara too," said Claudio. To his disappointment, Loredana gave no discernible response at learning of the happy coincidence.

"I'll be fine," Peppi assured them. "Thank you for offering. Now please, hurry back to your seats on the train before you both catch cold."

Loredana opened her purse and pulled out a small card. "Here," she said, pressing it into Peppi's hand, "my address in Pescara is on this. If you ever get lonely, call and you can come stay with my family for a while."

"Yes, that's a good idea," said Claudio, quickly producing a business card of his own. "Please, Signor Peppi, call me anytime. Let me know how you're doing."

"I'll tell you what," said Peppi. "Claudio, you give Loredana one of your cards, and Loredana, you give Claudio one of yours. This way if I ever contact one of you, you'll be able to let the other one know. How does that sound?"

"I think it's a great idea," said Claudio, holding up another business card. Loredana eyed him slyly before taking it.

"*I'll* call *you*," she said, not bothering to offer her own card in return. "*If* I ever need to."

Claudio sighed. "Well, at least that's a start."

Just then the conductor blew his whistle, calling for everyone to get on board. Loredana rushed to Peppi and gave him a hug and a kiss on each cheek.

"Buona fortuna, Signor Peppi," she said before pulling away.

Claudio took her hand and helped her up onto the train. The two hurried to their compartment and lowered the window as the train began to pull away from the station.

"Ciao, Signor Peppi!" they called. *"Arriverderci!"*

"Arriverderci!" Peppi called back as he waved them out of sight. Alone once more, he collected his bags and headed out of the station to find a room for the night.

CHAPTER EIGHT

Luca groaned when he heard the cock crowing out in the yard. He had been up late the night before and the bird's shrill cry pierced through his skull like the bit of an electric drill. He rolled over and tried to pull the covers up over his shoulders, but Filomena had already snatched them from him. To all appearances his wife was sound asleep, but when he tried to wrest a larger section of blanket from her grasp she held on with such tenacity that he was afraid the blanket might rip in two.

"Get out of bed, old man," she warned him. "It's Sunday morning. Leave me alone and go for your ride."

"I don't want to ride," moaned Luca. "The train to Milano is running through the middle of my head. I think I'm dying."

"That's what you get for drinking so much wine," she snipped. "You'd think that a man your age would know better by now."

"And one would think that you would have more compassion for your husband," he griped. The cock crowed again and Luca grimaced. He buried his face in the pillow to escape the agony. "If that animal makes another noise," he vowed, "I swear that we'll be having him for Sunday dinner this afternoon."

"Don't blame the bird for your foolishness," said Filomena, consolidating her grasp on the blanket. "Now go and let me sleep. Hurry, or they'll leave without you."

With another groan, Luca rolled over and let his legs drop off the edge of the bed. He sat up and set his feet on the floor. For a long time he simply sat there, holding his head in his hands. At last, though, he mustered the energy to stand. He trudged over to the dresser, pulled open a drawer, and began to dress.

When he had finished putting on his cycling shorts and jersey, Luca paused to assess himself in the mirror. If one ignored the wrinkled face and the thin crop of silver hair on his head, it would be easy to mistake him for a much younger man, he told himself. Yes, his stomach had taken on slightly more girth since the beginning of winter, but he still stood tall and straight, his shoulders and arms as strong as ever. But most gratifying to Luca were his legs. Even now they were just as lean and sinewy as when he raced his bicycle back in the old days. He liked the hard contours of his thighs and bulging calves. His were powerful legs, power built by untold thousands of kilometers of pedalling a bike, day after day, year after year. Luca loved his family and friends, his town and country; he loved his work, but it was cycling that kept him alive. It was as essential to him as breathing.

"You look wonderful," Filomena chided him from beneath the bed covers. "Now stop admiring yourself and finish dressing before you miss the group."

"My head hurts too much to be admiring myself," he replied. "But thanks for noticing me."

"Don't mention it."

Luca went downstairs and into the kitchen. It was chilly there. Even with his socks on he could feel the cold of the marble floor against the soles of his feet. He made coffee and sat down at the table to drink a cup while he nibbled on some biscotti. It was important to have at least a little something in his stomach, else he would never make it through the whole ride. Little by little, as he sipped his coffee and ate his biscotti, the banging in his head began to fade away. Before long he was feeling reinvigorated enough to entertain the thought of pedalling hard again. Luca took a last sip from his cup before leaving the kitchen to put on his bicycle shoes.

It was a brisk morning, but the Abruzzo sun shone warmly on Luca as he pedalled away from the house. He zipped up his jacket as he coasted down the drive past the modest two-story building that stood near the road at the end of the property. The building housed the factory in which his company made confetti, the delicious hard-shelled candy that was sold all over Italy. The company, a family business started generations ago, had been handed down to Luca when his father passed away. The business had given Luca everything he had: the clothes he wore, the roof over his head, the food on his table. Most important of all, it gave him the money to buy a new bicycle whenever he wanted, as well as the time to ride it. He was eternally grateful for that, and as he always did whenever he passed by the factory's front door, he made the sign of the cross and blew a kiss up to heaven as a gesture of thanks for his good fortune.

The group was assembled by the fountain when he finally rode onto the piazza. Years ago when he was young, Luca would have been the first one there, waiting for all the others instead of the other way around. But Luca had long ago relinquished his role as leader of the group. Still, he was greatly respected by all for the racing exploits of his youth. As always, he was greeted warmly by the younger riders when he rolled up alongside them. He soon joined in the idle chatter while they waited for the rest of the stragglers to appear before they headed off out of the village.

The first murmurings of *"Andiamo!"* were being made when someone recommended that they wait for one last rider that could be seen approaching from far down the road. Luca turned and gazed off into the distance to guess who it might be. Whoever it was, he was pedalling hard to get there on time. They decided to wait. Before long the rider had pedalled up the steep little hill that led into the piazza and up to the fountain where all the others immediately began to click their shoes onto their pedals.

Luca, however, paused and gazed through his dark sunglasses at the newcomer. He was an older rider, he saw, perhaps as old as himself, but he looked fit and trim. The jersey he wore was unfamiliar to Luca, but there was something vaguely familiar about the way the rider had climbed up the little hill before the piazza, something about his posture as he rolled up to the group.

For his part, the new rider sat on his bike, returning Luca's gaze, the side of his mouth curled up in the slightest hint of a smile. It was then that it dawned on Luca and he returned the half smile.

"Buon giorno, Peppi,*"* he said nonchalantly.

"Buon giorno, Luca,*"* Peppi replied.

"You know, I'm going to make you suffer today."

"I was hoping you'd say that."

Then they pedalled off together to catch up to the group.

CHAPTER NINE

"Let them go," said Luca. "They'll wait up for us on the other side."

They were pedalling up a steep section of road, struggling to keep pace with the lithe younger riders ahead who danced along effortlessly on the pedals. It had been weeks since Peppi last rode his bike with any regularity and months since he trained on any hills. His legs and lungs were on fire. His only comfort was the knowledge that Luca, judging by his labored breathing, was suffering just as much.

The ride had started out pleasantly enough. As they rode along out of town, Luca had introduced Peppi to the rest of the group. From their reaction, Peppi could tell that his name had been mentioned before. "That's Peppi," he had heard the younger riders whispering respectfully. "Luca's old teammate. He won a sack of races in his day." That he had been so well remembered gave Peppi a warm feeling inside.

Now, however, that comfortable feeling of warmth in Peppi's heart and soul had turned into the acute discomfort of his aching leg muscles as the road grew steeper still. He and Luca slowed to a crawl, so much so that the two were almost in danger of falling over sideways. It was only pride and sheer determination that spared them both from the humiliation of having to dismount and walk the last few meters to the top;

they would have preferred to drop dead on that very spot. Mercifully, the road leveled out as they reached the summit of the climb. They pedalled over the top and were greeted by the view of a long, gloriously flat road winding its way through the valley below.

"I think . . . you've suffered . . . enough . . . for today," declared Luca between gulps of air.

"There's . . . always . . . tomorrow," Peppi puffed in reply.

They coasted down the hill and gradually caught up to the other riders. By then the group had settled into a moderate tempo, allowing Peppi and Luca to cling to the back with a reasonable amount of effort. Soon they had recovered enough to join in the paceline. Peppi stayed behind Luca, letting him lead the way up to the front as he had done so often years ago when the two raced together. Luca had just reached the front of the line and was taking his pull into the wind when Peppi happened to look down for the first time at the rear derailleur of his friend's bicycle.

"Luca!" exclaimed Peppi. "You're using Shimano?"

"So what?" called Luca over his shoulder. He pulled off to the side to allow Peppi to pass to the front of the line.

"A nice Italian boy like you, using Japanese components instead of Campagnolo," said Peppi, clicking his tongue as he went by. "I don't believe it."

"Hey, welcome to the global economy," replied Luca with a shrug. "I would have thought a nice American boy like you would understand."

At that the two of them laughed. The others in the group smiled and laughed with them for it was good to see two old friends reunited after so many years. The whole crew pedalled on, jabbering all the while about little else but racing and riding, about derailleurs and pedals and gear sets and wheel hubs and about who was going to win the Giro that year. Those were the things most important to them at the moment; little else matters when you are riding a bike.

When they all finally returned to Villa San Giuseppe, it was nearing midday and the bright sun warmed the piazza as the riders rolled in. They gathered once more around the fountain and chatted a while longer before heading their separate ways for Sunday dinner. Before long only Peppi and Luca remained. They got off their bikes and sat on the steps by the fountain.

Peppi looked about the piazza, trying to reconcile his memories of the place with the scene now presented to his eyes.

"Things have changed," he said.

Luca looked about the piazza with him. "Everything changes," he replied. "But you know, at the same time, everything stays the same. Sometimes it all just looks different to you."

"But where did all these cars come from?" said Peppi. "When I left there were maybe one or two in the whole town. Now it looks like everyone has one."

"Ayyy, that was after the war when you left," said Luca with a wave of his hand. "No one had anything back then. Life is easier these days. If you'd stuck around, you might have a car or two of your own by now."

"I'd still prefer my bike," said Peppi.

Luca grinned and nodded in agreement. "Your Italian is still very good, by the way," he told Peppi. "I'm surprised you haven't forgotten it after all these years."

"You can take the boy out of Villa San Giuseppe, but it's hard to get Villa San Giuseppe out of the boy," said Peppi.

"Bravo," said Luca. Then he paused and gazed at his friend for a time. He nodded his head toward Peppi's hand.

"I see a ring on your finger, Peppi," he said, "but I don't hear you mention a wife."

Peppi looked down at his hand and shrugged. "I can't bring myself to take it off," he replied.

"I understand," said Luca. "Children?"

Peppi shook his head. "How about you?"

"Two," said Luca, unable to suppress a smile at the thought of his children. "A son and daughter, and two grandchildren! Who would have imagined, eh?"

"That's wonderful," said Peppi. "When do I get to meet them all?"

"Soon," said Luca, "but first, *amico mio,* tell me what finally brings you all the way back to visit Villa San Giuseppe after all these years?"

"I haven't come to visit," said Peppi. "I've come to stay."

"To *stay?*" said Luca, surprised but clearly delighted by the news. "But where, here in town?"

"I thought I'd live in the mulino," Peppi answered. "In the house where I grew up. It's still mine by right."

"Il mulino?" said Luca thoughtfully.

"Yes," said Peppi. "I want to go see it right now before I go back to Sulmona for my things. Why don't you come along, just in case I've forgotten the way."

"Well—yes, of course," said Luca, his brow furrowed. "But first, why don't we go to my house. My wife is making dinner. I can give you some dry clothes to put on, we can eat and talk, and later on I'll drive you back to Sulmona. Then we can go see the mulino."

"Okay," said Peppi. "A nice home-cooked meal sounds very good to me right now."

"*Va bene,*" said Luca, patting him on the back. "*Andiamo.*"

"I hope your wife won't mind having an unexpected guest."

"Don't worry," Luca assured him as they pedalled off. "You'll like my wife. She's the best cook in all Abruzzo!"

CHAPTER TEN

Luca and Peppi were discussing peppers and tomatoes and the cultivation of grapes when they finally came to the house a short time later. Luca lamented his lack of time to spend taking proper care of his garden.

"The factory keeps me busy almost every day," he complained to Peppi. "And then if I feel like riding my bike for a while—well, there just aren't enough hours to the day."

"You just need to get up earlier in the morning," Peppi chided him.

"You and my wife should get along very well," said Luca with a rueful sigh.

Filomena had seen them walking their bikes by the factory and up the path to the house. She assumed that her husband was dragging home to dinner another hungry straggler from his pack of cycling cronies. The extra plate was already set on the table by the time the two walked through the door.

Besides Filomena, Luca's son, Costanzo, was there with his wife, Maria, and their two teenage children, Gianni and Vittoria. Only Luca's daughter, Lucrezia, who had gone to visit friends in Pescara, was missing. When Luca first introduced Peppi, all of them, Filomena included, gaped at the newcomer as if they could not believe their eyes.

"*You* are Peppi?" said Gianni with great respect. "The bicycle racer?"

"I don't believe it," said his sister. "All these years I thought that you were just someone Papa Luca made up in his imagination."

"I've been gone a long time," said Peppi with a shrug. "It all seems like a dream even to me."

"Vittoria, Gianni, stop staring at him!" exclaimed Filomena. "Go sit down at the table. You too, Costanzo."

"But they're right," laughed Costanzo. "It's almost like we're meeting a ghost. My father's talked about you for so many years."

"That's what friends are for," said Luca happily. "Now, Peppi, let's get you some dry clothes and then we can all eat."

The long, perfectly choreographed meal that followed surpassed even Luca's lofty predictions. When everyone finally gathered around the dinner table, Luca poured the wine while Filomena brought out for appetizers a platter of bruschetta and another of fried olives stuffed with prosciutto. Soon after came the *pasta alla chitarra,* thin strands of pasta tossed in a savory sauce of pancetta, chopped tomatoes, olive oil, and cheese. *Il secondo piatto* consisted of tripe, the lining of the cow's stomach, boiled and served in a zesty tomato sauce. There is no more powerful reminder of days past than the aroma and flavors of the food one loves. Everything Peppi had tasted to that point, every morsel, had evoked some memory of his youth, but the tripe in particular pleased him for it had been one of his mother's specialties. He made a point of telling Filomena so as she was preparing to serve the main course of roasted lamb garnished with artichokes and fennel. Along with it she had prepared broccoli rabe and fried cardoons, a hearty, thistlelike vegetable that managed to flourish even in the chilly climate of the Abruzzi mountains. All in all, the meal was a staggering performance.

After dinner, while the men contemplated their bloated midsections, Maria and Vittoria cleared the dishes while Filomena prepared the coffee and dessert. Luca settled back in his chair and gave a contented sigh.

"What did I tell you, Peppi," he said, patting his stomach. "Is my wife the best cook in all Abruzzo or not?"

Peppi let out a contented sigh of his own, for it had been many weeks since he had eaten so robustly. He smiled and nodded in agreement as he eased back and looked up at the photographs displayed on the wall behind his friend. There were, he noticed, pictures from the early days when Luca was still racing and others from when he and Filomena first met. The wedding pictures dominated the center of the wall as did the pictures of the children and grandchildren.

Luca leaned back and looked over his shoulders at the photographs. "You're in one of those, you know," he said.

"Which one?" said Peppi.

Luca pointed to an old photograph hanging amidst several others taken years and years ago. Peppi stood and went to get a closer look. Tears came to his eyes when he saw it. It was a picture of Peppi and Luca after a race, their arms around each other's shoulders. They were smiling from ear to ear, so young, so full of strength and vitality.

"I remember that race," said Peppi. "It was our last one together. You won it easily."

"That's because you let me," replied Luca with a grin. "For once he gave me a leadout in the sprint instead of the other way around," he said to Costanzo and Gianni.

"It was the least I could do," said Peppi, still gazing at the photograph and the others around it. Looking at them reminded him of so many places that were once familiar to him, but about which he had since forgotten. Mostly, though, he studied the faces of the people and friends that he had known and loved so well, many of whom he knew were long gone by now. He turned from the wall and sat back down at the table.

"You have a beautiful family, Luca," said Peppi. "You too, Costanzo."

"Do you have children of your own?" asked Luca's son.

"No," answered Peppi. "My wife and I always wanted them, but none ever came along. That's just the way it goes sometimes in life." He looked at Costanzo and smiled. "So, do you work with your father?" he asked him.

"No," Costanzo answered to his surprise.

Luca let out a low grumble of irritation. "He works in Torino," he said ruefully. "Can you believe it? My son has a family business right here, but he decides to go work for strangers in Torino."

"I'm an engineer!" Costanzo protested, but with a laugh. "It's what you sent me to school for. There's nothing for me to do in a candy factory. Besides, you still have Lucrezia working for you."

"Uff," grunted Luca, rubbing his forehead. "It's more like I work for her." He looked at Peppi and shook his head. "I don't know what I'm going to do with these kids."

"I wouldn't worry," grinned Peppi. "I think you're all doing just fine."

Filomena brought out coffee to go along with a simple cornmeal cake and a plate of fruit. Vittoria and Maria set out some fresh plates and they all sat down to have dessert with the men.

"So, Peppi, you've made my husband very happy today with your visit," said Filomena. "And to think I almost couldn't get him out of bed on time for the ride this morning."

"I was sure he'd be there," said Peppi.

Luca laughed. "I wasn't."

"It was a good ride," said Peppi, "and a wonderful meal, Filomena. I couldn't have hoped for more on my first day here."

"Where are you staying?" asked Maria.

"In Sulmona," replied Peppi. "But I plan to move back into the house I grew up in. It's still in my name."

"Where is the house?" she asked.

"A little ways outside of town," explained Peppi. "Just down the road, if I remember correctly. It's been so long. Perhaps you've seen it. It has a little mulino attached to it."

They all glanced at one another.

"The mulino?" said Filomena, her eyes meeting Luca's.

"Yes," said Peppi. "You know, I'm really looking forward to seeing it again. For so long it was just a distant memory in the back of my mind, almost as if I had imagined it. I don't think I ever gave it a thought all the time I was in America. But now that I'm back here and so close to it, I'm starting to feel a little excited. Your husband promised to take me by to see it later on."

"Yes, yes, of course," said Luca expansively. "But first we'll finish our dessert and then watch the television a little, eh? The last stage of the Tour of the Mediterranean is on this afternoon. We should relax, it's been a long day."

By the time they had retired to the living room, the bicycle race was nearing the finish. Peppi watched with great interest for he had never before seen live television coverage of a bicycle race. Cycling was only just beginning to catch on as a spectator sport in America. Even then the broadcasts were almost always tape-delayed segments edited to fill up a thirty-minute program. It was engrossing to see the race in its entirety, to watch all the action unfolding as it happened.

The time passed quickly and before Peppi knew it the sky had started to darken. Luca stood and stretched his arms over his head as he gazed out the window. The sun had already dropped from sight, leaving in its path a great splash of purple and orange across the tops of the mountains.

"It's getting late," said Luca with a yawn. "Soon it will be dark. I should probably drive you back to Sulmona. I can help you get your things and you can stay here for the night."

"Yes," Filomena agreed. "That's a good idea. You're welcome to stay."

"Thank you, but that's not necessary," said Peppi. "I've imposed enough on you for the first day."

"Nonsense," said Filomena. "It's been a pleasure."

"If we leave now, maybe it will still be light enough to see the mulino," Peppi said hopefully.

"Well—we'll see," said Luca. "But first I just wanted to make one quick stop on the way."

With Peppi's bike secured to the roof of Luca's car, they left the house soon after. Luca drove them to the piazza and stopped outside the local bar.

"Come on," he told Peppi, "there are some people inside I want you to meet."

Luca led him into the bar and ordered a round of drinks for everyone. By then, word of Peppi's return had already spread around town. To his amazement, Peppi recognized several of the old, grizzled faces grinning at him as they all drank to his health to welcome him back to Villa San Giuseppe. The others were strangers to him, but they too welcomed him back as if he were a long lost relative. They stayed there till well into the night, drinking and talking and remembering, until it was time for Luca to bring Peppi back to Sulmona. By then it was too dark and late to visit the mulino, but as they stepped into his car, Luca vowed that they would ride their bicycles out to it first thing the next morning.

CHAPTER ELEVEN

Peppi saw Luca waiting for him by the fountain when he pedalled into the piazza. It was early and, like Peppi, he was bundled up to keep warm in the morning chill. He greeted Peppi with a nod and the two pedalled off together.

"Where are we going?" asked Peppi. "I know I've been gone a long time, but I still remember that the mulino is in the other direction."

"I know," Luca replied, "but I thought we'd go this way first so I can show you a little more of the area around the town. That will give me a chance to get a few extra kilometers in before I go to the factory."

Peppi let his friend lead the way. As anxious as he now was to see the mulino, he was content to follow along. Luca was right, it would be a good chance for him to reacquaint himself with the area. They rolled along at a gentle pace, spinning their legs easily to work out the stiffness left over from the previous day's ride. As they passed the houses, Luca pointed out the ones in which their childhood friends had grown up.

"There's Ernesto's old house," he said, gesturing to one home. "And there's Tomassino's," he said, pointing out another. "You remember Tomassino. His father was the baker. They moved out years ago. Last I heard, Tomassino had married some girl from Naples, but I don't know what's become of him since."

On they went through the outskirts of the village, waving as they passed the children awaiting the morning school bus. Before long the village was behind them and they rode off into the rolling countryside beyond. The sun shone brightly through the chilly morning air and though they pedalled along at a gentle cadence, they were soon feeling warm enough to unzip their jackets. They rode for a while without speaking, each content for the time being simply to listen to the hypnotic whirring of their gears as they turned the pedals over and over.

"I've been thinking," Luca finally said.

"What else is there for men of our age to do?" noted Peppi.

His friend chuckled. "You have a point. But seriously, I've been thinking about the mulino."

"What about it?" said Peppi.

"Well, it's just that the house has been abandoned for so many years. There's no electricity, no running water. How are you going to manage there?"

"I'll make do," replied Peppi. "I don't need much."

"Maybe so," Luca went on, "but no matter what, you'll need some time to make the place livable. So I was thinking that perhaps you could stay with us for a while."

"No," said Peppi, genuinely grateful for the offer. "I couldn't impose on you and your family like that."

"What imposition?" said Luca with a wave of his hand. "You forget that my family once lived above the factory when I was a boy. We still have a whole apartment upstairs just sitting there empty. Someone might as well use it. And it might just as well be you until you get settled."

"We'll see," said Peppi with a smile, "we'll see. Now take me to my mulino."

"Sure," said Luca softly. Then he made the sign of the cross and pedalled on ahead.

Peppi followed close behind, the anticipation within him starting to grow. So many years had passed since he left Villa San Giuseppe, but the image of his boyhood home that he had always carried in his heart and mind was as vivid as ever. He could still remember the road that led out of the village, through the valley, and up a long gentle hill. How could he not, for he had pedalled up it countless times! The mulino stood just over the crest of the hill, set back from the road where a little stream tumbled down from the mountainside. As a boy he had spent endless afternoons fishing in the stream or simply lying on its banks, gazing up at the clouds in the crystal blue Abruzzo sky. Sometimes his father would join him and the two would just sit there quietly listening to the water as it babbled past them. Those tranquil moments were some of his favorite times. When he wasn't playing by the water, Peppi loved to ride his bicycle into town to visit friends and family. He became a familiar sight, darting in and out of every street and alleyway in Villa San Giuseppe. Whenever his aunts and uncles came to visit, one of them would inevitably pat him on the head and say to his father, "Sandro, how long will it be before your son is champion of Italy!"

But not all had been fun and games for Peppi. As soon as he was old enough, he worked side-by-side with his parents in the mulino. He arose early and worked grinding the cornmeal each morning for a few hours before walking to school, dusting himself off the whole way as he went. After school he would return home to help fill the sacks and prepare them to be carted off to market the next day. It was hard, simple work that didn't make them rich, but it gave them enough to keep the family together with a roof over their heads and bread on the table. Only fools, Peppi's father often told him, wanted more than that from life.

As he had promised, Luca led him on a route that looped back through the village and out onto the road that led to the mulino. He suddenly slowed, though, and beckoned for Peppi to come up alongside.

"Are you sure you want to go out there right now?" he asked.

"Of course," Peppi replied. "Why wait?"

Luca pursed his lips. "I was just thinking that maybe it would be better to go back to Sulmona and get your things first. Then we could do it all in one trip."

"Don't worry, my friend," laughed Peppi. "I've brought next to nothing with me. I could carry it all here by myself on my bike. *Andiamo!*"

Luca sighed. "Whatever you say."

Peppi could feel his heart pounding as they rode on. It was all coming back to him and soon he realized that he recognized the twists and turns of the road. So much had changed, but so much had stayed the same. Before long the road straightened and gradually began the long climb that Peppi knew would crest at the mulino. He could contain himself no longer, and with a burst of energy that he had not felt in months, he rose off the saddle and sprinted ahead of Luca.

"Wait!" Luca cried after him. "Not so fast!"

But Peppi raced on toward the top of the hill, eager to see the roof of the mulino come into view as he drew near. He pedalled and pedalled as hard as he could until he felt the road starting to level off. He was near the top of the hill, but still the roof of the mulino was nowhere in sight. He was certain he should have seen it by now. Had he been mistaken that this was the road? Was the mulino farther along than he remembered? Peppi had his answer when he coasted over the crest of the hill and came to a stop.

His heart sank.

Peppi had not been mistaken, the mulino was right there, just where he remembered it, except what was once a proud, strong building was now nothing more than a pile of rubble. Peppi laid his bike down and stood there gaping at the scene.

Luca rolled up behind him and laid his bike next to Peppi's. "I didn't have the heart to tell you, my friend," he said sadly, patting him on the shoulder. "None of us did."

"But what happened?" said Peppi, bewildered.

"*Terremoto,*" sighed Luca, shaking his head. "An earthquake, the same one that knocked all the frescoes off the ceilings in Assisi. Around here it was next to nothing, a little rumble in the ground, barely an echo of the big one. But for some reason it hit this spot just right. Who knows, maybe the stream made the earth settle deep underneath the house. Or maybe there was a crack in the foundation. But whatever the reason, when the ground shook just that little bit, one wall fell and the rest caved in like a house of cards. Just incredible."

Still stunned, Peppi wandered closer, trying hard to rebuild in his mind the image of the mulino out of the shattered ruins that lay before him. Try as he might, Peppi could not force his imagination to do it, for his home was now nothing but a pile of rock and splintered beams. Even the great stone wheel of the mill was toppled over and half-buried.

Peppi walked to the back and gazed out toward the stream that still flowed lazily past the site. He sat down on the dry earth and leaned back against part of the crumbled wall. Closing his eyes, he thought of his childhood and he thought of Anna. He thought about how his life had brought him full circle to this spot and how everything he once cherished had now been destroyed. Peppi wanted to cry, but there were no more tears left in him.

Luca came to his side and sat down next to him. He said nothing, for he could think of no words that would comfort his friend.

Peppi opened his eyes and gazed off into the distance. "It's all gone now," he said, his voice heavy with the feeling of surrender. "Now what do I do?"

Luca looked off with him into the distance. "You come home with me," he said finally. "You sleep and eat and rest, and then you figure out a way."

"A way to do what?" said Peppi.

Luca stood and tugged on Peppi's arm. "A way to start over again," he said. Then he pulled Peppi up and led him back to his bicycle.

CHAPTER TWELVE

It was a little apartment, just one small bedroom, a kitchen, and a bathroom with a shower. A heavy, musty smell greeted them when Luca opened the door, for the apartment had been locked up and left unused for many years. All was still within. They were in the quiet part of the building. Most of the comings and goings in the factory downstairs took place on the opposite end. Below the apartment were the company offices and a few storage areas.

The shades were all drawn and the scant rays of sunlight that managed to filter their way in from the outside spread across the room like a dim, gray film. Luca tried the light switch, but the bulb overhead was dead. He stepped inside, parted the shades, and threw open one of the windows. A rush of fresh air and sunlight brought the room to life. Luca turned and beckoned Peppi in.

"It's not the Pitti Palace," he said with a shrug.

"I'm not royalty," Peppi replied. "This will do just fine."

"Good," smiled Luca. "Let's go get your things."

When they returned from Sulmona there was a great commotion in the factory. At first, as Peppi and Luca carried the luggage up the walkway, it sounded as if there were many people screaming at each other inside. As they drew nearer, however, it became clear that only one voice was doing most of the screaming.

"*Imbecilli!*" came the shrill cry of a woman's voice. "Are all of you fools!" The sound of doors slamming followed. Shortly thereafter, a smartly dressed woman with copper red hair and dark wild eyes burst from the building and stomped toward them in a blaze of fury.

"*O, Dio,*" muttered Luca.

"*Sono tutti imbecilli!*" the woman declared as she blew past Peppi and Luca like an express train barrelling down the tracks. "They are all idiots and I can't stand to look at them for another moment today. *You* deal with them!"

With that the woman hurled herself into a nearby car, started the engine, and tore away from the building in a cloud of dust.

"*Madonna mia,*" said Peppi. "Who was that?"

Luca looked down and shook his head. "Uff," he grunted. "That was Lucrezia—my daughter."

Peppi looked off into the distance at the car speeding away. "I think she's having a bad day," he remarked.

"That's bad news for us all," sighed Luca. "Let's go find out what happened."

They left Peppi's bags by the door and went inside. The workers were huddled at the far end of the factory, their voices raised in fits of mutual recrimination. At seeing Luca enter, they rushed over to him en masse, all of them beside themselves with anguish. Their hands open in supplication, their faces the very picture of contriteness, they all began pleading with him at the same time. Those who could not catch Luca's eye turned helplessly to Peppi, who could offer no other consolation than a sympathetic shrug.

"Please forgive us, Signor Luca!" some cried.

"It was all our fault," others admitted.

"It was an accident, we didn't mean it," cried others still.

Luca held his hand up for quiet. "Calm yourself," he implored them. *"Ch' è successo?* What happened?"

At that they all began talking at once again, each trying to tell his version of the story. Luca held his hand up again for quiet.

"One at a time," he told them, "one at a time!" He pointed to one of his supervisors. "You there, Enzo, you go first. Tell me what happened."

"It was an accident," cried Enzo, tears filling his eyes.

"I think we've pretty well established that fact," sighed Luca. "Now tell me all about it from the beginning."

"It all started first thing this morning," he began, "when they brought in the new shipment of boxes."

Enzo went on to recount the whole wretched tale. The boxes, he told Luca, through some act of God (for how else could these sort of things be explained?), had somehow gotten themselves switched. The boxes for the chocolate-filled candies were packed away where those for the vanilla-filled candies were normally stored, and vice versa. The workers began the day expecting to fill a large order of the chocolate-filled for the company's distributor in the Veneto region.

By this point in his telling of the story, the beads of sweat were rolling off poor Enzo's forehead. "We finished making the chocolate-filled and started to pack them into the boxes," he continued, his voice full of torment. "We'd been going for a while when your daughter came out of the office because she wanted to take a box of confetti to a friend. I said I'd get it right away for her, but when I brought her the box she said,

'No, Enzo, I don't want vanilla. I want chocolate.' *Dio mio,* that's when I knew something was wrong!"

"Let me guess," sighed Luca, giving Peppi a sideways glance. "You packed the chocolates in the vanilla boxes."

"Santo Giuseppe," cried Enzo, "when your daughter found out, I thought she was going to cut off our heads!"

Luca looked at him kindly. "Now now," he reassured them all, "I'm sure it wasn't as bad as all that. How many boxes did you fill before my daughter discovered what was happening?"

Enzo scratched the back of his neck. "Difficult to say," he replied sheepishly, a pained look coming over his face. "Thirty dozen, perhaps. Maybe a little more, maybe a little less." He cast his gaze down toward the floor and shook his head. "What a waste," he sighed.

At hearing the amount, Luca made a pained expression of his own. He gave a little cough and scratched his chin for a few moments. The workers gazed at him in suspense. "Well," he said at last, clearing his throat, "it's not the end of the world, is it? Life gives us lemons, we'll make lemonade."

"I'm not sure I know what you mean, Signor Luca," said Enzo.

"Don't worry," he said, patting Enzo on the shoulder, "it's an old American saying I once heard. Now tell me, besides being in the wrong boxes, is there anything wrong with the candies?"

"Nothing at all," Enzo assured him.

"And you followed the family recipe," Luca continued, "the one that was handed down to me from generation to generation?"

"To the letter," said Enzo with conviction.

"Then other than being in the wrong boxes, the candies you

made today are still of the highest quality, the quality that has made them popular all over Italy?" said Luca expansively.

"But of course!" replied Enzo with fierce pride. "We would produce nothing less."

"Then everything is okay," said Luca with a smile. "We'll just take those thirty dozen boxes and give them away at the schools or the churches. Or maybe there's some local charity that would love to have them to resell to raise money. We'll find a use for them. Nothing will go to waste."

The color was starting to come back into Enzo's face and an audible sigh of relief rippled through the workers all gathered around. "Are you sure, Signor Luca?" said Enzo, visibly grateful for the reprieve.

"I'm sure," said Luca. Then he gave them a stern gaze. "Now, you still have a big order to fill, so back to work, all of you!"

"Subito!" they answered in unison as they scurried back to their positions. *"Grazie, Signor Luca!"*

"And don't forget to use the right boxes this time!" Luca called after them.

Peppi stood by Luca's side and watched the workers return to their jobs. Soon the factory was humming again like a beehive.

"You handled that very well," said Peppi. "But your workers seem a little intimidated by your daughter."

"They're terrified of her," said Luca. "But you know, they love her too."

"That's a strange mix," said Peppi. "How did it come about?"

"It's a long story, my friend," he sighed. "I'll tell you about it another time. For now, let's get you settled in."

"D'accordo," Peppi agreed, and the two walked out to get his luggage.

"But thirty dozen boxes," Luca muttered to himself. "What imbeciles!"

After they brought the luggage to the apartment, Luca promised to send someone up to give the place a thorough cleaning. Peppi, though, insisted on taking care of things himself. The thought of Peppi doing a woman's work mortified Luca, but despite his protestations he could not make Peppi change his mind. He reluctantly gave in to Peppi's wishes and headed back to the house to change his clothes for work.

Peppi stood alone in the middle of the kitchen, assessing his new home. The years of disuse had left a healthy coating of dust over everything, but otherwise the apartment appeared to be in good repair. Peppi set himself to work right away. He threw open all the windows to air the place out while he began sweeping the floors. When he was finished he wiped down the woodwork and cupboards before turning his attention to the kitchen and bathroom sinks. The plumbing fixtures were quite old, but they all seemed to work when he turned on the water. A steady trickle of water, however, dripped from one of the faucets, so Peppi made a note to change all the washers.

Next he examined the old refrigerator that stood in the corner of the kitchen. He plugged it in and, much to his surprise, it sputtered to life. He left it running while he checked the little gas stove against the adjacent wall. All the burners seemed to be in working order. Both appliances needed a good cleaning, but he would get to that later. First he wanted to look over the few pieces of furniture in the apartment. The little kitchen table was flanked by two sturdy-looking chairs. Other than these there was only the bed and a small bureau in the bedroom. Peppi went in and sat on the mattress. It was old and musty like everything else in the apartment, but it seemed comfortable enough. He would buy a cover for it and it would do fine.

Later, after his new domicile had been rendered passably habitable, Peppi took a walk into the village to buy a few groceries, some light bulbs, and other provisions. Luca had invited him to dinner that evening, but Peppi had declined, explaining that he needed to be alone for a little while to adjust to things. Luca, though disappointed, understood.

On the way back from the village, Peppi's arms were beginning to ache from the strain of carrying the two bags of groceries he had purchased. It was then that he happened to pass a house in front of which its owner had left an old bicycle leaning up against the wall. The bike had a small *"da vendere"* sign taped to it. As he walked closer, Peppi could see that the bike had not been ridden in years. The tires were worn and the frame had spots of rust on it, but what interested him most was the basket suspended above the rear wheel. Peppi set down the groceries, went up to the front door, and gave it a knock.

"How much for the bike?" he asked when the door opened.

That night Peppi ate a simple meal of bread and cheese and a little fruit before spending some time fixing up the old bike he had purchased that afternoon. With a little lubricant to loosen the chain and maybe some new tires, it would be perfect for getting around on when he wanted to run an errand. When he was finished with it, he leaned the bike in the corner next to his Colnago. Between the two bicycles he had all the transportation he needed.

Before going to bed, Peppi sat at the kitchen table and wrote a letter to Angie as he had promised her he would do once he was settled into the mulino. He told her of his trip from Rome and how he had met up once again with Luca. He told her about finding the mulino in ruins, but assured her there was no need to worry; Luca had given him a place to stay. So, for the time being, he had a roof over his head and food on the table. One way or the other, it seemed that life would go on for him.

CHAPTER THIRTEEN

"What are you doing?"

The woman's brusque voice startled Peppi, causing him to drop the screwdriver he was using to tighten the hinges of the front door to the factory. He had noticed that they were loose the previous day when he walked in with Luca. The door had probably been hanging like that for months; it was practically ready to fall off. Repairing it, he knew, was one of those minor but annoying jobs that everyone always means to take care of as soon as they get the chance, but no one ever actually gets around to doing. Peppi wanted to make himself useful, so he decided to come down early and take care of it himself first thing that morning, before the workers began to arrive.

With the woman hovering ominously above him, Peppi picked up the screwdriver, gave the screw he was tightening one last quick turn, and stood. As he rose, his eyes could not help but be drawn to the sleek lines of the woman's slender legs. These eventually led his gaze upward across a graceful, curvaceous figure until finally Peppi found himself face to face with Lucrezia, Luca's daughter. He recognized her instantly from their brief encounter a day earlier when Lucrezia had stormed out of the factory.

"What are you doing?" she asked once more.

"Buon giorno, Signorina," Peppi replied, tipping his cap while

he tried to avoid her icy glare. "I was just fixing the door. It was getting ready to fall off, you know."

"Yes, I was well aware of that," she said testily. "But who are you? Who hired you?"

"I'm a friend of your father," said Peppi. "My name is—"

"I should have known," huffed Lucrezia before he had a chance to finish. "Just don't take all day to do it. The office will give you a check when you're done." She gave him a look of utter disdain and with a click of her tongue strode past him into the factory.

Slightly bemused, Peppi watched Lucrezia walk down the center aisle until she disappeared around the corner and the building reverberated with the echo of her office door slamming shut. He turned around to find one of the factory workers standing behind him. He too had been watching Lucrezia with admiring eyes.

"Bella, no?" he said with a big grin. "What legs! But look out, she's a force of nature."

"So I gather," Peppi said with a chuckle.

When he arrived a short while later that morning, Luca was mortified to find Peppi sweeping the floor by the entrance.

"Peppi!" he cried in horror, clutching his chest as if his heart were about to burst. "What in the name of God are you doing?"

Peppi leaned on the broom handle and smiled at his friend. "I'm just trying to earn my keep," he said.

"By sweeping the floors!"

"Well, somebody has to do it," said Peppi, nodding to the workers behind him, "and everyone else looks busy."

"Mannagia," said Luca, shaking his head. "My friend comes

back to Villa San Giuseppe after God knows how many years. His wife, may she rest in peace, is dead, his ancestral home destroyed, he has nowhere to go, and I'm supposed to put him to work sweeping floors so he can stay in a drafty old apartment that no one has used in a hundred years? What are you trying to do, make me look like some kind of *orco* in front of the rest of the village?"

"Of course not," laughed Peppi. "Please, don't worry, *amico mio.* I enjoy staying busy. It makes me feel useful."

Luca let out a grumble of consternation and took the broom from Peppi. He leaned it against the wall and put his arm around his friend's shoulders.

"Go back to your room and rest, Peppi," he said, guiding him toward the door. "Yesterday was a traumatic day for you, and for me as well. Take some time, get your feet settled on the earth again, and then we'll talk about how to keep you busy."

"Eh, maybe you're right," said Peppi. "I just wanted to help, that's all."

"You've helped already," said Luca with a big smile. "You don't know how much. So go now. And tonight you have dinner with us, no excuses."

"Okay," said Peppi, opening the door, "you go on to work now. I'll see you tonight."

"*Va bene,*" said Luca. He turned to go, but then stopped and gazed at the door. "Hey," he said brightly, "who fixed the hinges?"

Peppi answered with a shrug. Luca gave a shrug of his own and headed off to his office. As soon as he was out of sight, Peppi stepped back inside, grabbed the broom, and continued sweeping.

* * *

Filomena welcomed Peppi at the door when he arrived for dinner that evening. She ushered him in, fretting all the while about how he was doing after the previous day's shock.

"You poor thing," she said, shaking her head as she guided him to the living room. "My husband wanted so badly to tell you about the mulino before taking you out there, but he just couldn't bring himself to do it. Here, sit down and relax while I get you something to drink. Luca just went downstairs to get a bottle of wine. He'll be back in a minute. Luca! Peppi is here!"

Later, when the three sat down at the dinner table, Peppi noticed the extra setting at the place beside him.

"For my daughter Lucrezia," she said as she ladled out the minestrone. "That is, if she ever gets here. She's still down in that office of hers doing God only knows what."

Peppi glanced at the clock. "She certainly works long hours," he said.

"You're right," sighed Luca, "but there's no talking to her about it. The truth is, I'd be in trouble without her. Do you know that since I first let her start managing most of the daily operations our sales have almost tripled? She's relentless; she runs the place with an iron hand. But the workers all respect her because she herself works like a slave."

"She should work so hard at the rest of her life," observed Filomena with a hint of irritation in her voice. "The clock is running out, you know."

"Everything in its time," said Luca. He smiled and shrugged when he saw the questioning look on Peppi's face. "My daughter is forty-one and my wife is anxious for more grandchildren," he explained.

"Ah," said Peppi. "I understand. But your daughter is so attractive. Why hasn't she ever married?"

Luca was about to reply when the door opened and Lucrezia herself stepped inside. She carried a briefcase in one hand and an armful of files in the other. These she promptly dropped onto the kitchen counter before coming into the dining room. She stopped short when she saw Peppi at the table, her cheeks turning almost as red as her hair.

"Lucrezia, *finalmente,*" said Luca. "What have you been doing?"

"I had some things to finish up," she said, self-consciously pushing a strand of hair away from her face. "I didn't notice the time."

"Well, work is over, so come in and eat. This is my good friend, Peppi, the one I was telling you about last night."

"Hello again," said Peppi, hoping to put her at ease.

"You two have already met?" said Luca.

"Well, yes," murmured Lucrezia, "you might say we . . ."

"We had a nice chat this morning just before you arrived, Luca," said Peppi, giving her a smile.

"Lucrezia, don't stand there like a statue, go sit down!" Filomena ordered.

Lucrezia took her seat beside Peppi, reached over to the minestrone, and filled her bowl. She glanced at Peppi as she started to eat her soup.

"I'm sorry we didn't have the chance to talk longer this morning," she said awkwardly. "I was . . . in a hurry."

"No need to apologize, I understand," said Peppi.

"She's always in a hurry," said Filomena.

"The world is in a hurry," remarked Luca. Then he went off on a tangent, complaining about the pace of modern life, the cutthroat nature of the business world, and the pressures it all brought to bear on the modern family. He would have expounded further had Filomena not intervened by suggesting that he should run for parliament if he felt so strongly.

"This is what I have to put up with every night at dinner," she lamented while she cleared the bowls and set out the plates for the main course.

Lucrezia looked at Peppi and rolled her eyes. "And I have to listen to both of *them* every night at dinner," she said.

Peppi smiled, glad to hear Lucrezia speak to him, if only because it meant that his presence there had not entirely ruined her dinner. It was then that he observed the wedding ring on her finger. Luca had never answered him before when he asked why Lucrezia wasn't married. He saw no harm in asking now.

"Lucrezia, I couldn't help wondering about something," said Peppi. "I see that you wear a wedding ring, but I don't think I've heard mention of your husband."

Peppi immediately regretted bringing up the subject for a pall fell over the table. Luca gave a nervous cough and Filomena bit her lip. The two gazed with anxious eyes at their daughter, who stared vacantly at her plate. After what seemed an interminable silence, she pushed herself away from the table and stood.

"I don't talk about my husband," she said, barely above a whisper, "not with anyone—not ever. You'll excuse me now." Then she left the table and hurried out of the room.

"Lucrezia!" Filomena called. She looked upward with exasperated eyes, as if she were seeking divine guidance, before excusing herself to hurry out after her daughter.

Peppi looked helplessly at Luca. "I'm so sorry," he said. "I didn't mean to upset everyone."

"Don't worry," Luca reassured him with a wave of his hand. He let out a long sigh and shook his head. "It's not your fault, my friend. It's no one's fault really—except maybe God's. I should have told you sooner."

"Told me what?" said Peppi.

Luca beckoned for Peppi to pass him his glass. He filled it with wine and passed it back. "Lucrezia *was* married," he began, filling his own glass, "to a nice boy from Sulmona." He took a long sip of wine before continuing. "His name was Francesco. He had a good job working for his family's jewelry business. You should have seen the gifts he would bring to her after they first met! He worshipped my daughter, all the boys in town did. And she worshipped him in return. They seemed like a perfect match. So, to make a long story short, they finally ended up marrying. And it was a good marriage. They were very happy, and we were happy for them."

"What happened?" asked Peppi.

Luca took another long sip of wine and put his glass down. "Francesco travelled around quite a bit for business. He was driving home after a meeting in Napoli. It was a rainy night and the roads through these mountains are so dark. He couldn't see up ahead that the pavement was crumbling near the side of the road. He took the turn too fast and the car skidded off the embankment."

Luca stopped and stared sadly at his glass. He downed the rest of the wine and poured himself some more. "And that was that," he said with a shrug. *"Arriverderci, Francesco."*

"How long ago did it happen?" asked Peppi.

"Oh, almost ten years now," answered Luca, "but it seems like yesterday. Francesco was a good boy, and a good husband to my daughter. We were all heartbroken when it happened, naturally. But life goes on. We all got over it, everyone except Lucrezia, that is. To this day she won't say a word about it."

"And she's never found anyone else?"

"No," said Luca. "After it was all over, she just buried herself in work and has stayed there ever since. Sure, she has her friends, and now and then they'll try to introduce her to someone new, but Lucrezia won't let anyone get too close to her. It's like she's afraid to get hurt again."

"I know that feeling," said Peppi before taking a sip of his wine.

"We all come to know it, sooner or later," said Luca. "What can you do? That's just the way of things."

CHAPTER FOURTEEN

Angie opened the mailbox and pulled out the stack of mail piled inside. She flipped the box cover closed and headed back to the house, sifting through the assortment of bills and catalogs and credit card offers as she went. Most of it looked like junk mail, but then she saw the envelope from Italy.

"Finalmente," she sighed in relief.

Angie hurried back inside, tossed the junk mail in the trash, and sat down at the kitchen table. She ripped open the envelope and took out the letter.

"Hey, Carmine!" she called to her husband. "Come downstairs, we have a letter from Peppi."

By the time Carmine made it to the kitchen, Angie had already finished reading the letter. She motioned for him to sit down while she read it a second time. Dressed in his bathrobe and slippers, Carmine stood there scratching his side.

"What's he say?" he asked with a yawn.

"Shh! I'm almost through."

Carmine sat across from her and drummed his fingers on the table. He turned hopeful eyes to the coffeemaker on the counter, but to his disappointment he observed that it stood empty. "What's this?" he said, picking up the folded sheet of paper next to the envelope.

Angie reached out and snatched it from his hand. "That's not for you," she said testily.

"Then who's it for!" exclaimed Carmine, throwing up his hands.

"It's for his friends at the barber shop, Mister Nosy," she snipped.

"What, he's got something to tell his friends that he can't tell us?"

"No," said Angie with a grumble of irritation, "he says just about all the same things as he does in this letter."

"And how do you know that?"

"I read it. How do you think?"

Carmine rolled his eyes.

"Come on," he said, tugging her arm, "let me see what Peppi has to say for himself."

Angie finally gave him the letter. While he read, she got up and went to the telephone to call Delores. The line was busy, though, so she hung up the phone and waited to try again.

Carmine looked up at her.

"The mulino was destroyed?" he said in disbelief. "I thought you said the thing was built like a fortress."

"That's what they told me when I was a little girl!" cried Angie. "I never even saw the thing. Besides, even fortresses don't last forever."

"Geez, must have been a shock for him," said Carmine, turning his attention back to the letter. "To go all that way for nothing."

"Maybe now he'll come to his senses and come back home where he belongs," said Angie.

"I don't know," said Carmine thoughtfully. "I wouldn't bet on it. From what he writes, I'd say he's settling in there for good."

"What are you talking about?" said his wife, picking up the receiver. "You think he's going to spend the rest of his life cooped up in a little apartment out in the middle of nowhere?"

Carmine shrugged and went back to reading the letter while Angie dialed Delores's number again. Annoyingly, the line was still busy. She stood there by the telephone, waiting to try once more.

"Coffee would be nice," suggested Carmine from behind the letter.

Later, at the barber shop, Tony tried to read aloud the letter from Peppi that Carmine had dropped off. Doing so was no easy task given the constant interruptions from the others.

"So what else does he say?" asked Ralph eagerly. "Come on, Tony, keep reading!"

"Yeah, come on," agreed Gino and Sal.

"All right, all right," said Tony, waving his hand at them. "Gimme a chance here." He held up the letter to the light. "Okay, where was I? Here I am. He says, 'I met up with Luca on my first Sunday here just like I told you I would.' "

"How about that!" exclaimed Gino, laughing along with the others. "After how many years?"

Tony continued reading. " 'We went on a nice long ride with a big group of riders,' he says. 'I'm a little out of shape, but Luca and the others took it easy on me. Things have changed since I left, but the region is still as beautiful as I remembered.' "

"What about the mulino?" said Ralph.

"Hold on, let's see what he says," replied Tony. "Blah, blah, blah. Okay, here we go. 'I had dinner with Luca and his family that night,' he says. 'The next day we went out to see the mulino.' "

"I bet it was just like he remembered," said Ralph.

"Nah," said Sal. "The house you grew up in never looks the same when you go back and see it after you've grown up. It always looks way smaller. When I was a kid I thought our house in the old neighborhood was a castle. Now, when I drive by it sometimes, it looks like a little shack to me. I can't believe we all fit in it."

"Well, you certainly couldn't fit into it now with that gut of yours," said Gino.

"Are you guys gonna let me finish this letter or what?" said Tony.

"Go on, go on," said Ralph. "Keep reading."

"All right," Tony continued. " 'We rode our bikes out of the village but down a road I knew didn't lead to the mulino. Luca told me he just wanted to go for a longer ride, that we'd end up there later. All the while he kept saying that maybe we should go out to the mulino some other day. I couldn't figure out what was making him so anxious. It wasn't until we finally arrived there that I understood.' "

Tony paused, put the letter down, and rubbed his eyes.

"What is it?" said Sal. "What's the matter?"

"Come on," added Gino. "Let's hear the rest of it."

"If you say so," said Tony with a grim expression. He picked the letter back up. " 'The mulino had been destroyed by an earthquake,' " he read. " 'So now my home that I came all the way back to across the ocean is nothing but a pile of rocks.' "

Stunned by the news, they all sat there without speaking.

"*Che cozz'!*" cried Gino, breaking the silence. "All that friggin' way for nothing!"

"Can you believe it?" muttered Sal.

"But I don't understand," said Ralph. "How could something like this happen?"

The three of them carried on about the whole thing while Tony finished reading the letter to himself. When he was done, he folded it and tossed it into a drawer in the little desk he kept in the corner of the shop.

"But what's he going to do?" said Ralph. "Where's he going to live?"

"He says he's gonna stay with Luca for now," Tony replied. "Other than that, I guess he's gonna wait and see."

"Wait and see what?" said Gino. "He should get back on a plane and come home. What's to keep him there?"

"That's probably what he wants to wait and see," said Tony.

At that they all sat back once more and sulked in silence. The bell on the door jingled and a customer walked in for a haircut. Tony put on a smile and welcomed the gentleman. As he went to work, the others went back to reading the morning newspapers.

"The mulino," said Ralph, scanning the obituaries. "Destroyed. Can you believe it?"

"I can believe it," said Gino, opening up the sports section. "That's just Peppi's luck."

"Yeah," muttered Sal. "But you know what the worst part is?"

The other two looked at him and shrugged. Sal shook his head and picked up the front page.

"No polenta"—he sighed as he began to read—"with the *sausicc'*. . . and the rabes."

Sal looked up just in time to get hit in the face with the towel Tony had flung at him.

CHAPTER FIFTEEN

In the dream, Peppi saw Anna. Dressed all in white, she was standing far away from him across a great body of water. Despite the distance, Peppi felt that she was near to him in that way that's only possible in a dream. Happy, he waved and called to her.

A fierce gale was blowing now and the wind whipped the spray off the tops of the waves. Anna, her hair tossed wildly across her face, waved and called back to him. He could see that she was trying to tell him something, but try as he might, Peppi could not hear what she was saying. The waves swelled up, forcing Peppi to climb higher, but slowly Anna disappeared from sight.

When Peppi opened his eyes he found himself looking at the picture of Anna he kept on the table by the bed. He reached out to it and let his finger trace the outline of her face. His touch lingered there for a time before he finally sat up and looked over to the window where a soft warm breeze was nudging the drapes. The first rays of the morning sun splashed intermittently across the room. Slowly Peppi rose out of bed and walked across the floor. He pushed the drapes aside and opened the window.

Up the hill behind Luca's house, the rooster was making his usual morning commotion. Peppi yawned and gazed down below at the little courtyard behind the building. In the middle was a stone bench beneath an old arbor strangled by a sprawl of dry, withered grapevines that had been left untended for years. They would not stay withered for long, however, as it was obvious that the first hints of spring were in the air. Soon they would start growing again with renewed, if haphazard vigor.

Peppi let his gaze fall over the gardens that bordered the courtyard. Like the grapevines, they too lay in tangled disarray, the result of long neglect. Peppi understood how things had been allowed to degenerate into their present state. Gardens required much time and attention, both of which he knew were in short supply in Luca's busy life. Luca might easily have hired someone to take care of it all for him, but Peppi also understood that Luca was one of those men who felt that if life conspired to prevent them from doing certain things, then perhaps those things were best left undone altogether.

As Peppi looked over the scene it occurred to him how much the courtyard and gardens reminded him of his own backyard in America. He felt a familiar longing tugging at his heart. The early spring had always been a time when Peppi itched to get outside, to clean away the dead remnants of winter and make way for new life to appear. He loved to plunge his hands into the soft earth, to feel its cool richness as it ran through his fingers. He loved the feel of the warm sun on his shoulders as he planted and pruned and fussed over every detail of his garden. It was his chance to make things grow, to play for a little while at being the Creator.

Peppi longed to play that role again. He took a deep breath and let the morning's warmth fill him. Gazing at the gardens, a plan began to form in his head. In his mind he could see new bushes blossoming along the walls on the perimeter of the courtyard; he could see the grapes hanging neatly down from the arbor over the bench; he could see the flower beds bursting forth in their rightful splendor.

Peppi scratched his chin as he mulled it all over. He knew where all the gardening tools were stored. Whatever else he needed he could buy in town. Luca, however, would be a problem. He was sure to protest if Peppi asked his permission to take over the gardening duties on his behalf. That being the case, Peppi decided not to bother asking.

As eager as Peppi was to get to work on the gardens, however, he was equally anxious to get out on his bike and take a quick training ride. It was far too beautiful a morning to waste the opportunity, so he dressed quickly, filled his water bottles, and hurried downstairs with his Colnago.

The village was just coming to life as Peppi rolled along at a gentle pace past the bakery and across the piazza. The baker, as always, had already been at work for hours and the warm smell of freshly baked bread was everywhere. It blended pleasantly with the aroma of hot coffee wafting from the cafes and bars. Further along the shopkeepers were out in force, sweeping the sidewalks in front of their stores while the restaurant and trattoria owners set out their tables and chairs in anticipation of the rush of lunchtime patrons who would no doubt be eager to dine *al fresco* that afternoon. All around car engines were grumbling to life as commuters prepared to head off to work.

As Peppi neared the opposite side of the village, a motorist came up from behind and gave a friendly toot on the horn to let him know that the car was overtaking him. The driver swerved to the left to avoid Peppi as they approached the hill that descended from the piazza. To the right, the road hugged the narrow strip of sidewalk that bordered the houses. To the left, however, the ragged edge of the road gave way to a steep embankment that plunged down to the banks of the little stream below. The car skidded on the crumbling pavement, but the driver righted it in time to keep from tumbling over the edge.

Peppi shook his head as he watched the car speed away. Such brushes with fate were, he well knew, part of the daily routine of Italian drivers. The brief thrill of a near miss always provided the required rush of adrenaline that often got them through the day, or at least until their next cup of espresso.

As he coasted down the hill, Peppi drifted over to the left to take a closer look at the pavement near the edge of the road. Given its state of disrepair, it was only a matter of time before someone had an accident. He made a mental note to mention it to Luca. Then he pedalled off down the road, thinking all the way about Anna and his dream and how happy it had made him for a few sleepy moments. He looked up at the sun beaming down on the countryside. It was such a beautiful morning that he decided to stay out for a longer ride than he had originally planned, perhaps even take a spin past the mulino. What was the hurry? He had all day and the gardens would still be there when he returned.

CHAPTER SIXTEEN

Lucrezia looked out the window as she massaged the sides of her forehead. It had been a busy, hectic day; she had been on the run from the moment she rolled out of bed early that morning. First there was a meeting in Sulmona with one of the company's vendors. Later, she had to drive to Ancona to meet with one of the distributors. Next came a stop in Pescara to talk with a church group that was interested in taking some of the incorrectly boxed candies off the company's hands. That meeting took longer than expected, putting her behind schedule. She practically flew home along the roads through the mountains back to Villa San Giuseppe for a marketing meeting that afternoon in her office at the factory. Punctuality was a point of honor with Lucrezia. She demanded it of others as well as herself and she had been determined to arrive on time lest she lose face with her staff.

To no one's surprise, she made it with time to spare.

It was midafternoon now. The meeting had ended a few minutes earlier, but Lucrezia still had not found a free moment to eat or drink a thing all day. Her head was splitting.

Out in the courtyard, she saw a man on his knees, toiling away in the gardens. It had turned surprisingly warm that afternoon and the man had removed his shirt. Despite her headache, Lucrezia strained to see who it was, but the man's head was hidden from view in the bushes where he was working. It didn't matter, for what had really caught her eye was the way the rivulets of sweat rolling off his skin made his well-muscled back and shoulders glisten in the sun. For a moment she lost herself in a daydream as she stared at him. Distracted as she was, she didn't hear Filomena come into her office.

"You should go have something to eat," she said abruptly, interrupting her daughter's reverie.

Embarrassed, Lucrezia whirled away from the window, knocking a stack of files and other assorted papers from her desk onto the floor. Hurriedly, she stooped down to pick them up.

"You look terrible," her mother continued, standing over her. "You're too skinny, and see this mess, you're turning into a real *zolla* from not feeding your brain."

"Please, Mama," Lucrezia pleaded with a sigh. "I've had such a day today."

"Why? Where were you running around to today?" said Filomena.

"Sulmona, then Ancona, then later back to Pescara before I came back here," explained her daughter as she restored the stack of files and papers to their former spot on the desk. "I got stuck behind a pack of cyclists on the way and almost didn't make it back on time for my afternoon meeting. The bastards were spread across the road and wouldn't let me by for almost fifteen minutes. They drive me crazy sometimes."

"Mmm," purred Filomena. "They drive me crazy sometimes too, the way they look in those skin-tight suits they wear these days."

"Mama!" cried Lucrezia.

"What," scoffed her mother, "I'm supposed to be like you

and pretend that I don't notice when men look good? What do you think it was that first attracted me to your father, his intelligence and charm?"

"The way you talk sometimes," said Lucrezia with a shake of her head and an exasperated sigh. The truth of the matter, though, was that Lucrezia *did* notice men, but whenever she gave even a passing glance to one she found attractive, she was immediately beset by the anguished feeling that somehow she was betraying Francesco. Just that morning, she had lingered in bed, as she often did, remembering her husband. His touch. His smell. The feel of his body against hers. Even after almost ten years, it was all still so vivid in her mind.

Just the same, Lucrezia could not help admiring the sleek body of a very fit-looking cyclist she happened to pass a little while later as she zoomed across the piazza on the way to her first meeting of the day. Her eyes instinctively roamed across the outline of his back and shoulders, his well-rounded backside and the hard, sinewy legs that turned over the pedals with power and grace. As she passed the man, Lucrezia found herself trying to catch a glimpse of his face instead of watching the road. To her chagrin she inadvertently swerved too far to the left and came within inches of skidding off the embankment. The close call shook her awake and Lucrezia sped away from the village, tormented with guilt and self-loathing at the indiscretion. It was a terrible start to her day.

Now, those same guilty feelings had returned to haunt her as she glanced back out the window at the gardener. He was still half-concealed by the bushes, but she could see his strong arms and hands working away at the soil. Lucrezia sat down in her chair and tried to focus attention on her work.

"You need a man," said Filomena. "I'm your mother and it's

my job to tell you these things. You have to let go of Francesco and start to live your life again. There, I've said it."

"I don't want to talk about this," said Lucrezia, refusing to look up at her mother. She shuffled the papers around on her desk, pretending to be busy.

"Well, you have to talk about it," Filomena persisted. "You're still young now, but if you're not careful, someday you're going to wake up and realize that you've become an old woman with no one to share your life with. There's no need for you to live your life all alone. It's not natural and it's certainly not necessary. It's time to put away the black dress and start all over again."

Lucrezia made no reply but continued to look down at her desk, acting as though she was still working. Filomena folded her arms and scowled at her daughter. Exasperated, she threw up her hands and turned to go.

"Who did Papa hire to tend the gardens?" Lucrezia asked suddenly.

Filomena stopped and turned back around. "What do you mean?" she asked.

"The gardener out back in the courtyard," said Lucrezia without looking up, "when did Papa hire him? He said nothing to me about it."

Filomena stepped up to the window. "That's because he didn't hire anyone," she said, gazing out.

"Then who is that in the garden?"

"It's Peppi." Her mother laughed. "Who did you think it was?"

"Peppi?" said Lucrezia. She whirled around and looked out the window in time to see Peppi stand and pull on his shirt. Having finished for the day, he began to pick up his gardening

tools and toss them one by one into the wheelbarrow. As he was preparing to leave, he looked up and noticed the two women watching him from the window. With a smile, he tipped his cap to them and walked away, pushing the wheelbarrow ahead of him. Lucrezia gave a feeble wave in return.

"He certainly likes to keep busy," said Filomena. "I think it helps keep his mind off his wife. He's a lot like you in that respect."

Lucrezia rose and stood next to her mother. She continued to gaze out the window even after Peppi had disappeared around the corner.

"How old did you say he is?" she asked.

CHAPTER SEVENTEEN

One night, as Luca had predicted, it all finally caught up with Peppi.

It happened shortly after spring had settled in to stay and the transformation of the courtyard and gardens was nearly complete. The grapevines that once overwhelmed the arbor over the bench had been tamed and the flower beds restored to order. The bushes and shrubs along the wall were all pruned and the entire area around them thoroughly raked. It took many days of relentless effort, but in the end Peppi succeeded in getting it all back to the point where things could be maintained with a minimum of effort.

What was once an eyesore that everyone did his best to ignore soon became a favorite spot where the workers enjoyed passing their break times. Peppi planted many bulbs that would blossom later in the summer, but some of the early bloomers had already burst forth. The workers enjoyed strolling about the grounds, watching day by day as the new flowers sprang up. Even Luca, despite his protestations that Peppi was working too hard, was drawn there by the simple beauty and tranquility of the place. Lucrezia never ventured into the courtyard, but now and then, when he was working in the gardens, Peppi noticed her gazing out from her office at the arbor. Invariably she would turn away the moment she saw Peppi looking at her.

One afternoon, Luca came out to the courtyard while Peppi was weeding one of the flower beds. He stood over his friend and shook his head.

"It all looks beautiful, but you're doing too much, my friend," he told Peppi. "You need to go slower, rest more."

"Nonsense," said Peppi. "I love what I'm doing. Why should I rest?"

"Because you're an old enough athlete to know better," Luca tried to explain. "Life is like cycling. You train hard for a while, then take some time off to recover before doing more. That's how you grow stronger. But if you overtrain, don't give yourself time to recover, you end up weaker than when you started. You crash. And you, my friend, are riding for a serious crash."

"I feel strong as an ox these days," said Peppi with a smile.

"And you're as stubborn as one too," grumbled Luca. "I can't remember, were you this thickheaded when you left Villa San Giuseppe or was it something you developed in America?"

"America's a wonderful place," said Peppi with a smile. "You should visit it one day."

"Maybe in the next life," sighed Luca. "I've got too much to do around here right now."

"That's my point," said Peppi.

Luca glared at him for a moment before the two of them broke out in laughter. "Just promise me you'll take some time off," he said as he began to walk back to the factory.

"Maybe," Peppi called after him, "but first I thought I'd work on the landscaping out front."

"I don't want to hear it," said Luca, covering his ears.

That had been a week earlier. The trouble started a few days later when Peppi began work on the gardens around the front of the factory. He had slept poorly that previous night and he started the day with a nervous twinge in his stomach. Just the same, he accompanied Luca on a morning bike ride before starting work. He felt more tired than normal during the ride and found himself struggling to keep pace. It occurred to him afterwards that he had forgotten to eat breakfast, so he blamed his poor effort on his lack of proper pre-ride nutrition. Peppi promised himself that he would eat a more substantial lunch to make up for it.

By noon Peppi felt ravenous. When he finally sat down to lunch, he ate voraciously, but somehow he didn't feel satisfied. Nonetheless he returned to work that afternoon as usual and kept at it till almost sundown. That night Peppi went to bed exhausted and awoke the next morning feeling much the same, a pattern that would continue for the next several nights.

Though it had developed over many weeks, it seemed to Peppi in the days that followed that he had suddenly lost all his energy. He felt nervous and irritable all day and chastised himself for being lazy. In the hope that it might somehow snap him out of the doldrums, Peppi decided that what he needed was to press harder. So he sought out other projects to do in addition to the gardening. He repaired a window and painted a door. He kept an eye open for any opportunity to help at the factory, be it helping to stock inventory or loading one of the trucks, anything to stay busy.

This surge of intense activity briefly made him more productive, but soon things started to decline. In the mornings, Peppi had trouble deciding simple things like what clothes to put on or what to eat for breakfast. Throughout the day, he wasted time trying to make up his mind over easy little decisions that he would ordinarily make in an instant. Worse, as the days went by, he felt interminably sad and found his thoughts dwelling on Anna and the mulino and all the occasional sad events that are part of the fabric of every human life. Try as he might to shake those thoughts from his head, nothing helped, not even cycling. If anything, he felt worse on the bike than he could ever remember.

Things went on this way until one night when, after falling into a deep sleep, Peppi suddenly awoke in the middle of the night. Shivering, he sat up and wiped a thin sheen of sweat from his brow. His heart was pounding and an overwhelming sense of anxiety was gnawing at the pit of his stomach. He felt nauseous. He arose and went to the bathroom to throw some water on his face. This only served to make him feel dizzy.

Peppi went back to the bedroom and sat on the edge of the bed. He tried to tell himself that there was nothing wrong, that he was just coming down with the flu or some sort of stomach bug, but the more he thought about it the more nervous he became. Suddenly, he realized that he could not catch his breath, and the nervousness turned to panic. It lasted for several minutes and Peppi was certain that he was about to die, though he could not understand why. As quickly as it started, the episode passed and Peppi collapsed onto the bed. Exhausted, he stared at the ceiling for what seemed like hours before he finally drifted back into a fitful sleep.

CHAPTER EIGHTEEN

It was Lucrezia who first noticed that Peppi was missing the next day. The "old man," as she often referred to him, was quickly becoming something of a fixture around the factory and she had become accustomed to seeing him every morning when she arrived for work. He was always doing something, raking out the gardens or fiddling with a squeaky door hinge. Invariably he would greet her with a tip of his cap and a bright *"Buon giorno, Signorina!"* Invariably Lucrezia would barely acknowledge him, offering only a perfunctory *"Buon giorno"* of her own as she swept past him on the way to her office. It was the way she greeted just about everyone.

When she came to work that day and did not see Peppi, Lucrezia assumed that he was out back in the gardens somewhere or perhaps out riding his bicycle. The weather had turned beautiful, so who could blame him for not wanting to work? As the morning wore on, Lucrezia peeked out the window now and then, certain that she would catch a glimpse of him pruning the bushes or watering the flower beds, but still there was no sign of Peppi.

Just before lunchtime, Lucrezia emerged from her office to check up on how things were running out on the floor. She looked about; not seeing Peppi anywhere, she motioned to Enzo to come over. Enzo blanched, for more often than not, whenever Lucrezia called him over, it was not to exchange pleasantries.

"How are things running today, Enzo?" Lucrezia asked with a reasonable amount of geniality.

"Everything is fine, Signora Lucrezia," said Enzo. He was troubled by the soft tone of her voice and he waited nervously for the other shoe to drop. "We've got a big shipment going out later today," he added, "but other than that, things are going along as they should."

"And everything's in the right boxes today?" Lucrezia asked in a rare moment of playfulness.

"Absolutely!" exclaimed Enzo. "On the souls of my children."

"That's good," said Lucrezia. She looked over Enzo's shoulder at the other workers in the factory. "Where's the old man today?" she asked casually.

"Peppi?" said Enzo. "I don't know. We were all wondering the same thing just a little while ago. No one has seen him all morning. Do you want to speak with him? Should I send someone out to find him for you?"

"Don't be ridiculous," huffed Lucrezia, her earlier warmth vanishing like steam from a kettle. "I was only curious. I'm sure he'll turn up sooner or later." At that she turned away and walked back to her office.

Sooner turned into later and still Peppi did not appear. Luca arrived early that afternoon and, not seeing his friend, he asked Lucrezia if she knew where he might be.

"No one knows," she said indifferently. "We haven't seen him all day."

Luca rubbed his chin for a moment. "I'd better go check his room," he said.

* * *

Luca knocked on the door to the apartment and waited a moment. Not hearing any response, he knocked harder, but still nothing. He opened the door and leaned inside.

"Peppi?" he called.

From the bedroom came the stirring of bedcovers. Luca stepped inside and closed the door behind him.

"Peppi, it's me, Luca. What are you doing in bed at this time of day?"

"Go away," Peppi groaned. "I don't want to see anyone today."

Luca opened the bedroom door and gazed in at Peppi who was curled up beneath the blankets. "What's the matter?" he asked. "Are you sick?"

"I don't know what's wrong with me," Peppi answered. "It came over me last night. I'm exhausted and feel nervous all over. Every time I even think of moving or doing anything at all, I get all panicky. I think I've lost my mind."

Luca chuckled as he stood over him. "I told you this would happen," he said smugly. "You're not sick."

"What do you mean?" said Peppi.

"You're overtrained, *stupido,*" he answered. "You crashed."

"Crashed?"

"That's right. What have I been telling you all along? You needed to slow down, to rest. You wouldn't listen to me and this is what happens. You've stressed your mind and your body to the point where they're just not going to let you do it anymore."

"But how did it happen?" Peppi lamented. "I don't understand."

"Don't understand?" Luca snorted. "Let's see, first your wife dies, leaving you all alone. You leave your home, travel across the ocean to another continent where you decide to start your life over. Then you travel all the way back to the place of your birth only to find it destroyed by an earthquake. You end up living in this little hovel of an apartment and you work like a dog from sunup till sundown. All this—not to mention that you're not quite as young as you once were. Forgive me, *amico mio,* but you're not Superman. Nobody is. You've put yourself through a tremendous ordeal."

"But I didn't mean to do it," Peppi said unhappily.

"Nobody ever does."

"But when will it go away?"

"You didn't get like this overnight and it's not going to go away overnight either," said Luca. "And it won't go away at all unless you take care of it."

"What do I do for it?" said Peppi, pulling the covers more tightly around himself.

"Nothing," Luca answered. "You stay curled up on that bed and you don't think about anything or move a muscle until you're rested and ready to do it. It might take a few days, it might take a few weeks. Who knows, it might take a few months or more. No matter what, you can't rush it. It's time to start listening to your body again; you've been ignoring it for too long. It will let you know when the time is right."

Luca stayed for a while longer, lecturing Peppi further on the need for rest, reassuring him that if he did what he was told, he'd be back to his old self before he knew it. Once he was satisfied that he had made his point, Luca decided to leave Peppi alone to rest. He promised to have someone bring by some food later on even though Peppi complained that he felt too sick in the stomach to even think about eating.

"Don't worry, you'll get your appetite back," Luca assured him. Then he closed the door and returned to work.

Later that evening, after dinner, Filomena prepared a tray of food for Peppi while Luca leafed through the newspaper. "What do you think is really wrong with him?" she asked as she spooned out some leftover linguine into a bowl. "He seemed fine just a few days ago."

Luca shrugged. "He doesn't say it, but he misses his wife," he replied. "He's sad and he's tired. Those are the two worst things that a person can be, particularly a man."

"What, you think being sad and tired is any easier on a woman?" laughed his wife.

"Eh, it's different for a man," said Luca, tossing the newspaper onto the table. "Women can talk about things that make them sad much better than men—and that helps. But men, we just carry it all around with us like a sack of potatoes. We try to ignore it and sometimes, if we're strong enough, we get used to the weight of the sack and the sadness goes away on its own. But other times it just weighs on us, heavier and heavier, until it wears us down and eats away at our hearts and our souls. We try to ignore it by staying busy, which is the worst thing to do, because sooner or later it wears you down to the point where everything finally caves in. That's what happened to Peppi. He let it wear him down, so now he has to deal with it before he can go on and be happy again."

"My, you've become quite the psychologist in your old age," Filomena needled him.

"I've seen a thing or two in my time, *amore mia,*" chuckled her husband, "and I try to learn from what I see."

"Well, let's see if you can learn to carry this over to Peppi without spilling everything," said Filomena, covering the tray she had prepared with a cloth to keep everything warm. "Here, take it before it all gets cold."

Luca heaved a sigh. "Why is it that women are always telling me what to do?" he said, getting up from the table.

"Because they know what's best for you," his wife answered.

Luca chuckled again and picked up the tray. Filomena opened the door for him and turned on the outside light so that he would not stumble in the darkness on his way down to the factory.

"Hey," said Filomena as he was leaving, "do you think you'd miss me as much if I were gone?"

"I'll be missing you every minute I'm away from you till I get back from Peppi's," Luca said over his shoulder.

"Hah!" scoffed Filomena. "A likely story." She stood in the doorway and smiled as she watched her husband walk down the path. "And make sure he eats everything!" she called to him. Then she closed the door and went back to the kitchen to do the dishes.

CHAPTER NINETEEN

Early one afternoon, Peppi was sitting at his kitchen table. Still in bathrobe and slippers, he sipped a cup of coffee and stared out the window while he nibbled on a crust of bread. It was a warm, bright day with big puffy white clouds pasted against the blue Abruzzo sky. Peppi had been cooped up inside for the better part of a week and now he longed to feel the warmth of the sun on his face again. He took that as a sign that the deep vein of cold, nervous exhaustion within him was starting to thaw. He was getting better, just as Luca said he would.

Peppi yawned and stretched his arms over his head. He was contemplating getting dressed and perhaps taking a little stroll outside in the sun when suddenly he heard a loud commotion in the offices down below his rooms. There seemed to be a great deal of screaming going on, most of it being done by Lucrezia. Though muted by the floorboards, the shriek of her voice was unmistakable. By now Peppi, like everyone else, had grown accustomed to her occasional outbursts. He couldn't help chuckling, for he knew that somebody downstairs was catching an earful.

Peppi listened more closely, trying to guess who the unfortunate recipient of her wrath might be. He thought he could hear Luca's voice and perhaps one other, probably Enzo's. From the little he could make out, it sounded as if the two of them were pleading with Lucrezia about something, but obviously not having much success at it. Lucrezia, as one of the factory workers had once told him, was a force of nature when she was riled up. When the storm clouds swirled in around her it was not unusual for objects to start flying through the air. It came as no surprise, therefore, when Peppi heard the distinct sound of glass shattering. There was no way to know for sure, but he guessed that some object resting upon her desktop had found its way out into the courtyard through an unopened window. A moment later he heard the slamming of doors, and then all was quiet downstairs once more. Lucrezia's periodic squalls could be hellacious in their intensity, but more often than not they passed very quickly, like a thunderstorm in springtime. This one had evidently subsided.

After finishing his coffee, Peppi mustered the energy to get dressed. He thought of taking a walk, but he soon realized it was beyond him, so instead he sat for a while on the stairs outside his apartment. That brief taste of sunshine and fresh air was enough to tire him out. He went back in, stretched out on his bed once more, and took a little nap. He awoke later that afternoon to the sound of someone knocking on his door.

"Peppi, are you here?" he heard Luca call.

"*Sì*, come in," he answered through a yawn. "Where else would I be?"

Peppi rolled his legs off the bed and stood. When he came into the kitchen, Luca had already settled into a chair at the kitchen table and was looking over the derailleur on Peppi's bike.

"You know," Luca said thoughtfully, "if you're going to stick with Campagnolo on this bike, you should really think about upgrading to the ten-speed gruppo."

"If I ever ride my bike again," replied Peppi with another

yawn. He took out a carafe of red wine and filled two glasses. *"Ecco,"* he said, setting one of the glasses in front of Luca, "I think you need a little of this right about now. *Salute."*

"Salute," answered Luca, raising his glass. He took a good long sip, set the glass down, and let out a sigh. "I take it you heard all the uproar today," he said wearily.

"It was hard not to," said Peppi. "I thought for a moment that the roof was going to blow off."

"Tell you the truth, so did I," a laughing Luca said. He looked over at the counter and then to the refrigerator. "Hey, do you have any cheese?" he asked hopefully.

"Of course," said Peppi. "I've got some nice bread too. One of your workers dropped it off for me this morning."

"You read my mind."

"They're good people, you know, the ones you have working for you," said Peppi, setting the bread and cheese on the table.

"I'd be lost without them," Luca agreed.

Peppi opened the refrigerator once more and produced a stick of dry sausage, some roasted red peppers, and a plate of olives. He set these and a bottle of olive oil on the table alongside the bread and cheese. Luca took the loaf of bread and ripped off a healthy chunk. Peppi did the same. With the formalities dispensed with, the two of them set to work on the cheese and the sausage and the peppers and olives.

Luca smiled as he watched Peppi lop off a thick slice of sausage. "You're getting your appetite back," he noted with obvious satisfaction. "I told you it would happen."

Peppi took a bite of the sausage and let out a contented sigh. "I'm feeling better," he said with a shrug. "Still a little tired, but not so nervous anymore. I almost feel up to fixing that broken window in the office downstairs."

Luca caught the mischievous look in Peppi's eye. *"Mannagia,"* he groaned. "I thought she was going to crucify us all today."

"But why, *ch'è successo?"* asked Peppi. "Something bad?"

"It was nothing at all," said Luca. "Just a bunch of silly nonsense."

"Then why all the fuss?"

"Francesco's birthday," replied Luca with a shrug.

"Francesco?"

"It's this week," explained Luca. "Lucrezia always gets a little out of control right around this time every year. Now and in the autumn, when he had his accident, God rest him. Somehow, though, I always end up forgetting about it. It wasn't until late this morning that I remembered. I had just walked in and all the workers were in a state because my daughter had been cracking the whip since the moment they arrived. I asked one of them what the trouble was and they all pointed to the calendar on the wall. That's when it dawned on me and I knew in that moment that we were all in for a very long day, and probably one or two more."

"Poor girl," said Peppi.

"Poor *girl?"* huffed Luca. "What about poor me and the rest of them?"

"You'll survive," chuckled Peppi. "Besides, despite all the bluster, I can see that deep inside she loves you all. What's more, you all know it. Why else would you put up with her?"

Luca made no reply but instead swallowed another chunk of bread and cheese and washed it down with a gulp of wine. He poured himself another glassful and sat back in his chair.

"You have a point," he finally admitted. "But that doesn't make things any easier."

"Whoever said life was supposed to be easy?"

At that Luca laughed, but then his face grew more serious as he stared into his glass of wine. *"Povera ragazza,"* he muttered. "I just wish she could find someone, forget all this sadness and start all over again."

"It will happen someday," said Peppi.

"But when?"

"Whenever God decides the time is right."

"Well, I wish He'd hurry up and make up His mind," sighed Luca, "before the rest of us lose ours."

CHAPTER TWENTY

Maybe it was the wine, or perhaps he really was getting better, but Peppi went to bed early that night after Luca left and slept straight through till the morning, something he hadn't done in weeks. When he awoke the next day he felt reasonably refreshed, not yet his old self but definitely well on the way. Just the same he felt troubled, for he had awakened to the sound of someone softly crying outside. At first Peppi thought he had been dreaming, but when he opened his eyes and sat up, he heard it again. Anxious to see who it might be, he pulled his legs from beneath the covers, stretched them a little, and went to the window. He opened the shutters a crack and peered out at the morning sky.

It was very early; the top edge of the rising sun had barely cleared the crest of the mountains, but already Peppi could tell that it would be another warm day. Unlike the weather earlier in the week, however, there was a damp heaviness in the air now that clung to his skin like an old sweater. They were sure to get a thunderstorm before the end of the day. For now, though, all was quiet save for the sound of weeping coming from down below.

Peppi opened the shutters a little more and gazed down at the courtyard. There, beneath the arbor with its grapevines hanging down, surrounded by the gardens with the flowers just opening their petals to the morning light, sat Lucrezia. Oblivious to the beauty all around her, she stared blindly into the distance, her eyes and cheeks wet with tears. Clutching a picture frame tight to her heart, she rocked back and forth, sobbing uncontrollably now.

Transfixed, Peppi stood there and watched the pitiful scene from his window. He tried to turn away, but he could not take his eyes off her, for he recognized the deep anguish in her sobs, the inconsolable grief. The pain. They all reminded him of his own. But his pain was relatively new, the result of wounds that were still fresh. It struck him through to think that Lucrezia or anyone could still suffer so greatly from such old wounds, ones that should have healed long ago.

Peppi finally stepped away from the window, ashamed of himself for having spied on Lucrezia at such a vulnerable moment. He sat back on the bed and stared at the floor, trying not to listen, to allow her the privacy she obviously wanted. After a time, he turned and took the picture of Anna from the table beside the bed. He gazed at his wife, trying to recall everything about her. Her voice, the smell of her hair, the soft feel of her cheek. To his dismay, he found that already those precious memories were starting to fade.

With a sigh, Peppi lay back on the bed and rested the picture of Anna on the pillow beside him. He closed his eyes in the hope of falling asleep again, but by now sleep had been chased away by the light of the new day and the tender lament of Lucrezia's tears drifting up from the courtyard. Peppi tried rolling away from the window and burying his ears in the pillow, but it didn't help. Somehow that only seemed to make the sound and the light that much more insistent. Letting out a groan of consternation, he set Anna's picture back on the table, pulled himself out of bed, and dressed quickly.

Lucrezia was still there when Peppi peeked around the corner of the building. He stepped out onto the gravel path that led through the center of the courtyard and walked toward her. The crunching of the stones beneath his shoes alerted Lucrezia to his presence. At seeing Peppi approach, she jumped up and began to walk away.

"Buon giorno, Signorina," Peppi said with his usual warmth. "Forgive me for startling you. Please don't go."

Lucrezia stopped short in her tracks and turned slowly around. Still clutching the photograph, she looked at him with red-rimmed eyes. "You didn't startle me," she said tersely. "It's just that I was . . . what I mean to say is that I . . . How long were you there watching me?"

"Oh, I just came down a few moments ago," Peppi told her. "Please, go ahead and sit back down. I didn't come to bother you."

To his surprise, Lucrezia did sit back down on the bench, though she looked not at him but away toward the mountains. Peppi walked up to the bench and gestured to the space beside her.

"May I?" he asked.

Lucrezia responded with a shrug, as if to say that it made no difference to her one way or the other. Peppi took a seat. They sat for a long time in awkward silence.

"Che bella mattina, eh?" Peppi finally remarked. "It's a beautiful morning."

"I hadn't noticed," said Lucrezia, still gazing off into the distance. Abruptly she turned to him. "Are you sure you weren't over there hiding in the bushes, spying on me?" she said menacingly.

"Of course not," Peppi reassured her.

"Good," she said firmly, "because I don't like people who stick their noses into other people's business."

"I wouldn't dream of doing such a thing," said Peppi. At that Lucrezia seemed to relax a little. "No," he went on, "I wasn't hiding in the bushes. Actually I was watching you from my window."

Lucrezia let out a gasp of indignation. "How could you do such a thing!" she cried out.

"Well, it's very quiet here in the early morning," Peppi calmly explained, "and it was hard not to hear you. Don't be angry with me. You see, I saw you sitting here all alone and you looked so sad. To tell you the truth, I've been feeling alone and sad myself for some time now, and I just thought that maybe I'd come down and we could both sit here and be alone and sad together for a little while and maybe both of us would feel better."

Peppi looked into Lucrezia's eyes. He wasn't sure if what he saw in them was outrage or resignation. In either case, though, she did not get up and leave as he feared she might. Instead she slumped against the arbor and let out a long sigh. She suddenly looked as weary as he felt.

Peppi nodded to the picture in her hands. "May I have a look?" he said.

Very tentatively, as if she were holding a baby or some rare object of incalculable value, Lucrezia handed him the picture frame. Peppi held it up before him and studied the face of the young man in the picture.

"Your husband was a fine, strong-looking man," he said after a time. "I can see why you miss him so."

"Grazie," she murmured in reply. She looked about at the gardens with sad eyes. "Francesco and I, we used to sit here together all the time," she said. "It was beautiful then like it is now."

Peppi handed back the picture, reached inside his shirt, and withdrew his picture of Anna. He gazed lovingly at it for a few moments before passing it to Lucrezia.

Lucrezia sat up straight. "Your wife?" she said with genuine interest, taking it from his hands.

Peppi nodded in reply.

As Lucrezia gazed at the picture, her expression seemed to soften. "She was beautiful," she said after a few moments. "How long were you married?"

"I met Anna just after I went to America," Peppi told her. "We were married soon after."

"That's a good long time to be married."

"It went by in an instant."

"I know," sighed Lucrezia, "I know." She handed him back the picture. "Thank you for letting me see her."

"Prego."

Once again the two of them sat in silence for a time, listening to the incessant chatter of the birds and the whisper of the warm breeze. Lucrezia stared down at the ground before finally looking up and letting her eyes inspect Peppi more closely.

"You're a mess," she decided. "You look pale."

Peppi rubbed his unshaven chin and ran his hand back across his tousled hair. "I feel pale," he replied with a shrug.

"Have you been eating?"

"Not much," Peppi admitted. "Till now I haven't had much of an appetite. Lately all I do is sleep."

"I was like that after I lost Francesco," said Lucrezia. "All I wanted to do was sleep all the time so that I wouldn't feel anything. No matter how much I stayed in bed, though, I never felt rested. I was exhausted all the time."

"I know what you mean," Peppi nodded in agreement. "When I lost Anna it was like that for me. Everything went dark. I couldn't feel anything, not the sun on my face or the cold wind. People would talk to me, but it was like I couldn't hear them. I just walked around all day in a fog, as if—"

"As if you were half-asleep," Lucrezia said. "I know how that feels."

"Does that feeling ever go away?" asked Peppi.

"No," she answered, shaking her head sadly. "Not completely. It's always there inside you, especially when you're alone and it's quiet. That's why I work the way I do, because it's the only thing that makes me forget it for a while."

Peppi let out a little laugh. "I tried that too," he said. "It worked for a little while, but then I ended up flat on my back in bed for a week. The night it hit me, I thought I was dying."

"Something like that once happened to me too," said Lucrezia. "It came over me in the middle of the night. I thought my life was over."

"Did it frighten you?"

"No," she replied. "The thought of it was almost a relief. I didn't want to die, but I didn't care if I lived either." She turned and looked off into the distance once more. "I still don't," she added softly.

"Well it scared me," said Peppi. "Until that moment, I didn't care if I lived or died either. But as I sat there on the bed with my heart pounding and my head spinning, I suddenly realized that I was terrified, that I wasn't ready to die yet. When it passed, my body went limp like a piece of linguine that's been in the water too long. But, as exhausted as I was, I somehow felt better." He paused to see if she was listening to him. "Anyway," he said, "I don't know what God wants from me, but I know he doesn't want to see me above the clouds, at least not yet."

"Maybe he intends for you to go in the other direction," said Lucrezia, the first hint of a mischievous smile curling the corners of her mouth.

"I hadn't thought of that possibility," chuckled Peppi, "but I suppose you have a point. I'll have to think about that one." With that he stood and walked over to the garden to inspect the flower beds The weeds were starting to grow again and the flowers were wilted a bit from not being watered regularly.

"These gardens need work," he said.

"They miss you," said Lucrezia. "When do you think you'll feel up to spending time with them again?"

Peppi turned to go. "Soon," he said with a mischievous smile of his own, "but first I have a window to fix."

Just as Peppi had predicted, a tremendous thunderstorm ripped through the valley that afternoon. Great towering thunderheads rolled through the skies like giant bowling balls. The mountains echoed with their booming as they hurled crackling bolts of lightning that darted across the clouds in jagged, haphazard lines. When the rain arrived it came down in tremendous windswept torrents that lashed the trees and slammed against the houses. It seemed that all of nature was convulsed in fury.

Peppi stood at his window and looked out. A thrill of exhilaration surged through his body as he watched the dazzling spectacle unfold before him. The rain whipped through the window and the air was thick with the electric smell of the lightning. Peppi opened his arms wide and breathed deep, letting his body absorb all the energy nature would give him. He closed his eyes and let the bracing slap of the raindrops splash against his face, washing clean the pain and the sorrow and the tears. Deep within, in some way that he could not explain, he was being renewed. Peppi smiled, for in that very moment he realized that it was still good to be alive.

CHAPTER TWENTY-ONE

Peppi was standing outside in the bushes, measuring the window frame for a new pane of glass when Lucrezia walked into her office. He had arisen early that morning in the hope that he might get the job started and perhaps even finished without her ever noticing. Lucrezia, though, had been equally intent on getting an early start to her day. She hurried in and went directly to her desk.

"Buon giorno, Signorina!" Peppi called in through the broken pane.

The sound of his voice gave Lucrezia a start. She had not seen him at the window. *"O, Dio,"* she said, putting her hand to her heart. "I didn't see you there, Signor Peppi. *Buon giorno."*

"Mi dispiace, Signorina," said Peppi. "I didn't mean to startle you."

"No, that's all right," she said. "I was just preoccupied, that's all. I get like that in the mornings sometimes."

"You work too hard," said Peppi.

"You sound like my father."

"He's a wise man, your father."

Lucrezia gave him a half-smile and turned her attention back to the work on her desk. Meantime Peppi stretched out his tape and measured the bottom of the window frame. He scribbled down the length on a scrap of paper; then, with the pencil clenched between his teeth, he measured the height.

"Quite a storm yesterday," he said, scribbling down the other number.

"Dio mio!" exclaimed Lucrezia, facing him once more. "I thought the roof was going to blow off!"

"Me too," said Peppi with a smile. Then he beckoned for her to come to the window. *"Venga,"* he said, "I have a little something to give you."

"For me?" said Lucrezia. Her curiosity piqued, she stood and came to the window. "What is it?" she asked, gazing out.

Peppi reached down to his feet and picked up a small but hefty ceramic mug, the kind used to hold pens or paper clips or whatever else one might keep on a desk. It was splattered with mud from being left out in the rain, but otherwise it was in good repair.

"Here," he said, offering the mug up to her by way of the same broken window pane through which it had originally exited the building. "I don't know how it managed to find its way out into the garden, but I thought it might make a good paper weight."

Lucrezia gasped and broke out in an embarrassed, but delighted smile when she saw it. "I've been looking all over for that thing!" she exclaimed, taking the mug. "I made this when I was a little girl. It's one of my favorite things. How on earth did it ever manage to get out there?"

"I can't imagine," said Peppi.

Lucrezia wiped the mud off the mug and inspected it more closely. "It doesn't seem to be damaged at all," she said with relief. She turned her gaze to him and smiled once more. *"Grazie, Signor Peppi."*

"Prego," he replied, "but please, just call me Peppi."

"D'accordo," she said, still smiling.

"And you should do that more often."

"Cosa?"

"Show people your smile," Peppi said. "It's a shame to keep it hidden all the time."

"I'll try to remember," said Lucrezia. Then she went back to work and Peppi went off to buy a new pane of glass.

Pedalling into town and returning to replace the window pane took longer than Peppi had anticipated. As it turned out, the pane of glass he purchased was too big to fit securely in the basket on his bicycle. He had no choice other than to balance the glass against the back of his saddle while he walked the bike home. Along the way he stopped now and then to chat with the villagers he had come to know since returning from America. Everyone knew everything about everybody in a little place like Villa San Giuseppe. Invariably they asked how he was feeling and warned him about doing too much too soon.

By the time he returned to the factory and replaced the window pane, Peppi was feeling quite tired. After finishing up, he decided to follow Luca's advice, not to mention everyone else's in the village, about pacing himself more sensibly. He ate a light lunch then went to his bedroom and stretched out for a nap. Peppi came down later that afternoon to inspect the landscaping job he had only just started in front of the factory. As he descended the stairs he saw Enzo and Fabio, one of his co-workers, by the front door. The two were on their work break, puffing cigarettes while they traded shop talk.

"Hey, Peppi!" called Enzo at seeing Peppi come into view. *"Come 'stai?"*

"Eh, better than yesterday," said Peppi with a shrug, "but not as good as tomorrow, I hope."

"Bravo," said Fabio.

Peppi had always disliked the smell of cigarettes and he coughed when the breeze blew their smoke in his face. "Uff, don't you guys know that those are bad for you?" he said, fanning away the smoke with his hand.

"Ayyy, you stayed in America too long," laughed Enzo before taking another drag. "You guys worry too much over there."

"Maybe," said Peppi.

"Hey, Peppi, what did you think of that storm yesterday?" said Fabio. "I thought God was getting ready to knock down the mountains all around us."

"It certainly sounded that way," Peppi agreed. "It was quite a storm."

"Veramente," said Enzo, nodding. "Did you hear about that poor bastard in L'Aquila that got hit by the lightning?"

"No, I hadn't," replied Peppi.

"Get this," chuckled Fabio. "The guy's up on his roof, trying to fix the television antenna so he can watch the soccer match last night. It starts storming like crazy, but he doesn't come down because he hasn't finished yet and he really wants to watch the match. He finally gets the thing all plugged in just as the storm is at its worst. That's when he finally decides that he'd better get inside quick. But then he gets all the way down to the bottom of the ladder when he remembers he left his tools up on the roof. So what does the dope do? He goes back to get the tools! No sooner does he reach the top of the ladder than a big bolt of lightning comes down out of the sky and knocks him to the ground."

"That was God's way of showing him how stupid he is," noted Enzo.

"Dead?" asked Peppi.

"No," said Fabio, shaking his head. "Broke both legs, though. Just the same, he wouldn't let them take him to the hospital until after he watched the match. Can you believe it?"

"I'd forgotten how dedicated Italian soccer fans are," said Peppi.

They all shared a laugh, then Peppi went over to inspect the little garden he had started along the walkway that led to the front door while Enzo and Fabio continued to chatter. He knelt down and fussed with the soil around one of the flowers he had transplanted. Just then the door to the factory opened and Lucrezia came out.

"*Ciao, Enzo, ciao, Fabio,*" she said pleasantly.

"*Ciao, Signora,*" the two replied respectfully. They were accustomed to a more brusque greeting from Lucrezia and they glanced at each other with suspicious eyes.

"*Ciao, Peppi!*" she called, walking past them.

Peppi called back a greeting.

Enzo and Fabio watched with great interest as Lucrezia strolled over to Peppi. She stopped beside him and bent over his shoulder to take a look at the flowers. As she did so, the two strained to get a closer look at her backside.

"These are beautiful," she said, leaning over to breathe in the fragrance of the flowers.

"I hope to plant more soon," said Peppi.

"That would be nice," said Lucrezia. "Thank you for fixing my window, by the way, and also for finding my mug."

"Piacere mia, Signorina," said Peppi, smiling.

"Please, just call me Lucrezia," she said returning his smile.

"Okay," said Peppi.

Lucrezia hesitated for a moment as if she wanted to say something more. Instead she straightened up and started to walk away.

"Ciao, Peppi," she said, casting a glance over her shoulder.

"Ciao—Lucrezia," he replied.

Peppi knelt there in the garden and watched Lucrezia as she stepped into her car. When she drove away, he stood and kept watch until the car was out of sight. Then, humming a tune, he turned his attention back to the garden, completely forgetting that Enzo and Fabio were still there, observing the whole scene.

Enzo took a last puff from his cigarette and tossed the butt to the ground. "Know what I think?" he said, nudging Fabio with his elbow.

"What?"

"I think that guy in L'Aquila wasn't the only one to get hit by a thunderbolt."

CHAPTER TWENTY-TWO

One afternoon, Peppi decided to eat his lunch on the bench beneath the arbor in the courtyard. It was a bright, sunny day in early May and a brisk wind chased enormous white clouds across the sky. The factory protected the courtyard from the breeze, keeping it tranquil enough for Peppi to leaf through the sporting news in *La Gazzetta dello Sport* without the pages being blown about while he ate. For Peppi, one of the true delights of returning to Italy was the marvelous coverage competitive cycling received in the daily sports pages and on television. He couldn't get enough of it. As he happily scanned the results of the latest races, it occurred to Peppi that he was itching to start riding his bike again. He took that as a sign that he was almost fully recovered.

Peppi was just about to take his first bite of his provolone and prosciutto sandwich when he heard the familiar sound of Lucrezia's voice raised in anger. Apparently there had been some sort of mishap in the factory and she was letting everyone in the valley know about it. There ensued the usual sound of objects being tossed about and doors slamming.

Peppi put his sandwich down and waited, fully expecting that at any moment some object would come sailing through the window he had recently repaired. Instead, the back door to the factory opened and out stormed Lucrezia. She slammed

the door behind her and stomped over to the edge of the courtyard where she stopped and folded her arms. Looking up to the
sky, she took a deep breath and let it out with a long, weary
sigh. The energy seemed to drain out of her, and like a beaten
boxer, she let her arms droop down to her sides. It was then that
she looked up and saw Peppi sitting beneath the arbor.

"Oh, *Dio,*" she sighed again.

"Trouble today?" Peppi asked.

Lucrezia shrugged.

Peppi folded the newspaper and gestured for her to sit beside him. Lucrezia hesitated for a moment, then came over to
him.

"Here, have an olive," he said, offering her the bowl as she
sat down, "they always make me feel better. I don't know why."

Lucrezia took an olive and handed him back the bowl. "It's
the mono-unsaturated fats," she said tersely as she nibbled on
the olive.

"I beg your pardon."

"The unsaturated fats in the olives," she explained. "They've
done studies on them and the omega-3 fatty acids. Somehow
they interact with the central nervous system to elevate your
mood."

Peppi took a long look into the bowl. "Gee," he mused, "I
just thought it was because they taste good."

"That's another reason," said Lucrezia. She finished eating
the olive and tossed the pit into the bushes.

"Have another?" offered Peppi.

"No, *grazie,*" said Lucrezia. "I'm watching my weight."

"Ah, even here," chuckled Peppi before taking a bite of his
sandwich.

"What do you mean?"

"The women in America are always driving themselves crazy trying to lose weight," he told her. "They think that men want them all to be skinny like sticks, even though they're beautiful just the way they are."

"I don't care what men think," huffed Lucrezia. "Not anymore."

"Why not?"

"Because I could never love another man, not like I loved my husband, so why should I care what the rest of them think of me?"

"I guess you have a point," said Peppi. "But you're still young, anything could happen."

"No," she said miserably. "I might still be young enough, but my heart is dead inside me."

"Yes," said Peppi, "I know how that feels. Do you think that's why you get so angry sometimes?"

"I don't know why I get so upset," she admitted. "It just happens and there's nothing I can do about it."

"You could try eating more olives," Peppi suggested.

At that Lucrezia finally permitted herself to smile. She reached for the bowl and helped herself to another olive before getting up to go. "Maybe you're right," she said. "I'll give it a try."

"Good," said Peppi, pleased that he had managed to cheer her up a little. "Now go back to work and don't worry about it if you find yourself yelling a little now and then. It's good for you to let it out."

"I'll keep that in mind."

"But please, promise me no more broken windows!" he called after her as she walked back into the factory. "That glass is a real pain in the backside to carry on the bike."

Lucrezia waved over her shoulder as she stepped back inside. When the door closed behind her, Peppi turned his attention back to his prosciutto and provolone sandwich and *La Gazzetta dello Sport.* He contentedly munched away, unaware that Enzo and all the workers were lined up at the window inside the factory, watching him and Lucrezia. Enzo winked at the others who smiled and nodded in return. Then, upon hearing Lucrezia approach, they all scurried back to their places.

CHAPTER TWENTY-THREE

Peppi surprised Luca a few days later by joining him for the Sunday morning training ride. Luca could not have been more pleased, but he cautioned him to just "sit in" that day and let the others do the work at the front. The rest of the riders waiting in the piazza gave Peppi a hero's welcome when he rolled up to the fountain. It was good to see him out on his bicycle once more. Added to the group's delight was the general air of excitement over the start of the Giro D'Italia, Italy's greatest bicycle race. The race was scheduled to start that day in Rome and the riders could think or talk of little else. Along with them, the rest of the country would be mesmerized for the next three weeks as the drama of the race unfolded.

"Andiamo!" shouted one of the riders.

"Forza L'Italia!" cried another.

With that they all clicked their shoes onto the pedals and swept out of the piazza onto the open road. The group zipped along at an enthusiastic pace before settling into a more moderate tempo. Protected as he was in the cocoon of riders surrounding him, Peppi rolled along comfortably. The feel of the wind in his face and the warmth of the sun energized him as did the sound of the gears spinning on all the bikes. That sound had always been something special to Peppi. It reminded him of a giant beehive, full of life and energy, just buzzing along down the road. After a while he got the urge to test himself and he started to follow the line of riders up toward the front. At seeing him move through the pack, one of the younger riders pulled up alongside and wagged a finger of disapproval at him.

"*Troppo duro alla testa!*" he admonished Peppi.

"He's right, it's too hard up there," added another. "Stay in the pack for a few rides until you get your legs back."

Reluctantly, Peppi obeyed what he knew was wise advice. With a smile and a shrug he drifted back into the safety of the group. Luca pedalled up alongside and gave him a nudge in the ribs.

"Don't feel bad," he said with a big smile. "They're just looking out for you."

"I know," grumbled Peppi. "I appreciate it. But when I'm back in form, I'll drop all of them."

"Hah!" laughed Luca. "Now I know you're feeling better!"

Later in the ride, Peppi and Luca dropped off from the group and pedalled down a different road that bypassed the more arduous terrain the younger riders were planning to challenge that morning. Had Luca insisted, Peppi would have braved the difficult climbs ahead, but he was just as happy rolling along the flat roads at a leisurely pace. For his part, Luca seemed equally content to avoid the suffering that would inevitably have followed if they had stayed with the group. The two pedalled along, talking and laughing as they traded war stories from races past. It was not much longer before they decided to plot a course back toward Villa San Giuseppe. It was then that Peppi realized that one possible route would take them by the mulino.

"Come on," he said, turning down a new road, "I want to visit my home."

When they arrived at the ruins they coasted up to the edge of the property and stopped. Straddling his bike, Peppi leaned his elbows onto the handlebars and gazed over the pile of rubble that was once his home. Not much had changed from his last visit other than the grass around it, which had grown taller.

"What are your plans for the place?" asked Luca.

"I don't know," admitted Peppi. "For the time being, I thought maybe I'd put a tomato garden in over there in the back where my father had his garden. It gets some nice sun there. I'm sure the soil is still good."

"Nobody's planted anything there for years," noted Luca. "The soil probably doesn't need anything at all, maybe a little manure and some lime, but that's it. Come to think of it, my own garden could use some."

Peppi smiled and nodded, and for a moment the two just stood there in silence, enjoying the tranquility of the spot.

"By the way," Luca said at last, "I've been meaning to thank you."

"Thank me? For what?" replied Peppi.

"For whatever it was that you said to Lucrezia out in the courtyard the other day when it looked like she was just about ready to murder us all."

"I didn't tell her anything," said Peppi with a shrug. "I just gave her a few olives."

"Well, whatever it was, it worked," said Luca. "These past few days she's been a different person. I've actually seen her smile once or twice. It's like a miracle."

"It's the mono-unsaturated fats and the omega-3 fatty acids," said Peppi.

"The *what?*"

"The olives," chuckled Peppi. "All that stuff in them does something good to your brain."

"I would have thought it was just because they taste good."

"That's another reason."

"Olives," chuckled Luca, shaking his head. "Who would have thought?" He clicked his shoe back onto the pedal and turned his bike toward the road. "Come on," he said to Peppi, "let's go home and have dinner. Filomena's expecting you. We can watch the Giro prologue while we eat."

"Sounds good to me," said Peppi, following him. "Just make sure she serves olives. I'm in a good mood today and I want to stay that way."

"Eh, whatever you want," said Luca, and the two pedalled away down the road.

CHAPTER TWENTY-FOUR

Lucrezia was helping Filomena put dinner on the table when Peppi arrived at the door. Costanzo was there with Maria and the kids. They took their seats while Luca pulled the television in from the living room and set it up at the far end of the table so that they could all watch the beginning of the race while they ate. Luca could barely contain his glee as he beckoned for Peppi to take the seat across from him.

"Sit, sit," he said excitedly, "they're just getting ready to send the first rider off in the prologue."

Lucrezia nodded a hello at Peppi, but otherwise said nothing at seeing him come in. She put the big bowl of pasta she was carrying on the table and returned to the kitchen to help her mother finish preparing the meal. She soon returned with Filomena. The two women filled the pasta bowls and everyone settled down to eat and watch the race.

The prologue of the Giro D'Italia is Act One of a three-week drama full of triumphs, tragedies, politics, and, above all, passion. It mesmerizes cycling fans—and cycling fans are among the most rabid sports fans in the world, for they hold one great advantage over devotees of other sports. Whereas most professional athletes compete in constructed arenas where they are, for the most part, safely separated from the mob of spectators, cyclists compete out on the open road, an arm's length from the crowds that line the sidewalks as they whiz by. Cycling fans can reach out and touch their heroes, especially when the race enters the mountains and the competitors drag themselves up toward the clouds, often at a snail's pace. That is where the real fans, the *tifosi,* come out to watch the races. They line the steep mountain roads, leaving a path no wider than the back of one's hand for their heroes to pedal through. They paint the names of their favorite riders on the road. They paint their faces to match their national flags. They run alongside the cyclists wobbling up the road, screaming in their ears, exhorting them to pedal harder, to stay ahead of the chasing pack, to catch the rider just up the road, or perhaps just to help them survive to race another day.

Unlike most of the long, arduous stages of the Giro, where all the riders leave the starting line together and the first man to the finish line wins, the prologue is a short time trial, an individual race against the clock over a course of perhaps only three or four miles.

But it is three or four miles of sheer agony!

The riders go off one at a time at two- or three-minute intervals. This is their showcase, their introduction onto the stage, and for those three or four miles they tear apart their hearts and legs and lungs in a desperate attempt to show the cycling world that they have come to Italy ready to race. In many ways a time trial is the sport at its most basic and most brutal. It is not for nothing that they call it *la corsa di verità,* the race of truth.

As they gobbled down their food, the men took turns commenting on the riders as they entered the start house, noting the aerodynamic equipment each used.

"Not like in the old days, eh, Peppi?" Luca said for the benefit of Costanzo and Gianni. "Back when we were young you raced with the same bike every day no matter if it was a time trial or a mountain stage or a race on the flat roads. None of these special wheels and crazy handlebars they use today. We raced like men!"

"Yes, that's why you went so much slower," remarked Gianni.

Luca gave his grandson a withering look before bursting out in laughter along with the others. "Is that so?" he chortled. "Suppose you get on your bike and I'll get on mine and we'll see who pedals up the climbs faster."

"Nonno, I'd drop you in a minute," boasted Gianni.

More laughter ensued and then they turned their attention back to the prologue.

"Speaking of climbs, that reminds me, Peppi," said Luca. "Did I tell you about the stage to Abettone?"

"What about it?"

"They're going over the San Pellegrino this year," he told Peppi. "A group of us are planning to ride the climb ahead of the race. It's a little tradition we started a few years back. We always try to do at least one of the Giro climbs."

"You're not planning on doing it, are you?" Maria asked Costanzo.

"No," he told his wife, "I wouldn't make it half way up."

"You're smart," said Filomena. "Not like these other ones. They all want to see who can be the first one to croak on the mountain."

"It's not that bad," scoffed Luca. "You just have to set a nice easy tempo. Besides, the *tifosi* are always there to give you a little push to keep you going."

"Don't listen to him, Peppi," said Lucrezia with an edge of concern in her voice. "It's much more difficult than he makes it sound."

"I don't know," said Peppi. "It sounds like fun."

"It is!" exclaimed Luca. "Practically everyone in the group is planning to do it. We'll all ride up, and later on we'll have a little picnic on the mountain and watch the race go by."

"That's if any of you are still breathing," said Filomena.

"Don't listen to them, Peppi," said Luca with a wave of his hand. "Let's watch the race. We'll talk more about it later."

After dinner Luca rolled the television back into the living room so that the men could relax and digest while they watched the rest of the race. Meantime Maria and Vittoria helped clear the table while Lucrezia and Filomena started the dishes. Alone in the kitchen with her for a few moments, Filomena looked at her daughter as she scrubbed one of the big pots.

"What's wrong?" she asked.

"What makes you think something's wrong?" said Lucrezia.

"I'm your mother, I know these things," replied Filomena. "Besides, you've barely said a word since dinner."

"There's nothing wrong," said Lucrezia testily.

"Then what is it?"

Lucrezia tossed the sponge she was using into the sink and turned to her mother. "I just think it's a bad idea," she said.

"What is?"

"Papa taking Peppi up that mountain," she said.

"So do I," huffed Filomena. "But you know how men are. There's no talking to them about these things. They have to show off for the women, as if any of us care. Besides, what do you care if Peppi goes?"

"I don't," said Lucrezia awkwardly. "It's just that . . ."

"What?"

"It's just that he was sick and he's just starting to get better. I'd hate to see him get hurt for no good reason, that's all."

"If you don't want to see it, don't go," said Filomena in a matter-of-fact tone.

"I'll go if I want!" cried Lucrezia, slamming the pot she'd been washing down into the sink. Then she stormed out of the kitchen in a fury.

Later, after the prologue had finished and everyone had left, Luca came into the kitchen to see if there were any leftovers to pick at.

"What happened with Lucrezia before?" he asked as he peered into the refrigerator. "I heard her yelling about something."

"Who knows?" said Filomena. "She was just in one of her snits. You know how moody she gets."

"Hmm," grunted Luca, spying a plate of leftover veal, "maybe we should try to get her to eat more olives."

CHAPTER TWENTY-FIVE

The road to the summit of the San Pellegrino in Alpe starts far below in a lush, pleasant valley in the midst of the Apennines. Over the next twelve and one half kilometers, it climbs steadily toward the five-thousand-foot peak at an average gradient of ten percent. What that means is that the road rises one foot for every ten feet of pedalling for nearly eight miles. To get an idea of what a ten percent grade looks like, one might take a ruler, tilt one end up an inch or so, then draw an imaginary line along the ruler to some point in the distance. One soon sees that the imaginary line rises at an incredible rate!

It is the excruciating finale of the climb, however—the last two kilometers—that attracts the *tifosi,* the maniacal fans of competitive cycling who turn out to cheer the racers up the mountain. There the road goes straight up toward the sky at a staggering twenty percent grade! That is where the pedals turn over at an agonizingly slow tempo.

Each rider has his own style for getting up the mountain, his own method of survival. Some riders stay seated, their upper bodies relaxed and motionless to conserve energy as they make their way up the mountain. Others stand on the pedals and thrash about on the bicycle, desperate to find the energy for each successive pedal stroke. The one thing they all have in common, even the leaders who seem to defy gravity itself, is their suffering. Though the air gets thinner and colder as the riders near the summit, the sweat still pours out of them, leaving white splotches of salt across their faces and jerseys. They gaze with blank expressions at the road ahead, their red-rimmed eyes fixed on the pavement directly in front of them. To look further up the daunting climb toward the summit is an invitation to despair. Here is where real cyclists earn their keep. Their lungs burn and their legs cry for mercy, but they pedal on, for this is where the true contenders of the Giro come out and show themselves.

Peppi knew full well that he was not a contender for the Giro crown that year. His name would not be inscribed in any record book noting that he was one of hundreds of amateur riders, fit and unfit alike, who were foolish enough to pedal their bicycles up that ridiculously steep mountain road to the summit of the San Pellegrino in Alpe that day. He knew that no matter how soon he finished there would be no reward, monetary or otherwise. No medal, no commemorative patch, no certificate verifying the deed. Nothing. *Niente.*

Peppi knew all this and yet, as he struggled up the last few kilometers of the climb, his legs aching, his body ready to topple over sideways at any moment, he would have preferred to die than to get off his bike and walk, even though walking would most likely have been faster. Instead, Peppi kept his gaze glued to Luca's rear wheel just in front of him. As if hypnotized by its rotation, he focused all his mind and body into keeping pace with it; but try as he might the wheel kept slipping away from him. Now and then, Luca would look over his shoulder and slow down so that Peppi could catch up, but each successive effort to keep pace was starting to take its toll.

Peppi looked up at the mob of spectators along the road.

The frenetic scene surpassed anything he had ever imagined. There were people everywhere, eating and drinking and singing and dancing. Youngsters waved their nations' flags and chanted the names of their favorite riders while they tried to out-sing the fans from other countries. To be sure, the majority of the fans were Italian, but there were also sizable contingents from all of Europe and across the globe. As he gazed in wonder at the spectacle, it seemed to Peppi that all the world was woven into this colorful tapestry on the mountain.

To Peppi's surprise, the *tifosi* cheered each of the amateurs with almost as much zeal as they showed for the *maglia rosa,* the pink jersey worn each day by the Giro's leader. Some of them sat by the road and called out words of encouragement as the amateurs toiled away up the climb. Others ran along beside them, screaming in their ears, exhorting them to push harder. At one point, a man dressed as a red devil trotted up next to Peppi.

"Die! Die!" the devil screamed at him, shaking his pitchfork for emphasis.

For a moment Peppi was stunned, for he could not understand what this satanic impersonator wanted of him—he was already dying. As it was, he expected to see Anna waiting for him at the top of the climb. Then Peppi smiled and laughed despite the pain. He realized that the devil was not screaming the English word die, but the Italian word *dai,* meaning *give.* He was exhorting Peppi to give all of himself to the effort, all his heart and soul. That moment of levity was enough to give Peppi a burst of energy. He stood up on the pedals and moved up alongside Luca.

"Coraggio!" the devil called after Peppi, giving his backside a healthy push to send him on his way.

"Dio mio!" puffed Peppi, "these people are nuts!"

"Don't worry," laughed Luca, "you're doing great. How are you feeling?"

"My legs are getting ready to fall off."

"Don't give up," said Luca, "take a look at that."

Peppi looked up ahead and saw the banner over the road that told them that they were one kilometer from the top. From there on the crowd grew even thicker, but the end was now definitely in sight.

"Finalmente," gasped Peppi.

It was then that Luca and Peppi, despite their years, overtook a small group of younger riders struggling up the climb. Peppi tucked in behind Luca and the two pedalled as far as possible over to the side of the road to get by them. One of the riders, though, was having a particularly hard time of it. He wobbled and weaved, doing all he could to stay upright. For a moment he lost his concentration and veered into Peppi's path. Their wheels crossed and both riders went down hard on the pavement.

At hearing that awful scratching sound of metal and man against the road, Luca squeezed his brakes and jumped off his bicycle. He hurried back to help his friend, but by now Peppi and the other rider were engulfed by a group of fans who had picked them up and set them on their feet. Peppi had taken the worst of the fall. His shorts were torn and his forearm was badly scraped, but all in all he would survive. The other rider was practically in tears, apologizing to Peppi for causing the mishap.

"Colpa mia!" he cried. *"Mi dispiace!"*

"Don't worry," Peppi told him, giving him a pat on the

shoulder. "These things happen, my friend. Besides, I needed the rest."

At that bit of bravado the crowd around them broke out in laughter. *"Bravo!"* they all cried. Then they helped Peppi and the other rider back onto their bikes and everyone took turns pushing them along to get them started back up toward the summit.

"Hey Peppi, you're a hero now!" laughed Luca as they resumed the ascent. "I bet they'll remember that crash better than anything else they see the pros do today."

"Well, I know *I'll* remember it," said Peppi, giving his forearm a quick look as they pedalled on.

Pandemonium reigned at the top of the climb. At crossing under the banner that marked the summit, some riders would dismount and raise their bikes overhead in a triumphant salute to the cycling gods. Others would pedal over the top, blowing kisses to the crowd as they passed. The rest, Peppi and Luca among them, were content to simply get off their bikes and wade through the crowd in search of their families and friends.

"There they are," said Luca, pointing to an open spot up away from the road where the group from Villa San Giuseppe had set up camp. Filomena and Lucrezia were there, calling and waving to them as they waited with the others for the last few stragglers to make it up the mountain before the real race came through. As Peppi and Luca drew near, though, the smiles on the women's faces disappeared.

"Dio mio!" cried Lucrezia at seeing the nasty scrape on Peppi's arm.

"What happened?" said Filomena.

"A little accident," shrugged Peppi, "nothing serious."

"Don't worry, he's a hero now," said Luca, giving Peppi a wink. "Anyone else would have quit."

"Who cares about heroes!" yelled Filomena, giving her husband a slap across the shoulder. "I told you something like this might happen. Didn't I say just yesterday that . . . that . . ."

Filomena's tirade halted when she noticed that Lucrezia had taken Peppi by the arm and guided him over to the blanket they had laid out on the ground. There her daughter made him sit while their friends gathered around to pat Peppi on the back and hear the story of how it all had happened. Meantime Lucrezia opened a bottle of water and began to clean the wound on Peppi's arm.

"Ouch!" Peppi winced, pulling his arm away. "That stings."

"That's what you get for listening to my father instead of to me," she chided him. "Now be still while I clean this or you'll end up with an infection."

While she continued to scold him, Lucrezia meticulously picked out the bits of gravel that were imbedded in Peppi's skin. When she finished, she took a cloth napkin and used it as a bandage to cover the wound. Then she ordered Peppi to stay there and relax while she got him something to eat and drink.

Filomena watched with keen interest as her daughter fussed over Peppi. She let her gaze alternate between the two. Lucrezia was giving him an earful, but in that way that women do only to men they truly care about. For his part, Peppi was offering no resistance whatsoever to all the attention.

It was a very interesting situation.

Luca, meantime, was not paying any attention at all to the scene unfolding behind him. "You were saying," he said to his wife, interrupting her ruminations.

"Never mind what I was saying!" Filomena exclaimed, giving him another whack. "I've got more important things on my mind right now." Then she took her husband's arm and led him over to the blanket where she would be able to keep a closer eye on things as they developed.

That night, after they had left the madness of the Giro behind and returned home, Luca drove Peppi and the two women into Sulmona for dinner to celebrate their adventure on the mountain. After a hearty meal and a few carafes of wine, they all went for a stroll around the city's piazza. It was a cool but pleasant evening with a soft breeze drifting down from the mountains. As always on a Saturday night, the piazza was filled with people, young and old alike. In the middle of the piazza a statue of Ovid kept a contemplative watch over the proceedings. At the feet of the Roman poet sat a group of teenagers singing love ballads along with a young boy strumming the guitar.

Luca was in fine spirits as he ambled along, talking nonstop with Peppi about the Giro. "You know, some might say that the Tour de France has more prestige," he was saying, "but the Giro has more of the soul, the real spirit of cycling."

"What makes you say that?" asked Peppi.

"Don't let him get started," said Filomena, walking with Lucrezia a few steps behind. "He'll bend your ear for the rest of the night if you let him."

"But it's true," said Luca, coming to a stop. "You know yourself, Filomena. Tell Peppi about the day we all went to watch Andrea from Introdacqua the last time the Giro came through here."

"You tell him," sighed Filomena, rolling her eyes for Lucrezia's benefit.

"You had to see it," Luca began. "The group let Andrea pedal up ahead so that he could stop and say hello to all his family and friends who had come out to watch him race. They do the same thing sometimes in the Tour when the race goes through a rider's home town. But what's different about the Giro is that this time all the riders ended up stopping, not just Andrea, because Filomena and some of the other women had baked a load of pastries for them. It was incredible: almost two hundred guys on bicycles pull over and start gobbling down all the sweets they can get their hands on. Even the guys on the motorcycles and the race commissars grabbed a couple! Then one of the racers pedals off with a tray of cannoli and starts serving them to the other riders as they went along. It was great! You just don't see that sort of thing in any other race—only the Giro."

The four of them continued their walk until they came to the edge of the piazza. Just across from it was a little park where they sat down on the edge of one of the fountains. Peppi leaned over and smiled when he saw the brightly colored fish swimming about in the pools. Lucrezia turned in time to see the smile on his face.

"What is it?" she said, looking with him into the pool.

"I was just remembering when I was a little boy," said Peppi. "My parents used to bring me here sometimes and I would always get soaking wet trying to reach in and catch the fish."

"How sweet," said Lucrezia, still gazing into the pool. "You must have been so cute."

Peppi made no reply, but simply smiled and stared with her at the tranquil water.

Filomena, meantime, jumped up, took Luca by the arm, and tugged him away from the fountain.

"What are you doing, *amore mia?*" he said to his wife as she made him walk with her down the path by the other fountains in the park.

Filomena looked back over her shoulder to see if Lucrezia and Peppi had even noticed that they had left. "I'm doing whatever it takes," she said firmly. Then she smiled, coiled her arm around Luca's, and the two walked on together.

Left to themselves, Lucrezia and Peppi sat by the fountain chatting about the day's adventures. It was a good long while before either noticed that Filomena and Luca had disappeared. Peppi finally turned and looked about to see where they might have gone to.

"I wonder where your parents are?" he said.

"Don't worry about those two," said Lucrezia, "I'm sure they haven't wandered far."

She regarded Peppi for a moment before reaching out to touch him lightly on the elbow. "How is your arm feeling, by the way?" she asked, sounding concerned. "That was a nasty fall you took today."

"It's a little sore," Peppi admitted, flexing his arm, "but not too bad. Thankfully I received some very good medical attention after I made it to the top of the mountain. You would have made a very good nurse," he added.

"A nurse?" Lucrezia replied, feigning indignation. "Why not a doctor? Are you a chauvinist?"

"Oh no, never," said Peppi. "It's just that—"

"Just what?" said Lucrezia. She looked quite pleased with herself for having made him squirm a bit.

Peppi caught the mischievous gleam in her eye. "Doctor or nurse, you would get along very well in America," he said with a chuckle. "Over there the women don't let men get away with anything either."

"And why should they?" she replied smugly.

Peppi could only offer a shrug in response. Lucrezia gave him a nudge to show that she was just teasing him, and they both laughed.

"So tell me," she asked, "do you miss America?"

"Sometimes," Peppi answered. "I lived there most of my life, so I left a lot of myself behind, if you know what I mean."

Lucrezia leaned forward and rested her chin upon her hand. "I would like to visit America someday," she said. "Do you think you would ever go back?"

"To live? No," said Peppi, shaking his head, "I don't think so."

"How about just to visit?"

"Eh, who knows?" he shrugged. "I doubt it, but then again it wasn't so long ago that I would never have imagined coming back here. But for the moment, I'm very happy right where I am."

"So am I," she said.

Lucrezia looked out to the other side of the park where a pair of young lovers had just sat down together on a bench. The two, she saw, were off together in a blissful world of their own and before long their arms were entwined in an impassioned embrace. It was a tender scene that stirred something within Lucrezia, an old yearning that she knew still lived in her despite her best attempts to push it from her consciousness. She let slip a sigh and looked back at Peppi. By now, he too had taken notice of the couple. As he watched them, Lucrezia let her eyes study the rugged profile of his face. Just then Peppi broke out in a smile and his eyes became aglow with a merriment that she had never seen in them before. There was something irresistible about it and she found herself smiling too.

"What is it?" she asked him. "What's so funny?"

"Those two over there should be more careful," Peppi said, nodding at the couple, who at this point were kissing each other quite dramatically. "The way things are going they might both wind up needing dental work."

"Hey, sometimes love hurts," joked Lucrezia.

"Yes, I've heard that," laughed Peppi, "but they say it's still worth it."

As he said this, Peppi turned back to face her and for the first time the two gazed directly at one another.

"So they say," said Lucrezia, her eyes meeting his.

Peppi returned her gaze, unsure of what it was he saw in her eyes—and of what she saw in his. Lucrezia lifted her hand and, for a hypnotic moment, he was certain that she was going to touch his face. The moment passed quickly, though, and Lucrezia came back to herself. Looking a bit flustered, she stood and gave his shirtsleeve a tug.

"Come on," she said, "let's go find my parents before they get lost somewhere."

As Peppi stood he saw a brilliant full moon rising over the mountains in the distance. At the sight of it he gave a sigh of his own. *"Che bella notte,"* he said. "What a beautiful night."

"Yes, it truly is," said Lucrezia.

Peppi smiled and gave her a nod. He let her slip her arm through his and together the two strolled off into the moonlight.

CHAPTER TWENTY-SIX

One day, after the three frenzied weeks of the Giro had passed and June's warm weather had settled in to stay, a letter came to the post office in the village addressed to:

Signor Peppi
Il Mulino
Villa San Giuseppe

By this time the men in the local post office knew that Peppi was the American who lived in the apartment above Luca's factory; they tucked the letter in with the bundle of business correspondence that would be delivered to the factory later that morning.

Peppi was out back working in the gardens when Lucrezia came out with the letter.

"Peppi, you have some mail," she called.

At hearing her approach, Peppi stood and brushed the dirt off his hands and knees. "From America?" he said, wiping his hands on his trousers.

"No, Pescara."

"Pescara?" said Peppi. "Who's sending me letters from Pescara?"

"Open it and see."

"Please, you do it for me," said Peppi. "My hands are a mess right now."

Lucrezia opened the envelope, pulled out the engraved card inside, and began to read. "It's a wedding invitation," she announced.

"To whose wedding?" asked Peppi, now totally perplexed.

"Let's see . . . two people named Loredana and Claudio."

Peppi scratched his head, repeating the names to himself. Then he suddenly remembered. "Of course, Loredana and Claudio!" he exclaimed. "Now I remember. Who would have thought?"

"Who are they?" asked Lucrezia.

"Two young friends of mine. I met them on the train," said Peppi. "When are they getting married?"

"In three weeks."

"And they want me to come," mused Peppi. "That's nice of them to invite me. But my word, they only just met this past winter."

"Remember, this is Italy, Peppi," said Lucrezia, looking over the invitation. "Things happen fast when people fall in love here."

Peppi nodded. "I guess so."

Lucrezia tucked the invitation back into the envelope and handed it to Peppi. "So, will you go?" she asked. "The shore at Pescara is beautiful this time of year."

Peppi shook his head. "No, I don't think so."

"But why not?"

Peppi walked over to the bench beneath the arbor and sat down. "I don't know," he said with a shrug. "Anna and I were married in June. Our anniversary is coming up soon."

"I didn't know that," said Lucrezia. She walked up beside him. "May I?" she asked, gesturing to the bench.

"Of course," said Peppi, dusting the spot off for her.

Lucrezia sat next to him and gazed past him into the distance for a time without speaking. In her eyes Peppi could see the colorful reflection of the flower beds behind him.

"Francesco and I were married in July," Lucrezia said wistfully. "Don't ask me why we waited till the middle of the summer. Even now I don't know why. *Mannagia*, it was so hot that day! Our anniversary will be coming up soon too."

"Should I start to measure the window panes again?" asked Peppi.

"No, you don't have to worry about the windows," replied Lucrezia, swatting him on the arm with the back of her hand. "But I think you should go to the wedding. It would be good for you."

"I don't know," said Peppi, "I'm not sure if I'm ready yet for that sort of thing again. And don't forget, I don't even have a car to drive there. Besides, I'd feel funny going all alone even if I did."

"Hmm," sighed Lucrezia. "I know what you mean."

Peppi stared at the envelope. "Then again, maybe I should go," he said thoughtfully. "I haven't been to mass since Anna's funeral. It's probably time I went."

"Weddings and funerals are the only times I go to church these days," said Lucrezia.

Peppi nodded to show he understood. Patting her shoulder, he stood and tucked the invitation into his back pocket. Then he walked away toward the flower beds.

"So, what are you going to do?" said Lucrezia.

"Well, for now I'm going to finish weeding the garden," he replied. "Then I'm going to take a nap. I'll worry about the wedding later on."

That evening after dinner, Peppi walked up to Luca's house to watch the news, something he liked to do once or twice a week. In truth, Luca and Filomena would have welcomed him every night if he wanted to come, but Peppi didn't like to intrude too much. As he strolled up the path, it occurred to him that in addition to going back to church on a more regular basis, it was probably about time he bought himself a television for the apartment. He made a mental note to look into it soon.

When Peppi came in, Luca and Filomena were in the living room. Filomena was just turning the television on while Luca read the newspaper. He looked up from his reading and gave Peppi a nod.

"Any good news?" said Peppi.

"None in here," Luca replied, tossing the paper aside in favor of *La Gazzetta dello Sport.* "But sit and watch. Maybe they'll tell us about something worth listening to on the television."

"We can only hope," said Peppi.

"*Ciao,* Peppi," said Filomena, taking a seat on the sofa. "It's a warm night. Would you like a beer or glass of wine?"

"No, thank you, Filomena. I'm fine."

"Didn't see much of you today, Peppi," said Luca from behind the sporting news. "What were you up to today?"

"Shh!" shushed Filomena. "I'm trying to hear the news."

"I was around, doing a little gardening this morning," Peppi said softly in reply to Luca's question. "Got some mail today that surprised me."

"A letter from America?" said Luca aloud.

"Hey, do you mind? I'm trying to listen," said Filomena, flinging a sofa cushion at her husband. *"Sta zita!"*

Peppi stood and moved his chair closer to Luca so that they might talk more quietly. "No, it was a wedding invitation from Pescara," he whispered.

"A wedding invitation?" said Filomena, suddenly turning away from the television. "Who from?"

"Would you mind not speaking so loudly?" said Luca. "I'm trying to read the sporting news."

"Watch yourself, *Signore,*" his wife said menacingly before turning her attention back to Peppi. "Who do you know in Pescara, Peppi?"

Peppi told them the story of how he had met Loredana and Claudio on the train from Rome. It was a nice memory and he laughed after telling them the story, for he never would have dreamed that the two would end up married.

"Well, it was nice of them to invite you to the wedding," said Filomena when he had finished. "Will you go?"

"No," Peppi explained. "I don't think so. It's a long way and I really don't feel like going alone to something like that anyway."

"Who says you have to go alone?" she replied. "Did the invitation say only you were invited?"

"Well, now that you mention it," said Peppi, "the card inside did say Signor Peppi and guest."

"There!" said Filomena, slapping her hand down on the table. "I told you, you don't have to go alone. Take somebody with you. It will be good for you."

"Who on earth around here would want to go to a wedding in Pescara with me?" said Peppi, grinning.

"Don't even look at me," said Luca from behind *La Gazzetta*.

"Who's asking you?" said Filomena. "Now, don't you worry about it, Peppi. Lucrezia will go with you."

Peppi squirmed uneasily in the chair. "Oh, but I really don't think . . ." Peppi began to say, but just then the door opened and Lucrezia herself came in carrying her usual load of paperwork from the office.

"Here she is now," said Filomena. "Lucrezia, come in here."

Lucrezia dumped her work on the kitchen counter and came into the living room.

"Ciao, Peppi, *"* she said at seeing him.

"Lucrezia," her mother began, "Peppi has been invited to a wedding."

"I know," Lucrezia replied.

"You do? Well, good, because I told Peppi that you would go with him."

Lucrezia shot a look at her mother that would have stopped a rhinoceros. She folded her arms and tapped her foot. Peppi was certain that hostilities were about to commence.

"Don't worry," Peppi told her. "You don't have to come. I knew you wouldn't want to. Please, don't give it another thought."

"Of course she wants to go," said Filomena before her daughter had a chance to open her mouth.

To Peppi's surprise, Lucrezia's scowl turned into a small but detectable grin. "I'll tell you what," she said in the tone of voice she might use when negotiating a new sales agreement or perhaps trying to finagle a better price from a vendor, "I'll go with you to the wedding, but under one condition."

"Which is?" said Peppi.

"You *have* to let me help you buy some new clothes," she

said, shaking her head in disbelief. "I refuse to go anywhere with you unless you get a new suit and definitely some new shoes."

"She's right," said Luca, lowering the sports page for only a moment. "I didn't want to say it, but I can't believe the things they let you Americans walk around wearing. It's appalling."

"You know, you're not the first person in Italy to tell me that," sighed Peppi.

"Then we have a deal?" said Lucrezia.

"Do I have a choice?"

"No, not really," said Lucrezia playfully. "Not if you want a ride to Pescara." Then she turned and sashayed out of the room.

"Looks like you have a date," said Luca. "I hope your intentions are honorable. I don't want any mischief."

"Well, I'll be taking her to church," laughed Peppi. "I don't think we can get into too much mischief there."

No, thought Filomena, but it's a start.

CHAPTER TWENTY-SEVEN

The morning of the wedding, Peppi arose early. The ceremony was to take place at noon, so Lucrezia had made him promise to be ready by nine-thirty to give them plenty of time to make the drive to Pescara. By Peppi's reckoning, especially taking into account the way that Lucrezia liked to drive, that would get them to the church a half hour or so early. He would have preferred to arrive just on time, but he supposed it was better to give themselves a little cushion.

Peppi went into the kitchen and made himself some coffee. As he sat at the table with his cup, he nibbled a biscotti while he looked over at the new suit hanging on the bedroom door. Below on the floor sat the box containing his new shoes. The new shirt and tie were already laid out on the bed.

Though he preferred to live simply, Peppi was quite secure financially. Just the same, he let out a sigh at the thought of the money he had spent on the clothes. Lucrezia had taken him to Michele's, the only men's clothing shop in Villa San Giuseppe. The fact that the shop was located in a little out-of-the-way town high in the Abruzzi mountains made it no less expensive. The prices rivalled anything Peppi might have found in Milan. When they walked in together, Lucrezia had beckoned for the owner.

"Michele," she had announced with great solemnity, "in three weeks I must accompany this man to a wedding in Pescara. I don't wish to be embarrassed, so *per favore,* do *something* with him!"

"Si, subito, Signorina!" said Michele with a quick bow of his head. He turned to Peppi, narrowed his gaze, and looked him up and down like a sculptor inspecting a fresh, unchiseled piece of marble for the first time. He frowned at what he saw, particularly Peppi's shoes. "Turn, please," he said, shaking his head in disbelief.

Peppi turned around, allowing the tailor to scrutinize his back and shoulders. For a time, Michele stood there, scratching his chin thoughtfully while he assessed the situation. "You brought him in just in time, Signorina Lucrezia," he said at last. "If he had stayed dressed like this for much longer, the damage might have been irreversible."

"I agree," replied Lucrezia, straight-faced. "That's why I brought him to you right away."

Michele turned and gestured for them to follow. "Please, take him this way," he told her, leading them to the fitting room. "You are very fortunate. Just this morning I got in some nice new fabrics that would be perfect for a summer suit. I'll get some samples for you to look at while I take his measurements."

Peppi dutifully stood there in silence while the tailor measured his arms and legs and neck and shoulders. There wasn't much else for him to do for Lucrezia was running the show. She and Michele talked nonstop the whole time, debating the merits of one fabric over another and deciding which styles would look best on Peppi. It was almost as if they were dressing a mannequin. Now and then, though, Lucrezia would look up at Peppi and give him a brief smile before refocusing her attention on the serious business at hand. Peppi could not complain, for it was obvious that she was thoroughly enjoying herself. That had made him feel happy.

After breakfast, Peppi showered and dressed. When he came downstairs from his apartment, Lucrezia was already standing by the car, waiting for him. As always, she was dressed to perfection, but this day she looked softer, more feminine, not so businesslike. Instead of pulling her hair back tightly, she had let it fall down naturally to her shoulders. She wore a simple silk blouse and matching skirt. Lucrezia had that Italian sense of style that gave her a simple but elegant look that stopped men in their tracks.

Peppi gulped when he saw her for he suddenly realized how very out of place he would feel next to her. At seeing him approach, though, she allayed his fears by flashing him a brilliant smile. She lowered her sunglasses to get a better look at him.

"*Ciao, bello,*" she said with an approving nod, gesturing for him to turn about so that she could get the whole effect. "Now *that's* more like it."

"You don't think the slacks fit too tight?" said Peppi.

"This is Italy, Peppi," she laughed. "Slacks are supposed to fit tight."

"But I feel like Tom Jones," sighed Peppi.

"Who?"

"Never mind," he said. "I'll get used to them. *Andiamo.*"

They climbed into the car. As he buckled himself in, Peppi could not help but notice Lucrezia's long slender legs as she revved the engine. He quickly looked away and directed his gaze straight ahead. "Remember, not too fast," he told her. "I'm an old man, you know."

"You're not so old," she replied mischievously. Then she put the car in gear, stepped on the accelerator, and sped away from the house and down the road.

They were on their way.

CHAPTER TWENTY-EIGHT

As Peppi had expected, they arrived in Pescara well before the start of the wedding. It was a warm, pleasant day with a gentle breeze drifting in off the nearby Adriatic. To pass the time until the ceremony began, Lucrezia suggested that they take a stroll around the piazza outside the church. As they ambled along, chatting about the weather and peeking into the windows of the shops, Peppi realized that there was something very familiar about the place. He stopped suddenly and looked out across the piazza.

"I remember now," he said, breaking out in a smile.

"Remember what?" asked Lucrezia.

"I raced through this piazza once years ago, your father too. It was during a circuit race. We passed through here at least three or four times. I knew the church looked familiar. I remember because right in front of it I punctured a tire on the last lap and I had to walk my bike to the finish."

"You're just like my father," laughed Lucrezia. "How can the two of you remember such things from so long ago?"

"We old cyclists remember everything," grinned Peppi, "especially races we might have won."

They walked on until they came to a street vendor selling cold beverages from a little cart with a colorful umbrella overhead. Peppi bought two bottles of lemonade while Lucrezia secured them a free spot on a nearby bench. They sat there for a time in silence, sipping their lemonades while they watched the people come and go.

"Francesco was a cyclist," Lucrezia said at last.

"I didn't know that," said Peppi. "Did he race?"

"As much as he could before we were married, but then his business started to take up too much of his time. But still he liked to ride and train as often as he could."

"Your father must have liked that about him," said Peppi.

"Yes," she said with a wistful smile. "He was always trying to get Francesco to ride with him on the weekends. Sometimes I think that the only reason my father gave us his blessing so quickly when we decided to get married was that he wanted someone else in the family to ride his bike with."

"That's entirely possible," said Peppi. Then he looked back to the church and saw that the wedding guests were starting to arrive. "Speaking of getting married," he said with a nod toward the church, "I think it's time for us to go."

There was still plenty of time before the start of the ceremony when they entered the church. Peppi helped Lucrezia choose a place for them to sit then left her for a few moments. It was his first time in church since Anna's funeral and he thought it would be nice to light a candle for her. He walked to the little alcove on the side aisle of the church where the rows of candles flickered in the dim light. Only two remained that had yet to be lit that day. He took a piece of straw and used it to light one of the two. Then, after tucking a sum of lira that far exceeded the suggested offering into the little metal box, he knelt on one of the two kneelers and began to pray for his wife.

A few moments later, Lucrezia appeared at his side. She took one of the thin pieces of straw, held it into the flame of the candle Peppi had just lit, and used it to light a candle of her own for Francesco. When the candle had flamed to life, she reached into her pocketbook to find some money to put into the offertory box. Peppi, though, reached out to stop her.

"Don't bother," he whispered, touching her arm, "I put plenty in for both of us."

Lucrezia nodded her thanks, took her place on the other kneeler, and the two of them bowed their heads in prayer.

CHAPTER TWENTY-NINE

"Signor Peppi, you look wonderful!" exclaimed Loredana, throwing her arms around Peppi's neck.

They were at the reception on a beautiful terrace overlooking the sparkling Adriatic Sea. In the corner a quartet played while the other wedding guests who had already passed through the receiving line sipped their cocktails and nibbled on the antipasti. One and all wore sunglasses for it was a bright, gorgeous day. The air was full of laughter and talk as everyone took turns gazing out at the sundrenched beach below.

"Thank you so much for coming today," Loredana gushed as she kissed Peppi's cheeks.

"Thank you for inviting me," said Peppi.

"How could we not invite the man who brought the two of us together?" said Claudio, giving Peppi an embrace of his own. "You're family to us now!"

Embarrassed by all the sudden attention, Peppi gestured to Lucrezia. "This is Lucrezia," he told them, "a good friend of mine. I couldn't have come today if it weren't for her."

"Thank you for coming," said Loredana, "and for bringing Signor Peppi. It means so much to us."

"It was my pleasure," said Lucrezia with a genuine smile. "Congratulations to both of you. Your wedding ceremony was beautiful and I just love your gown, Loredana. You have to tell me, was it made by a local designer?"

While Lucrezia and Loredana discussed bridal fashions, Claudio gave Peppi a pat on the shoulder. "Signor Peppi, my wife is right, you look very sharp in that suit," he said with a nod of admiration, "and what great shoes!"

"I had a little help picking things out," Peppi admitted.

"From your . . . friend?" said Claudio, giving Peppi an inquisitive look.

Peppi responded with a shrug.

Claudio leaned closer so that the others wouldn't hear. "She is very beautiful, Signor Peppi," he said with a knowing smile. "I'm happy for you."

Peppi blushed. "Oh, it's not what you think," he said quickly. "At least, not what I think you are thinking."

"I was only thinking the best," Claudio assured him. He gave Peppi a conspiratorial wink before turning his attention back to the bride.

Later, after dinner had been served, the quartet gave way to a ten-piece band and the dancing began. Lucrezia and Peppi stayed off to the side at a little table from which they could watch the festivities. Lucrezia gazed pensively out at the dance floor where Loredana and Claudio were taking their first official dance as husband and wife.

"They make a nice couple, don't you think?" said Peppi.

"Very nice," she agreed. "They're so young and happy and with so much in front of them. It's almost like watching two people being born, if you know what I mean."

"I never thought of it that way, but I suppose you're right," said Peppi. "They *are* starting a whole new life, so I guess that it is like being reborn in a way."

"Strange, isn't it?" she continued. "Life always seems to be beginning then ending then beginning again, all within itself. It keeps changing and it's like we're always happy and sad at the same time."

"It's hard to feel one if you haven't felt the other," observed Peppi. "I think a little sadness now and then makes the happier times like these that much sweeter. It's not healthy to be one or the other all the time."

Peppi paused and looked at her. "I couldn't help noticing some tears in your eyes during the ceremony today," he said after a moment. "It made me sorry for making you come here today."

"Nonsense," said Lucrezia, touching his hand. "You can't pay attention to me at times like these. It happens to me all the time at weddings. I start to think about my own wedding day, wishing I could do it all over again, wishing Francesco were still here, wishing that we had never waited so long to start having children. It all comes out. You must have felt that way at least a little too."

"I suppose everyone does who has ever been married," said Peppi. "So you're not sorry you came?"

"Not at all," she said, smiling. "I've had a wonderful time. But I was a little concerned when you convinced me to go up to communion with you at mass. I haven't taken communion in years and I haven't been to confession either. I thought for sure that the walls were going to start shaking or a lightning bolt was going to fall down from the sky and strike me."

"No," chuckled Peppi, "you had nothing to worry about. God doesn't hold grudges—so long as you don't hold one against Him."

Lucrezia looked back out to the dance floor where the other

couples had started to join Loredana and Claudio. "That's the real trick," she replied. "Isn't it?"

Just then Peppi heard his name being called. He looked over at the dance floor and saw that it was Loredana and Claudio calling to him. They beckoned for him and Lucrezia to join them on the dance floor. Peppi turned nervous eyes to Lucrezia.

"I'm a terrible dancer," she said with a pained expression. "If you want to dance with me, you'll do it at your own risk."

Peppi pushed his chair away from the table and stood. "I don't want to disappoint them," he said, reaching for her hand. Then he guided her to the dance floor amidst the applause of the entire wedding party. Claudio gave a nod to the band leader and the music started once more, a slow melodic waltz.

"Are you sure you want to do this?" asked Lucrezia as Peppi very tentatively took her hand and slipped his arm around her waist. "I really don't know what I'm doing on a dance floor."

"Don't worry," Peppi answered. "I'm not so sure of what I'm doing either. Just follow my lead—and try not to step on my new shoes."

Lucrezia and Peppi remained at the reception, dancing and enjoying the music until the time came for Loredana and Claudio to bid farewell to everyone and hurry off to start their honeymoon. As he watched the newlyweds leave in a flurry of hugs and kisses, it occurred to Peppi that the day had passed very quickly. He was glad for not having given in to his initial reluctance to attend the wedding. All in all it had been a wonderful diversion. He was equally gladdened to see that Lucrezia had enjoyed herself as well. Now that it was time to go, he was surprised to find that he felt a little let down, as if inside he wished that the festivities could still go on.

It was well past nightfall by the time he and Lucrezia finally strolled back to the car and started on the way back home.

"It will be very late by the time we reach Villa San Giuseppe," noted Lucrezia as she started the car. "Do you think my parents will be up waiting for me when I get home?" she added playfully.

"It's entirely possible," chuckled Peppi. "They still worry about you, you know."

"Ayyy, I know," sighed Lucrezia. "Sometimes they act like I'm still sixteen."

"Well, you certainly dance like you're still sixteen," said Peppi with a smile.

"Hah!" laughed Lucrezia. "I don't know if that's an insult or a compliment."

"It's a compliment," Peppi assured her. "Believe me, it's a compliment."

The remark seemed to please Lucrezia and a look of satisfaction came over her face as she steered the car toward the autostrada. With a sly grin she stepped hard on the accelerator, jolting both of them back against their seats.

"Hey!" said Peppi through his laughter. "If I had wanted to fly I would have gone to the airport."

"But think of all the fun you would have missed," she said.

The engine gave a roar and the car sped off down the highway.

An hour or so into their journey home, the two decided to stop for coffee. It was nighttime and there was still quite a long drive ahead of them, so it seemed like a good idea to take a little break along the way. Lucrezia pulled off the highway into a little *paese* named Montevecchio. It was a quiet village, but there were still plenty of people strolling about when the two walked onto the piazza. When Lucrezia spied an empty table at a little outdoor café, they hurried over to take it before someone else had the chance. Before long a waiter brought them coffee and the pair settled back to watch the people come and go.

"What a beautiful night," noted Peppi as he sipped his coffee.

"Yes," Lucrezia agreed, "it was a beautiful day as well. I'm happy things worked out so nicely for your friends."

"They're your friends now too," said Peppi.

Lucrezia smiled and looked out across the piazza. There a group of teenage boys were sitting on the stairs to the church, talking and laughing among themselves as they ogled the girls passing by.

"Sometimes it seems to me like yesterday when I was one of those girls walking past all the boys back home," she mused.

"Well," chuckled Peppi, "I have to admit that for me it seems a little bit longer than yesterday when I was one of those boys on the steps."

"I can just imagine you back then"—she laughed—"and my father too!"

"Ah, now those were the days," Peppi sighed.

Peppi and Lucrezia stayed there for quite a while just talking and enjoying the evening. It was late and they had far to drive, but neither seemed in a hurry to leave. Finally, though, when Lucrezia let out a little yawn, Peppi knew that it was time for them to get on their way.

Lucrezia yawned again when they returned to the car. *"Dio,* I'm so tired all of a sudden."

"Then why don't you let me drive the rest of the way," offered Peppi, reaching for the keys in her hand.

"Do you know how?" said Lucrezia, holding them back. "I've never seen you on anything but a bicycle."

Peppi gave her a look of indignation. "Trust me, Signorina," he told her. "I'm a very good driver. We may not get there as fast as we would if you were behind the wheel, but we'll get there."

Lucrezia gave him a skeptical look of her own, but finally relinquished the keys.

"Well, just don't run into anything," she told him, trying her best to stifle another a yawn, "or I'll be very upset."

"I'll be careful," he promised.

Lucrezia said very little once they were on their way, and after a while said nothing at all. Peppi wondered what it was that had suddenly made her so quiet until he looked over and saw that she had simply nodded off to sleep. She was out like a light. Peppi laughed to himself and started to reach over to turn on the radio. Some quiet music, he thought, would keep him company for the rest of the ride. Just then, however, Lucrezia gave a soft moan, curled her legs up, and to his surprise leaned over and rested her head against his shoulder. No longer able to move his arm, for he feared that to do so might wake her, Peppi forgot all about the radio. Instead, he just smiled and hummed a song to himself while Lucrezia slept and the two drew nearer and nearer to home.

CHAPTER THIRTY

Lucrezia yawned and sat up on the edge of the bed. She stretched her arms over her head for a moment, stood, and looked out the bedroom window to the mountains in the east. To her surprise, she discovered that she had slept well into midmorning, early enough for most people to arise on a Sunday morning, but not Lucrezia. Most mornings she awoke with the birds, sometimes even before the sun had a chance to peek over the mountaintops or the rooster to crow. On those mornings, a low, thin white carpet of mist would cling to the cool, dark ground, making the world outside a dreamy place half between sleeping and waking. It was her favorite time of the day.

By now, though, the mist had long disappeared, chased away by the warming rays of the morning summer sun. With another yawn, she turned away from the window and sat back on the edge of the bed. She felt too tired to start her day, but too restless to go back to sleep. It was the aroma of freshly brewed coffee that finally tugged her out of bed for good. She put on her robe and slippers and walked wearily to the kitchen.

As Lucrezia had suspected, Filomena was there at the table sipping her first cup of coffee of the day. Lucrezia smiled, for she knew that daily life for her mother, and most Italians for that matter, could not begin otherwise. For them, caffeine was an essential nutrient. The mere thought of starting a day without the bracing jolt of a good cup of coffee was beyond comprehension. She gave her mother a nod and went to the stove to pour herself a cup.

"You're up early today," she said as the dark, warm brew filled the cup.

"And you're up late," Filomena replied, barely looking up from the magazine she was leafing through.

"Papa out for his ride?"

"Mm-hmm," nodded her mother. "He left just a few minutes before you got out of bed." She turned the page of the magazine. "I didn't hear you come in last night. What time did you get home? It must have been late."

Lucrezia brought her mug to the table and sat down. She said nothing at first but simply gazed out the window as she drank her coffee.

"We stopped for a coffee on the way home," she said after a time. "It was a long ride, so we decided to stop and take a break."

"That was sensible," noted her mother, still focused on her magazine.

"We got to talking," Lucrezia went on with a yawn. "The time passed so quickly."

"That can happen," said Filomena.

Lucrezia stretched out her legs and flexed her feet and toes. *"Dio mio,"* she winced, "my legs are aching today. I'm not used to dancing anymore."

Filomena peeked over the page she was reading, took a sip from her cup, and studied her daughter for a moment. "Sounds like you two really enjoyed yourselves," she said before hiding once more behind the magazine.

Lucrezia slammed her cup down. *"Cosa?"* she said, glaring at her mother. "What are you trying to say?"

"What do you mean, what am I trying to say?"

"You know exactly what I mean," fumed Lucrezia. "I know from that voice of yours. I can tell when you're trying to say something. What have you been doing, waiting out here for me to get up so you can start something first thing in the morning?"

"I haven't been waiting to start anything. I've just been sitting here reading my magazine."

"Well you're reading it upside down!"

Filomena's face reddened and she tossed the magazine aside. "I was looking at an advertisement, that's all. I don't see why you're acting so upset. What did I say, anyway? I only said it sounded like you two enjoyed yourselves. What was wrong with that?"

Lucrezia scowled at her. "What, are you trying to say that we *weren't* supposed to enjoy ourselves?"

"Of course not, just the opposite!" said her mother, throwing her hands up. "It's natural for a man and a woman to enjoy each other's company."

"Then why don't you just come out and say what's really on your mind?" said Lucrezia.

"Maybe you should come out and say what's really on *your* mind," Filomena replied, locking eyeballs with her daughter.

"I haven't got anything on my mind!"

"Well, it's about time you did have something on your mind," cried Filomena, slamming her hand down on the table, "something other than running that stupid candy factory at the bottom of the hill!"

"What on earth are you talking about, Mama?"

"What do you think I'm talking about? I'm talking about you and that cyclist who's living two flights of stairs above the office you work in every day."

"Me and *Peppi*?" answered Lucrezia, gaping at her mother.

"Ayyy, don't act like you don't know," said Filomena with a wave of her hand. "You know exactly what's going on."

"No, I don't know, *madre mia*," huffed her daughter. "Why don't you explain it for me."

"What's to explain? You're a woman, he's a man. Figure it out for yourself."

"*Ma, tu sei pazza, Mama!*" Lucrezia exclaimed, jumping up from her seat. "You're crazy!"

"You're right, I am crazy!" Filomena shot back. "What a mistake we made, your father and I, letting you come back here after poor Francesco died. We should have made you keep your old apartment in the city and forced you to start your life over again. Instead we let you come back here and hide yourself where no one can find you."

Lucrezia stood in the middle of the kitchen, glaring at her mother. "Is that what this is all about," she said, suddenly calm, like the calm before a tumultuous storm, "you want me to move out?"

"No," said Filomena, shaking her head. "All I've wanted for you is to find another man. I want you to be happy. I told you before, it's time to put away the black dress. You can't go on mourning Francesco forever. *He* wouldn't want you to."

"But, Mama, listen to yourself. Are you telling me I should start my life over with *Peppi*?"

"Why not?"

"Please, Mama, he's Papa's friend," cried Lucrezia. "Have you forgotten that? And besides, I'm too young for him—or he's too old for me."

"So what?" said her mother. "He's strong and fit. And believe me, there's nothing old about the way he looks at you—or you at him. Anyone with eyes can see what's happening between you two."

"There's nothing happening between us! We're two people who have both lost someone they once loved, and now we've become friends. What's wrong with that?"

Filomena stood and brought her cup to the sink. "Trust me on this, *figlia mia*," she said as she rinsed it out. "Men and women aren't supposed to be friends. They're supposed to be lovers and husbands and wives. It's what makes the world go around, in case *you've* forgotten that."

"And *you* make my head go around," snapped Lucrezia, holding her forehead. She collapsed wearily onto a chair, then suddenly sat up straight. "You haven't talked about this to Papa, have you?" she said, clearly alarmed by the prospect. "He hasn't said anything to Peppi, has he?"

"Please," said Filomena with a dismissive gesture. "Men almost never figure these things out for themselves. Your father is as blind to all of this as Peppi. It amazes me sometimes how stupid men can be."

Lucrezia stood up once more. "I can't talk about this anymore," she said as she started to leave the kitchen.

"Go to him," Filomena called after her. "Go today, don't wait. Just let it happen."

Lucrezia whirled around. "I won't," she said, gritting her teeth.

"But why!" cried her mother.

"Because I'm not ready!" she screamed back. "And because . . . and because I'm afraid!"

"Afraid of what?"

"That he'll die, all right, Mama? There, I've said it. I lost one man and look what it did to me. Once was enough. I can't give my heart to someone again knowing it could all end tomorrow."

Filomena stood there with her arms crossed. "Lucrezia," she said very softly, "listen to me. There are no guarantees in this life. You of all people should understand that. Young man, old man, it makes no difference. If God wants him, He takes him. So Peppi's no spring chicken. Maybe he's got ten years left in him. Maybe he's got twenty or thirty. Or maybe he's only got one. But if it means one good year of happiness for you, isn't it worth it?"

Lucrezia covered her ears and turned away. "I told you, I don't want to talk about this anymore!" she said, hurrying to her room.

"But where are you going?"

"I'm going to take a shower," she cried, "and then tomorrow I'm going to Milano!" With that she slammed her bedroom door so hard that a painting fell off the corridor wall.

"L'amore," Filomena said, shaking her head in wonder. "Who can figure it out?"

CHAPTER THIRTY-ONE

Peppi shifted the chain of the bike to a smaller gear. The hill they were ascending was not particularly steep, but just the same he was having trouble keeping up with Luca and the rest of the group. Taking several deep breaths, Peppi sat up straight, relaxed his back and shoulders, and did his best to spin his legs at a nice even cadence. Nothing seemed to help, though, and he drifted further and further back. At last, Luca looked over his shoulder. At seeing his friend struggling behind, he sat up and waited for Peppi to catch up to him.

"Cosa fai oggi, Peppi?" he chided him. "What are you doing back there?"

"Mannagia," Peppi groaned, "I'm really suffering today. I just don't have the legs."

"Eh, what did you expect? That's what you get for staying out till all hours of the night. You should have stayed in bed this morning."

"What, and miss all this fun?" Peppi grumbled.

"Hah!" Luca laughed. "It's days like these that will turn you back into a tough *Abruzzese.*"

"Or maybe a dead one," Peppi replied.

"Don't worry," Luca told him. "We can turn off from the group and stick to the valley today if you like."

"Only if you insist," puffed Peppi.

As they approached the foot of the mountains where the roads would start to climb in earnest, Peppi and Luca bade the rest of the group farewell before turning off onto a flatter road that would wind its way through the valley. Peppi led the way, for by now he had once more become familiar with most of the roads throughout the region. He was in the mood for a leisurely ride, so he chose a route that would take them by the mulino.

The fresh coolness of the mountain air that had greeted them when they first set out from the piazza early that morning had vanished. By now the sun had climbed high into the cloudless sky and was beating down upon them. The sweat rolled off both men's arms and legs. As if on cue, they reached for their water bottles and squirted a few drops on their faces and across the back of their necks before taking a swig. They were both thankful that they had chosen to avoid the arduous mountain roads that day.

It was nearing midday when they finally came to the mulino. Peppi dismounted his bike and leaned it against what remained of the front wall. Luca, though, stayed by the edge of the road. He clicked out of his pedals, straddled his bike, and rested his elbows on the handlebars.

"Where are you going?" he called after Peppi, who had wandered off to the other side of the building.

"*I pommodori!*" Peppi replied. "I want to see how my tomatoes are doing."

The prospect of having fresh garden tomatoes again one day soon was enough to motivate Luca into joining Peppi. He leaned his bike up against Peppi's and hurried off to see how matters stood in the tomato garden.

Peppi was already fussing with the plants by the time Luca arrived. Kneeling in the soil, he went from plant to plant, meticulously pruning away with his fingers any unwanted branches or yellowing leaves. It was important to constantly trim off the little offshoots, the suckers as Peppi called them, otherwise the plants would never grow to their full potential. By limiting the number of branches, the plants might bear slightly less fruit, but the tomatoes would be lush and full and bursting with flavor. Judging by the number of little yellow flowers blossoming on the branches, there would be an ample crop.

"Your plants are doing very well here," Luca observed. "How are you keeping them watered?"

"From the river," said Peppi, nodding his head toward the little stream tumbling down from the mountains nearby. "I just fill up a bucket or two and that's all they need."

"Good," said Luca approvingly. "That water is the purest in all Italy. It's the best thing for them."

"I know," smiled Peppi. "I grew up drinking it, remember?"

"Just remember not to give them too much or it will break their skin when the tomatoes start to grow," Luca warned him. He let out a sigh and looked with longing eyes at the garden. *"Dio!"* he cried. "I can't wait. I can almost taste them already!"

"Who says you're going to get any?" Peppi teased him.

"Ayyy, I'll come and steal them in the night if I have to," said Luca, and the two of them laughed. Luca sat down at the edge of the garden and watched while Peppi pulled up some weeds that had dared to start growing between the plants.

"I don't get out here often enough," said Peppi when he was finished. "This garden needs a lot more attention." He straightened up and let his gaze roam across the property. Except for the well-ordered space of the tomato garden, everything was in disarray. "The whole place needs a lot more attention," he added ruefully.

"What are your plans for the place?" asked Luca.

"I don't know yet," Peppi admitted. "I've thought about trying to rebuild the house, but I don't know if I'm ready for that kind of project."

"Why bother?" said Luca. "Sell the land and leave the work to someone else. There are plenty of people who would love to have a house on a spot like this. Why give yourself *agita?*"

Peppi looked about and smiled. "I couldn't let it go," he said, "not yet."

"Eh," shrugged Luca, "everything in its time." Letting out a grumble of irritation, he settled back on one elbow and stretched out his legs.

"What's the matter?" asked Peppi.

"I was thinking about tomorrow."

"What about it?"

"I have to go to Milano, so do Filomena and Lucrezia."

"What's in Milano?" said Peppi, sitting next to him.

"A trade show that starts on Wednesday," Luca lamented. "I hate it. Five days of smiling and trying to act sweeter than the candy we sell. Even that's not so bad by itself, but then afterwards we leave to make our annual trip around the country to meet with vendors and all our distributors. It's just one of those things that has to be done."

"How long will you be gone?" said Peppi.

"Two weeks," groaned Luca. "Two long, hot weeks, but when we get back, that's it! Filomena and I head straight to the ocean to get an early start on the *ferragosto*. Meantime, Lucrezia will come back and finish up whatever needs to be done here before she starts her vacation. You'll have to come stay with us. We have a nice little place on the beach in Alba Adriatica. There's an extra room, so you'll be comfortable."

"But what will you do with the factory in August?" asked Peppi.

"We shut it down completely," explained Luca. "It's the only civilized thing to do. Who can work in this heat? It's barbaric to even make them try."

"In America we have something called air conditioning," noted Peppi.

"An equally barbaric invention," scoffed Luca. "Terrible for the lungs, to go from hot air to cold air then back again. Better to just let our bodies adapt to nature."

Peppi grinned and looked off into the distance. High above the treetops, a hawk floated along, drawing a wide gentle circle through the air. The effortless grace of such large birds had always fascinated Peppi. Seeing this one brought back to mind the many lazy summer hours that he had passed as a boy, lying on his back in this same grass, staring up into the same azure sky. How many dreams had he dreamt in those carefree days when it was simply too hot to work in the mill? How often had he wished he could be up there soaring with the hawks, gliding away to wherever the winds wished to take him?

"So you'll be gone two weeks," mused Peppi, a sad, faraway look coming into his eyes. "Lucrezia too."

Luca studied his friend for a moment. "You two have become good friends, haven't you?" he said.

Peppi gave a shrug. "We have some things in common," he

said. "I guess it helps both of us to have someone to talk to about them."

"It's good," said Luca, patting him on the shoulder. "I can see my daughter finally coming out of her shell. I have you to thank for that. But of course, you'll be thankful she's away these next few weeks. Her wedding anniversary is coming up, so, trust me, it's better that she's away."

"Should I expect to hear some rumblings coming from the north?" joked Peppi.

"Don't laugh. Keep an eye on the headlines," Luca quipped. He plucked a blade of grass from the ground and clenched it between his teeth. "But she'll be all right," he said. "To tell you the truth, I think Lucrezia plans this trip for this time every year just so she'll have something to take her mind off of Francesco."

Peppi looked back into the distance in time to see the hawk suddenly dive out of the sky. No doubt it had spotted its prey on the ground and was zooming in for the kill. In a flash the majestic bird disappeared from sight amongst the trees.

Peppi stretched his arms over his head for a moment and got to his feet. "Come on," he said, giving Luca a tug to help him up. "Let's get going again before our legs stiffen up."

"Who cares?" laughed Luca. "It's all downhill from here to Villa San Giuseppe. We can practically coast the whole way."

The two walked back to their bikes. As they clicked into their pedals, Luca looked back over his shoulder at the garden. "You know, Peppi, maybe you're right about not getting rid of the place just yet," he said. "You've got good soil with tomatoes growing and fresh mountain water flowing nearby. I think there might be a lot more life left in the old place after all."

"It all depends on how much life is left in the old *man,*" said Peppi. Luca nodded his head in agreement and the two rolled off toward home.

CHAPTER THIRTY-TWO

"Ciao, Peppi!" called Enzo. *"Come va?"*

Peppi answered with a shrug and a yawn as he trudged down the steps from his apartment. He had just arisen from his *siesta* and he was feeling a bit grumpy. He wasn't sure why he felt that way; he had slept well enough after eating a good lunch. Perhaps it was the heat of the July afternoon. Peppi had forgotten how hot the summer days could get in his native land. It would take some time for his body to reacclimate to the sultry weather.

Three days had already passed since Peppi had seen Lucrezia and her parents off to Milano. Their departure had been an exercise in organized chaos. While Filomena hastily prepared some pasta salads, panini, and other provisions for the long ride, Lucrezia and Luca had scurried about the factory, issuing the inevitable last minute flurry of frantic instructions to Enzo and the rest of the staff. For his part, Peppi helped carry out their luggage and stowed it in the trunk of the car for them. Aside from that, he stood on the sidelines and simply watched the spectacle. When the time had come for them to finally leave and the three had installed themselves in the car, Luca had rolled down the car window and beckoned for Peppi.

"You'll have to look after the place for me while we're gone," his friend told him.

"I'll try," Peppi replied.

"Don't worry, nothing much happens this time of year," Luca went on. "Just remember, you must come and stay with us at the ocean when all of this nonsense is over. Till then you have the key to the house, so feel free to go up and cook dinner or watch television or sleep there if you like."

"Grazie," said Peppi. "Now go before you waste the whole day here." He looked inside the car to say good-bye to Filomena and Lucrezia. *"Buon viaggio, tutti,"* he said.

"Ciao, Peppi,*"* Lucrezia replied before turning her attention back to the contents of her briefcase, which were by now spread out across the backseat. She seemed to have barely noticed Peppi, but as the car pulled out of the drive, she looked out the back window and nodded good-bye to him before they drove out of sight.

Now, with the absence of the boss and the presence of the heat, things in and around the factory were moving in slow motion. Enzo and Fabio were sitting on the front step, their backs pressed up against the door to take advantage of the shadow cast by the factory. To Peppi's astonishment, they were contentedly puffing away on cigarettes as they always did during their break time. He shook his head in disgust at them as he approached.

"It must be a hundred degrees outside," he said. "Why would anyone want to stick a piece of burning paper in his mouth on such a day?"

The other two men nodded and smiled.

"It's the menthol," answered Fabio, exhaling a long, lazy plume of smoke. "It gives the tobacco a nice cool taste."

Peppi shook his head once more and sat down next to them.

He stretched out his legs and let out another yawn. "How are things in the factory today?" he asked.

"Like Dante's Inferno," groaned Enzo. *"Grazie Dio,* we won't be in there too much longer. Two more weeks and then we're closed for August."

"Then what will you do with all your spare time?" said Peppi.

"Sleep—as much as possible every day," chuckled Fabio. "Then of course at night . . ." he let the words drift away on a sigh as he gestured with his hands to form the hourglass shape of a woman.

"Heh, nice to be single and free," grunted Enzo.

"What about you, Peppi?" said Fabio.

Peppi looked out across the drive to the gardens he had started in the spring. The flowers and shrubs were starting to wilt in the blistering sun. They would all need a good watering before the end of the day. "I don't know," he finally answered. "I guess I'll find something to keep me busy."

"Peppi, it's the summer," Fabio kidded him. "The only thing you need to keep you busy this time of year is a woman."

"Don't you ever think about anything else?" said Enzo.

"Not if I can help it."

Enzo looked over at Peppi, who was still gazing out toward the flowers. "You know, Peppi," he said, giving his cohort a nudge and a wink, "Fabio might be right. Maybe you *should* go out and find yourself a nice woman. A bed gets cold at night when you're sleeping all alone. It's no good."

"A cold bed doesn't sound so bad right about now," grumbled Peppi, wiping a bead of sweat off his brow. "As for you, Fabio, you might benefit from a cold shower."

"Hot or cold, it doesn't bother me," laughed Fabio, "just so long as I have someone in there with me to scrub my back."

"You can't win with him, Peppi," chuckled Enzo. "It's not even worth trying."

Peppi rubbed his chin and looked up at the sun. He was feeling restless, anxious to do something productive, but the afternoon heat made it near impossible to do anything but hide in the shade until the early evening came.

"So, Peppi, what do you think of the Tour de France so far?" said Enzo, referring to the French version of the Giro D'Italia. The Tour had started just a few days earlier. "Have you followed much of it?" he asked.

"No, not yet," shrugged Peppi. "The flat stages at the beginning don't interest me much. I'll start paying attention when they get to the mountains."

"Me, I'm just the opposite," said Fabio between puffs on his cigarette. "I love the flat stages because that's where you get all the best sprint finishes. In the mountains they just crawl along. It's boring to watch."

"Eh, to each his own," said Peppi, getting back to his feet. He stood there for a moment, gazing off toward the horizon. "One good thing at least," he said.

"What's that?" said Enzo.

"This hot weather will be good for my tomatoes," Peppi replied, "so long as I keep them watered."

"Yes, but be careful, Peppi," cautioned Fabio. "If you water them too much you'll break their skins."

"*Grazie,* Fabio," said Peppi, "but I've already been warned about that." Peppi gave them a nod and headed off to the back of the building to check on things in the courtyard.

"What's with him today?" said Fabio as they watched him go.

"What do you think?" snickered Enzo, flicking away his cigarette butt. "He's getting tired of that cold bed of his."

Peppi wanted to make sure that the flowers had a good drink, so he waited until almost sundown before he watered the gardens. In the cool of the evening the water would have a chance to soak deep into the soil to the roots of the plants instead of evaporating right away in the scorching heat of the midday sun. For good measure, he would water them again in the morning before the heat returned.

When he had finished watering the gardens, Peppi went back to his apartment to prepare supper for himself. As the sun disappeared behind the mountains, the temperature outside mercifully cooled. Inside, however, the warm air was still trapped. Peppi peeled off his shirt and left it hanging on the chair while he prepared for himself a salad to have with some bread and a little cheese. It was much too hot to eat anything more substantial. He set his simple meal down at the table, opened a bottle of mineral water, and sat down to eat.

As he ate, Peppi became acutely aware of the stillness of the descending night and the quiet of his apartment. Surrounded by this silence, it occurred to him that even the crunching of the lettuce between his teeth overwhelmed any sounds that might have drifted in from the world outside his window. When he stopped chewing, he was sure that he could hear his own heart beating. It was an odd feeling and, for the first time since returning to Villa San Giuseppe, he felt truly alone.

Peppi put his fork down and let his thoughts drift back to America, to a dinner he had eaten on another warm summer's night many years earlier. That night, however, he had not been dining all alone. Anna had been with him then. It was a breathless, sultry night, as he recalled, and they had decided to brave the mosquitoes by eating dinner on the little stone table beneath the grapevines in the back garden. To ward off the bugs, Peppi had encircled the table with a ring of citronella candles. It was the soft glow of those candles on Anna's face, the reflection of the tiny flames dancing in her eyes, that he most remembered from that night. In that gentle light, she had looked as young and beautiful to him as the day they first met.

"It's not polite to stare, you know," he remembered Anna telling him.

Later that night, after they had made love, Peppi could not have imagined feeling more content and at peace as he felt in that moment. As he lay beside her in bed, caressing her cheek, she had looked up at him and smiled.

"You're still staring," she had said.

"I'll never stop staring," he had promised her.

It was a beautiful memory, but somehow it only deepened his sense of isolation. He gave a sigh and tried to think of other things. His thoughts drifted to Milano, and he wondered how Lucrezia was managing at the trade show. It struck him then that thinking of her made him feel equally lonely. He glanced over at his bicycle and decided that perhaps it would be better at that moment to get out of his apartment and not to think of women at all. He ate his meal quickly, and when he had finished he took the key Luca had given him and trudged up to the house to watch the evening recap of the Tour de France.

CHAPTER THIRTY-THREE

A curious thing happened one afternoon a few days later when Peppi rode out to the mulino to check on his tomato garden. Tending to the garden had become something of a daily obsession since Lucrezia and her parents had left for Milano. There was next to nothing happening at the factory, so the quest for a bumper crop of tomatoes gave him something around which he could build his day and focus his energy.

By now the plants in the garden were supported by the rows of stakes Peppi had pounded into the ground. As he went from plant to plant each day, tying each one to its stake as it grew taller and taller, Peppi would meticulously prune each branch. When that task was completed, he would turn his attention to the soil and attack any upstart weeds without mercy. Finally, when he was satisfied that all was as it should be in the garden, he would walk to the river to fill the buckets with water for the plants. Afterwards, he would sit for a time and admire his work, all the while telling himself that he must be patient, that in time he and the others would enjoy the fruits of his labors.

As he pedalled up the hill toward the mulino that afternoon, Peppi was daydreaming about how delicious his tomatoes would be. When he crested the hill just before his ancestral home, he was greeted by the sight of a hawk perched upon the highest section of wall that had yet to totally collapse. Peppi pedalled to a stop at the edge of the road and straddled the bike. To his surprise, the hawk did not fly away at seeing him approach, but instead remained there observing him with dark, fearless eyes.

Peppi lowered his sunglasses and gazed back. It was another torrid but breezy day. As man and bird regarded one another, a hot, dry wind whistled through the ruins of the mulino and across the long waving grass. Peppi rested his bike on the ground and slowly stepped closer to get a better look at the hawk and perhaps to see just what it was up to. It was then that he suddenly recalled the hawk he had seen soaring through the sky that day with Luca. He wondered if this hawk and that one could be one and the same.

Peppi took off his helmet and laid it next to the bike. He inched closer still until the hawk opened its wings as if it were about to take flight. Peppi stopped in his tracks and the bird resumed its previous impassive stance.

"What is it you want, my friend?" Peppi called to it. "What are you doing here in my wreck of a mulino?"

The hawk made no move other than to scratch at the stone wall with one of its talons before suddenly raising its head. It opened its beak wide and let out a long, shrill screech that gave Peppi a start. Just as suddenly, the hawk spread its wings, and with a few powerful flaps it effortlessly soared away from the mulino. Holding his hand up to shield his eyes from the glare of the sun, Peppi stood there watching the mysterious bird fly away until it had glided out of sight.

Now, Peppi had lived virtually all of his adult life in America, but he had grown up in the isolated highlands of central Italy where superstition still ran very deep. Peppi, however, never considered himself particularly superstitious. Just the same, though, he upheld tradition by always keeping a broom by the door to his home, an ancient trick to keep away witches who, should they want to enter one's house during the night, must first waste all the dark hours before dawn counting the bristles. Not surprisingly, the strange encounter with this natural predator had left him troubled. Despite the insistence of his intellect that it had all occurred by chance, his emotions told him that their meeting on that spot at that time had nothing to do with mere coincidence. It was an omen, but of what type he could not guess. Peppi continued to look up into the sky, wondering all the while what meaning there was to be found in it all.

Turning his gaze back to the Earth, Peppi stepped inside the crumbling walls of the mulino to examine the spot where the hawk had perched. The rock, he soon saw, still bore the faint scratches left behind by the bird's claws. He passed his hand over them, feeling the rough texture of the rock against his fingertips. Turning, he looked around at the remains of the mulino. He had pecked about the rubble more than once, sifting through the broken fragments of wall and ceiling, searching for any artifacts of his former life there. Aside from a few forks and knives and other utensils, he had never found anything of true interest amidst the debris. Over the years just about everything else had been taken from the abandoned homestead by vandals or mischievous youngsters.

Leaning back against the wall, Peppi let his eyes continue to roam about the place as he puzzled over the eerie incident with the hawk. He had just made up his mind to go check on the tomato garden when the weight of his hand against the wall caused a small section of rock and plaster to crumble and fall.

Peppi looked down. There by his foot, tucked beneath the

shattered remains of one of the ceiling beams, he saw the faint glint of some small object reflecting the sun. When he stooped down to get a closer look, he realized that what he had seen was the edge of a small oval picture frame lying half buried beneath the beam. Very carefully, he reached down and tugged the frame free from its hiding place. Miraculously, the frame and glass were in perfect condition. When Peppi dusted off the glass and held up the picture, his lonely heart soared a thousand times higher than any hawk had ever flown. Behind the glass was a photograph of Peppi's mother and father, a very old photograph he suddenly now remembered very well, for it had always rested on the mantel above their fireplace.

Stunned by this discovery, he sat down against the wall and beheld the photograph. How young and strong and beautiful his parents looked! Tears of joy welled in Peppi's eyes and a thousand memories flooded his mind. It was if he were holding in his hand some sort of portal to the past through which he could suddenly see all the people and places he once knew and loved so well as a child. Common, everyday events he had long ago forgotten burst into his memory. He remembered watching his father and mother toil away in the mulino, never once complaining, for they were happy to have productive work to sustain them. He remembered riding in the back of the wagon atop the sacks of grain on their way to the market. He remembered holidays when the house was filled with aunts and uncles and cousins and friends, all long gone now or scattered to the four winds. In particular, though, Peppi remembered a stormy night, late one spring, when the thunder boomed so loud that he feared the mountaintops would topple down upon them. His mother had tucked her frightened son into bed that night while his father secured the windows. "Don't worry, *figlio mio, vananon',*" she had comforted him. "You'll always be safe in this house because your father and I will always be here watching over you." Peppi closed his eyes and smiled as he recalled his mother's words. In that moment, he knew in his heart, for the very first time, that he had truly done the right thing in returning to Italy.

Afterwards, when Peppi had finished tending to the garden, he tucked the picture frame safely into the back pocket of his cycling jersey. As he mounted his bike, he happened to look up into the sky where he once again saw the hawk circling high above him. To his delight, a second soon joined it and the two birds floated gracefully along, held aloft on the breath of that hot summer's day. Peppi made the sign of the cross and blew them a kiss. Then he turned and pedalled home, mindful all the way of the precious newfound treasure he carried with him.

"It's a sign," declared Fabio with some authority after Peppi recounted the story of the hawk later that afternoon.

"What kind of sign?" said Enzo, not at all confident in Fabio's ability to interpret such phenomena.

"It's a sign from God, what else would it be?" Fabio replied. Some of the other workers who had gathered around to hear the story nodded in agreement.

"But what do you think God is trying to tell me?" asked Peppi, as skeptical as Enzo of Fabio's perspicacity. "What's it all supposed to mean?"

"Think about it," said Fabio, striking a contemplative pose. "The mulino was the place of your birth, where you started your life, and now you've come back to it. You've come full circle, but your life hasn't ended yet. You've just ended up back at the beginning. You see, your life is like a big circle. Even the picture you found of your parents is shaped like a circle."

"It's an oval," Enzo pointed out.

"Oval, circle, what's the difference?" said Fabio. "Wherever you start on it you end up back in the same place."

"But you still haven't told me what it all means," said Peppi with a smile. "What is God trying to tell me?"

Fabio scratched his chin thoughtfully. "If you asked me," he finally replied, "I'd say He's trying to tell you that your life isn't over, that it's time to make another circle."

"What are you saying?" scoffed Enzo. "He's supposed to go back to America again? He comes all the way over here and now you think God wants to send him back there?"

"I didn't say that he had to make the *same* circle," said Fabio, anxious to defend his theory. "Maybe it's time for a different circle, a brand new one."

"And maybe it's time for you to get out of the sun and get back to work," said his supervisor. "Come on, everyone, back inside. We still have lots to do today. Signora Lucrezia will be calling soon to see how things are going and I don't want to have to lie to her."

With a communal groan, Fabio and the others obeyed Enzo and went back into the factory to finish their work for the day. When the door closed behind them, Enzo turned to Peppi and gave him a nod.

"What do you think, Peppi?" he said. "Do you think maybe Fabio is right, that it really was a message from God?"

Peppi shrugged. "Who knows?" he said. "Maybe it was all just a nice coincidence. Either way, I'm happy to have my parents back."

With that Peppi started to make his way up the stairs to his apartment. He paused and looked back at Enzo, who had yet to go back inside the factory.

"Does Signorina Lucrezia call every day?" he asked.

Enzo smiled. "Without fail," he chuckled. "God help me if I'm not there to take the call."

"I hope things are going well for them in Milano," said Peppi, starting up the stairs once more.

With an impish sparkle in his eye, Enzo watched him go. "I'll tell her you were asking for her," he called up the stairs. Then he went back into the factory to wait by the telephone.

CHAPTER THIRTY-FOUR

The days dragged.

With little else to do to keep himself occupied, Peppi passed the long, hot afternoons watching the daily coverage of the Tour de France on Luca's television. It was a welcome diversion, but somehow the race did not stir in him the same passion as had the Giro. Even the dramatic mountain stages failed to thrill him as they ordinarily might. Still, each day Peppi watched the action closely, for he knew that Enzo and the others were hungry for news about how the Italian racers were faring. Now and then he would walk down to the factory to give everyone an update on what the race leaders were doing and to fill them in on any new stories of interest floating around about the *peloton*.

In every major bicycle tour, one must understand, there is always one controversy or another swirling around the periphery of the race. Racers on one team complain about the tactics of those on another team. Sometimes racers on the same team squabble because their team leader is not faring as well as expected. Other times a particular rider fares much *better* than expected, fueling rumors that he has used some illicit substance to improve his performance. Perhaps one of the race leaders was observed late at night, out on the town with some movie starlet, when he should have been fast asleep in bed, recovering for the next day's stage. All of these stories and others are just part of the ongoing drama, threads woven into the overall fabric of the race. They are what make the experience of the Tour or the Giro so captivating, even when the actual racing might be lackluster.

Despite having already watched most of the day's racing, Peppi generally went up to Luca's house each evening to watch the news and the nightly recap of the race. By now, however, the Tour had wound its way out of the Alps and back onto the flatlands of France. The overall leader had, for all intents and purposes, already been decided in the mountains. All that was left were the few remaining stages for the has-beens and might-have-beens to fight for in the few days before the race reached Paris. The drama was over.

Just the same, Peppi trudged up the path to Luca's house one night to watch the day's proceedings on the television. He had already lost the little interest he had in the race days ago, but the routine of watching it had become something of a comfort to him. It helped him fall asleep at night. He was just making himself comfortable in front of the television when the telephone rang unexpectedly. To his surprise, it was Luca.

"Ah, I knew I would find you watching the Tour," said Luca when Peppi answered.

"What else is there for an old man to do at night around here?" replied Peppi, happy to hear his friend's voice once again. "Have you had time to watch any of it yourself?"

"Not much during the day," Luca admitted, "but I've watched the highlights every night. What did you think of the Alps?"

For a few minutes they chatted enthusiastically about the race, sharing their views on the riders and their teams, the tactics they used, and why they succeeded or failed. Before long, though, the conversation turned to the subject of tomatoes. How were things turning out in Peppi's garden? Luca wanted to know. Peppi apprised him of the status of the tomato garden where, he was happy to report, a healthy crop of luscious green tomatoes was bursting forth from his plants. It wouldn't be long before they slowly ripened into a deep, delicious red.

Luca sounded very pleased by the news. "I can taste them already!" he exclaimed. "But tell me, Peppi, what's this business I hear about you talking to a hawk?"

"How on earth did you hear about that!" laughed Peppi.

"Lucrezia," Luca answered.

"Lucrezia?"

"Yes," Luca told him, chuckling. "One day when she was talking on the telephone to Enzo, she happened to ask about you."

"Really?" said Peppi, unsure of why he felt so pleased about such a trifle. "What did Enzo tell her?"

"He told her 'the old man is doing fine, but he was getting lonely, so he decided to talk to the birds because no one else would listen to him.' "

Peppi could not contain his laughter, for he could well imagine Enzo saying those very words. He made a mental note to put Enzo on the spot about it the first chance he got. Then he recounted for Luca the whole story of what had happened that afternoon at the mulino.

"It's an omen," said Luca with great gravity when Peppi had finished the tale.

"Yes, that's what everyone says," replied Peppi. "But an omen of what?"

"Ah, now that's the question," said Luca. Peppi could picture him on the other end of the line, scratching his chin thoughtfully. "It's so difficult to say with these things," his friend went on. "But at least we know it's a good omen, Peppi. I mean, finding the photograph of your parents was a wonderful thing. I can't see how you could read anything bad into it."

"I hope you're right," said Peppi. "But no matter what, it made me very happy."

"Good," said Luca before letting out a sigh. "So, tell me the truth, Peppi," he asked, "how are things really going in the factory? I know Lucrezia has been calling every day, but you know how it is. When the cat's away, the mice all play. Sometimes you don't get the whole story."

"Don't worry," Peppi told him. "I've been cracking the whip here since you left. The place is running even better than it was before."

"Hah!" chortled Luca. "In that case I'll have to make you a manager when I get back. We're going to need all the good help we can get."

"Sounds like your trip to Milano was a success," said Peppi.

"Not bad," replied Luca. "I think it will help business."

"And how are your wife and daughter?" Peppi asked. "I didn't hear any rumbling from the north."

"No," said Luca. "Things have been surprisingly calm on that front. Lucrezia's anniversary came and went without a peep. To tell you the truth, though, it was even worse. Filomena and I kept waiting for Lucrezia to tear our heads off, at least once, but it never happened. She's been restless, though, and a little moody. I think maybe she's finally starting to reconcile herself with what happened to poor Francesco. Maybe she's getting ready to move on with her life. God knows, it's taken her long enough. But who can say? Anyway, I think she'll be happy to get home tomorrow."

"Tomorrow?" said Peppi, much surprised. "I thought she wouldn't be back till the beginning of next week."

"That's the real reason I called," said Luca. "Some of the people we had planned to visit were already at the trade show, so when it was over we were able to travel about and make some of our other stops sooner than we had planned. Right about now there's not much left for Lucrezia to do but go home and close up the factory for a month while Filomena and I take the train to the beach. That's why I wanted to call you ahead of time, to make sure the coast was clear, if you know what I mean."

"I'm sure everything in the factory is fine," Peppi told him, despite having observed firsthand the somnambulant pace of things since Luca had been away. "Just the same, I'll pass the word along first thing tomorrow to make sure."

"*Grazie, amico mio,*" said Luca. "You know, just having you there makes me feel better about things."

"*Piacere mia,*" replied Peppi. "Anything to help."

Later, when he had finished talking to Luca, Peppi hung up the phone, turned off the television, and went straight back to his apartment. The doldrums of the past two weeks had suddenly vanished like a dream at the first light of dawn. He was anxious now to get to bed as quickly as possible for he would need to arise with the sun the next morning. There was much, he realized, that he wanted to do before Lucrezia came home and little time to do it. But he wasn't worried. If anything, the prospect of a busy day ahead gladdened him. He laid his head on the pillow that night and drifted off to sleep with his heart full of anticipation.

CHAPTER THIRTY-FIVE

"That's not funny, Peppi," said Enzo, crushing out his cigarette. "Don't even joke like that."

"I'm not joking," said Peppi. "She's coming back today. I spoke with her father just last night on the telephone."

They were standing at the front door to the factory. It was early morning and the rest of the workers were just straggling in like war-weary troops on their way to the front. The incessant heat of the past few weeks had taken its toll; just arriving at work to start their day was something of an accomplishment. Like any good field commander, Enzo knew when to push his troops and when to go easy. He was a compassionate supervisor, so he had carefully analyzed the work that needed to be completed to shut down the factory for August and the amount of time allotted to do it. With that in mind, he set a reasonable pace for his charges with the goal of having everything finished just in time for Lucrezia's return. Until that very moment, he had been serene, perfectly content in the knowledge that all was going along right on schedule. When he realized, however, that Peppi might be in earnest, that Lucrezia was indeed returning early, Enzo's face turned ashen.

"You *are* joking, right, Peppi?" he said, his voice full of dread. "Please tell me you're joking."

Peppi winced and replied with a shake of his head.

"Dio in cielo!" Enzo cried. "She'll murder us all!"

With no time to waste, Enzo fled into the factory to raise the alarm. There soon ensued the clamor of lamentation and profanity one might expect in such a desperate situation. From the cries of despair and wails of mutual recrimination, one might have thought that the end of the world was coming.

Peppi ducked his head inside the door to get a peek at the scene. Pandemonium, he saw, reigned supreme. Workers were running back and forth, their arms laden with boxes of confetti that had been stacked in haphazard piles and now needed to be stowed neatly away with the rest of the inventory. Now and then the workers collided with one another, causing them to drop their loads and spill out the contents onto the floor. With rags in their hands, others climbed atop the machinery and began hastily wiping everything down. Poor Enzo stood amidst the confusion, trying vainly to bring some semblance of order to the sudden frenzy of activity that swirled about him. Frantically he screamed out instructions, waving his arms and hands for emphasis like a conductor at the crescendo of a symphony.

"The vats!" he cried, making no attempt whatsoever to hide his sense of panic. "Clean the vats first, *then* wipe down the machinery!" He paused when he saw Peppi observing him from the door with sympathetic eyes. "It will take a miracle to finish before she arrives," he lamented, "a miracle."

The best Peppi could offer was a shrug. Just then, as the noise and confusion reached its apogee, the shrill ringing of the office telephone pierced the air. All activity stopped and dead silence fell over the factory.

The telephone rang again.

Enzo turned dejected eyes to Peppi, shook his head, and

marched off to answer it while the others held their breath. *"Buon giorno, Signora Lucrezia,"* his voice echoed throughout the factory. One could almost hear the communal gulp that followed those words.

Grim-faced, but finally composed, Enzo emerged from the office a short time later. He walked out before them, looking like a man who had resigned himself to the fact that his fate was now sealed and there was nothing he could do about it.

"Three o'clock," he told them. "She'll be back by three o'clock."

The full gravity of the situation set in and no one spoke until Fabio finally stepped forward. "We can do it, Enzo!" he cried. "We can do it if we all work together. We won't let you down!" His words rallied his co-workers and before Enzo could mutter another word, the previous chaos resumed.

Peppi came inside and did whatever he could to help with the cause. Before long, though, he left them, for he wanted to tend to the front gardens and the courtyard before Lucrezia came home. He wasn't sure why, but somehow it had become very important to him that things should be looking their best when she arrived. As he walked out the front door, Peppi stopped and gave Enzo a salute to wish him good luck. Enzo rolled his eyes in reply and looked up to heaven, his hands folded in supplication.

Outdoors, it was another scorching day, and the beads of sweat rolled off Peppi's forehead as he set himself to work in the gardens beneath the midmorning sun. Now and then a stray cloud would wander by overhead and cast its cooling shadow over him. The relief was always brief, though, and the sun felt that much hotter on his shoulders when it reappeared. Despite the heat, Peppi whistled a cheerful tune as he went along pruning the bushes and weeding the flower beds. He liked the warm weather and he felt happy to be busy with a clear purpose once again.

Afterwards, Peppi went out back to the courtyard and spent some time raking around the arbor and fussing with the grapevines coiled about it. The flower beds, he noted, were still in good shape for he had kept them well watered. Once he was satisfied that things were looking as good as might be expected, Peppi sat down on the bench beneath the arbor to take a short break. As he cast his gaze about at the gardens, he thought that it might be a nice idea to pick some flowers to leave on Lucrezia's desk, just to welcome her back. When he went back inside, he would look around the factory to see if he could lay his hands on a vase.

Noontime was fast approaching and Peppi felt a twinge of hunger in his stomach. His first impulse was to go upstairs to his apartment and fix himself a light lunch. His thoughts, though, turned to Enzo and the workers inside the factory. With the deadline of Lucrezia's return hanging over their heads like a guillotine, they would certainly not be taking any siestas that day. Peppi felt sorry for them, and guilty at being able to relax and enjoy his lunch when they could not. Without giving another thought to his stomach, he collected the gardening tools, stowed them away, and went back inside the factory to see how things were progressing.

"Let's face it," said Enzo when Peppi returned, "it would take an act of God for us to finish everything before she gets back. My only hope is that we have the place close enough to being finished that she won't notice where things are a little rough around the edges, if you know what I mean."

"Is there anything I can do to help?" Peppi offered.

"You could go to church and pray for us," Enzo suggested with a wry smile.

"Is that all?" said Peppi, patting him on the shoulder.

Enzo sighed and shook his head. "At this point, it would help as much as anything."

"Okay," chuckled Peppi, "I'll do it. But first I need to take a look around."

"What are you looking for?" said Enzo.

"A vase."

Peppi walked off to the back offices to begin his search. He soon discovered that there were no vases to be found in any of the offices and there was nothing suitable in any of the closets or storage areas in the factory. He stood for a moment in the middle of the factory floor, wondering where he might look next. That's when it occurred to him that if he could not find a vase, he should just go out and buy a new one. With that in mind, he bid farewell once more to Enzo and his cohorts and headed off into town on his bicycle.

Despite the heat of the afternoon sun, a surprising number of people were strolling about on the piazza when Peppi pedalled into town on his rusty old bike with the basket. Most were old women looking after their grandchildren while the parents were off at work. The children kicked soccer balls and gleefully chased each other around the piazza while their grandmothers passed the time gossiping among themselves. Peppi smiled, for the scene might easily have been one out of his own childhood. The world had turned many times since he left for America so many years ago, but things in his hometown had not truly changed all that much.

Peppi rode across the piazza and turned down a narrow cobblestoned alleyway that wound its way through one of the adjoining neighborhoods. The air was distinctly cooler there because the stone buildings on either side kept the street in shadow most of the day. Just being out of the sun made a refreshing change. Peppi pedalled a short way down the street before he spied the *"aperto"* flag in front of the little gift shop he sought. He was pleased to find it open, having feared that the owner might already be taking his *siesta*.

"You're lucky," said Enrico, the gift shop's owner, when Peppi came in. "I was just about to close the place and go home for lunch."

"I won't keep you long," Peppi promised him. "I just came in for one small thing."

"Take your time, take your time," Enrico urged him, giving him a wink. "Buy as many things as you want. We have plenty! My stomach can always wait."

"Thank you," chuckled Peppi, "but all I need is a vase to put some flowers in. Nothing too fancy. Just something simple."

"I have just the thing," said Enrico without hesitation. He turned and went off to the back of the shop. A few moments later he returned carrying a simple white vase large enough to hold a good-sized arrangement of flowers. He held it up for Peppi to inspect.

Peppi smiled and nodded.

"Perfetto," he said.

Later, with the vase bundled up in brown paper to protect it on the ride home, Peppi carefully walked his bike back out the alley so as not to jostle the basket on the cobblestones. When he came back out into the sunlight, he paused at the edge of the piazza. The bells in the church tower across the way had just chimed one o'clock, and the women and children were all making their way home for lunch. Peppi was feeling hungry and thirsty himself, so he began to walk his bike over to the bar to buy a bottle of mineral water to sustain him on the ride home. As he pushed the bike along, he happened to look down the road that led down the hill and away from the village.

Off in the distance he saw a tiny glint of sunlight. He stopped and gazed intently at it until it became clear that what he had seen was the sun reflecting off an approaching automobile. Judging by the speed at which the car was zooming along, Peppi knew in an instant that it must be Lucrezia. Her breakneck driving style was unmistakable. Peppi let out a laugh, but it should have come as no surprise to him that she would make it home nearly two hours early.

With no time left to get home before her, Peppi put the flowers and the vase out of his mind and stood there watching as the car sped closer and closer to the village. For a brief time, he lost view of it as the road disappeared from sight behind the buildings that encircled the piazza. Not long after, though, he heard the growl of a car engine. Peppi looked down the road just in time to see the car turn the corner and start the climb up the hill to the piazza. As luck would have it, Lucrezia looked up ahead and saw Peppi standing there. To his delight, her face broke out in a great smile when her gaze met his. She put her hand out the window and waved.

It was then that something happened that would forever alter the final course of Peppi's life. As he lifted his hand to wave back, something moving off to the side caught his attention. It was a soccer ball, he realized, rolling off the piazza— and into the car's path. Directly behind, a little boy who had squirmed free from his mother's grasp, chased after it. Oblivious to the danger until it was too late, the child darted out into the road. At the sight of the oncoming car, he froze in his tracks like a fawn. With no time to stop, Lucrezia instinctively swerved the car hard to her right. Miraculously, she avoided the boy, and the ball glanced harmlessly off the car's fender. The car, though, had veered far off the edge of the road.

People in circumstances such as this often recount that the experience seemed to take place in slow motion. In Peppi's case, however, his mind raced at the speed of light to the conclusion before the event had actually taken place. In a flash, he envisioned the crumbling pavement on the edge of the road, the pavement he had noticed so many weeks ago and had intended to do something about. He saw it giving way beneath the weight of the car, the rear wheel spinning and spewing bits of dirt and rock out the back as it tried to gain traction. He saw Lucrezia futilely trying to right the car before it was too late.

He saw the inevitable.

Despite Lucrezia's best efforts to steer the car back onto the road, its momentum caused it to skid and slide sideways down the embankment. For an agonizing instant, it teetered there on two wheels. Lucrezia let out a scream of terror just before the car toppled over and dropped from sight. It rolled down the rest of the embankment until it came to a crashing halt on the dry, rocky riverbed below. For a moment all was still. Then the back end of the car burst into flames.

CHAPTER THIRTY-SIX

Once, when Peppi was young, he rode his bicycle in a regional cycling championship that took place just a few towns over from Villa San Giuseppe. The race course was not particularly arduous, as it travelled through the nearby valleys over predominately flat and rolling roads. Just the same it was a fast, furious race. With no leg-shattering climbs to break the field apart, the final outcome was decided by a frantic mass sprint to the finish.

By that age, Peppi had developed into a formidable sprinter. Like all good sprinters, he knew how to handle himself without fear during the frenetic final moments of a race when everything happened with breathtaking speed, when the slightest misjudgment could cost one the race or, worse, cause a serious crash. He understood that, at the crucial moment, a successful sprinter doesn't think, he simply acts on instinct. Somehow or other on that particular day, Peppi managed to weave his way through the maze of man and machine hurtling down the road. The tiniest of gaps opened between two riders in front of him. At the last moment, he dashed through the breach and sprinted across the finish line a whisker ahead of the next closest rider.

Afterwards, a friend asked him to describe the victory and how the final few hundred meters of the race had played out.

Peppi shrugged and said that it was just luck that he had seen an open lane to the finish. He could offer no other explanation because, right at the moment, he could remember next to nothing else about how he had gotten himself to the finish line other than the fact that he simply wanted to get there first. It was quite often that way for him after such races. Not until much later on, perhaps as he lay in bed at night, could Peppi replay the whole thing in his mind and dissect each and every second with any clarity. In the heat of battle, though, it was all just a blur.

That was how things were for Peppi, so many years later, on that blazing hot afternoon on the piazza in Villa San Giuseppe when Lucrezia's car tumbled off the road. He had no conception of how he suddenly found himself at the bottom of the steep embankment, struggling over the rocks to get to the car. He did not know or care what had become of his bicycle and the flower vase. He was oblivious to the women and children screaming in horror up above. All Peppi knew in that moment was that he wanted to get there first.

The car had rolled over onto the driver's side. When Peppi reached it, he saw that the fire that had broken out in the rear was now advancing with terrifying speed toward the front. He knelt and looked in through the windshield. All he could see was the top of Lucrezia's head. To his dismay, she didn't appear to be moving, and for a terrible moment Peppi was sure she was dead. Just as quickly, he realized that he was wrong. Lucrezia was not dead but looking down at her lap. Her body was folded up like a baby in the womb. Though she couldn't lift her arms, her hands were working frantically to unbuckle her seat belt. Unable to release it, she looked up in panic just in time to see Peppi climbing up onto the passenger's side of the car.

"Save me, Peppi!" she screamed in terror.

Balancing himself atop the car, Peppi tried desperately to pull open the passenger door. With the sides of the door caved in and the roof crumpled by the impact of the crash, it refused to give. Peppi tried and tried to wrench it free, but it was of no use. By now the flames had spread to the backseat and he knew that it was only a matter of moments before they reached the front—and Lucrezia was consumed.

Peppi stood there for a moment, his mind feverishly trying to sort out what to do next. Maddeningly, he could hear Lucrezia screaming his name just a few feet away, but he could not reach her. Suddenly the car shifted slightly and Peppi slipped and fell to the ground. He cracked his knee hard against a rock, but oddly he never felt the pain. Instead, at that crucial moment, instinct took over. With time running out and nothing else to do, Peppi staggered to his feet, lifted the same rock, and used it to smash the windshield.

The glass shattered into thousands of tiny pellets that fell to the ground like drops of water spilling from a bucket.

"Save me, Peppi!" Lucrezia screamed again in panic. "I can feel the fire! Don't let me die! Please don't let me die!"

With the flames licking at the front seat like the tongue of a snake, Peppi reached in and tried to grab Lucrezia by the shoulders. He managed to push aside the shoulder harness, but try as he might, he could not get a firm hold of her. At last he grabbed her unceremoniously by the head and pulled with all his might. Lucrezia let out a shriek of protest.

"You have to help me!" Peppi cried.

"How?"

"Push with your legs!"

"I can't!"

"Try!"

Lucrezia arched forward and tried to push with her legs. It was a weak effort, the most she could give, but it was just enough to make her budge a tiny bit. Peppi slipped one hand under her arm.

"Again!" he screamed.

Now the tears were streaming down Lucrezia's face as she struggled to free herself. "Don't let me die, Peppi!" she begged him. "Please, I want to live!"

"Then push!"

Lucrezia tried again. This time Peppi managed to reach over her back and get both hands under her arms beneath her shoulders. Little by little, as she wriggled her waist out of the seat belt, he began to slide her out over the dashboard.

"One more push," he told her, his voice calmer now, his mind totally focused despite the searing heat of the flames against the tops of his hands and arms. "Just one more push."

Crying out in agony from the strain, like a mother in labor, Lucrezia gathered herself and gave one last push. It moved her enough so that Peppi could now stand and put his legs and back into the effort. With his hands clasped firmly around her, he dug in his heels and pulled with every bit of strength he possessed. Steadily, Lucrezia's head then shoulders emerged from the car. With one final try, Peppi pulled the rest of her free just as the fire engulfed the front seat.

The violent effort, combined with her sudden release, sent the two of them sprawling side-by-side to the ground. Shivering from fright, Lucrezia immediately curled into a ball like a new-born child trying to stay warm. "Don't let me die, Peppi," she murmured.

Wasting no time, Peppi swept her up into his arms.

"Please don't let me die, Peppi," she sobbed over and over again as he carried her up and away from the burning wreck. "I want to live, Peppi. I want to *live!*"

Peppi cradled her close as he carried her up away from the burning wreck. "I won't let you die," he told her gently. "I promise."

At hearing the crash and the cries of the women, some of the men who worked in town, and others who just happened to be home that afternoon, had come running to the piazza. They scrambled down the embankment to help Peppi carry Lucrezia. One of the men offered to carry her the rest of the way, but Lucrezia kept her arms wrapped tightly around Peppi's neck.

By the time they reached the top of the embankment they could hear the wail of a siren. In all the confusion, only Enrico, the shopkeeper, had the presence of mind to run back to his shop and call for help. The crowd moved aside to allow the ambulance through when it finally screamed into the piazza and the two rescue workers jumped out.

Peppi never once let go of Lucrezia until the moment he laid her safely down on the stretcher. While one of the rescue workers strapped her in securely, the other turned to Peppi, whose face had by now lost all color.

"Are you okay?" he asked. "Maybe you should come along too."

"No, I'm fine," Peppi insisted. "Just take care of the girl."

No sooner had the ambulance driven away with Lucrezia when, down below the piazza, her car exploded into a ball of fire, chasing everyone away from the edge of the embankment.

Then they all mobbed around Peppi, patting him on the back and mussing up his hair to congratulate him on his heroics. Cries of *Bravo! Bravo!* filled the air.

In response, Peppi could only shrug and give a modest smile. Like any true cyclist, the first words out of his mouth were, "Where is my bike?"

Everyone laughed at his bravura, then Peppi collapsed to the ground out of sheer exhaustion.

CHAPTER THIRTY-SEVEN

When news of the accident reached Luca and Filomena shortly after it happened, they dropped everything and raced home from Alba Adriatica. Despite assurances that Lucrezia did not appear to have been seriously injured, the two of them were beside themselves with worry; the long, nervous ride home was an agonizing ordeal. Early that evening, when they finally arrived at the hospital in Sulmona where Lucrezia had been taken, Luca and Filomena rushed inside only to discover that their daughter had already checked herself out and gone home.

"What do you mean, you let her check out?" Filomena screamed. "She was just in a terrible accident! What kind of hospital is this?"

"Well," the doctor tried to explain, "except for a few cuts and bruises and some soreness in her neck, she had no other injuries or complaints. It was actually quite miraculous, judging by the account she gave of her accident. I think she was mostly just very shaken up by the whole thing, which of course was very understandable. All the same, you should know that I did want her to stay overnight for observation, but she would have none of it. She kept insisting that she had work to do in the morning and that she wanted to go home. We all tried to convince her, but your daughter is very . . . well, shall we say, strong-minded?"

"Oh, so you noticed?" Luca sighed.

"Yes," the doctor continued, "and the older gentleman, who I understand pulled your daughter from the car, was much the same story. He refused to be taken in the ambulance, but someone else brought him in shortly after your daughter arrived."

"You must be talking about Peppi," said Filomena with concern.

"I have the man's name as a Signor Peppino," said the doctor, consulting his notes.

"That's him," said Luca. "Is he okay?"

"Other than a nasty contusion on his knee and a few cuts and scratches, he seemed to be fine. Again, however, I would have preferred that he also remain here overnight, just to be safe. But, like your daughter, he insisted that he preferred to go home."

"That's Peppi all over," said Luca.

"If you ask me, the two of them need a good slap in the head," Filomena added. With that thought in mind, she directed her husband to the door and the two drove home to Villa San Giuseppe.

To anyone who knew her well, it should have come as no surprise when Lucrezia showed up for work at her usual hour the following morning. Just the same, all the workers gaped in delighted astonishment when she strode into the factory. By the time Lucrezia had made it halfway to her office, the entire staff had gathered around her, everyone smiling and trying to talk to her at the same time. Even Enzo, who only one day earlier had been praying for a miracle to delay Lucrezia's return, had tears in his eyes. They were all overjoyed that she had emerged from her terrible accident alive and well.

Fortune indeed had smiled upon Lucrezia. Other than having been frightened out of her wits, miraculously she had only a few minor bumps and bruises to show from her tumble down the embankment. Still, she walked to her office at a distinctly slower pace than the one at which she normally tore through the factory. From the occasional wince and the weak smile she gave Enzo and the rest of the workers gathered around her, it was obvious that she was feeling more discomfort than she cared to let on.

"You should stay home and rest, Signorina Lucrezia," one of the older women who worked in the factory gently admonished her. "We can take care of things here today. Please go home before you make yourself sick."

"Ayyy, you sound just like my parents," Lucrezia said with a wave of her hand.

"And she doesn't listen to us either," said Luca who had come out of his office when he heard the commotion. He gave his daughter a look of consternation and shook his head.

"Don't worry, everybody, I'm fine," his daughter replied, rolling her eyes for the benefit of the others. "But come on now, let's all get to work so we can finish up and start enjoying the rest of our summer!"

It was as gentle an order as Lucrezia had ever issued to her staff, but they were all delighted to obey. Just as they were returning to their posts, however, the door to the factory opened and Peppi limped inside. A round of cheers went up. Soon all the workers were mobbed around Peppi, just as they had done to Lucrezia, giving him a hero's welcome.

"I only came in to find a paper bag," Peppi said, embarrassed by all the attention. "I want to go pick some tomatoes from my garden."

Luca looked on and smiled. The minor delay in getting his troops back to work was a small price to pay considering the debt of gratitude he owed his friend. He gave Peppi a nod and let him enjoy the spotlight for a few moments. Lucrezia, on the other hand, turned and retreated to her office without so much as a glance at Peppi. Luca was startled by her sudden departure from the scene. Peppi, however, seemed unfazed. Although he had surely seen Lucrezia's strange behavior, Peppi gave no sign of surprise or displeasure. Once the tumult died down and everyone returned to work, he found the paper bag he was looking for and went on his way as quickly as had Lucrezia.

That was the way things went for the next few days. As was to be expected, Lucrezia still went to the office every morning, ignoring her mother's advice to stay home and rest. For his part, Peppi kept himself busy as always. Thankfully, both of them seemed to be recovering from the bumps and bruises they had sustained in the accident.

Still, there was something strange in the air, a feeling of tension and anticipation like the calm before an approaching storm. Luca could feel it. He noticed it whenever he mentioned Peppi's name to Lucrezia. She would immediately clam up or try to change the subject. Not only that, but she seemed to go out of her way to avoid Peppi altogether. Whenever they encountered one another, Lucrezia barely gave him the time of day. Luca had long ago become accustomed to his daughter's inscrutable mood swings. All the same, he was appalled that she did not demonstrate at least a little sense of gratitude to the man who had saved her life.

Luca might have chastised his daughter for her aloofness had it not been for the fact that Peppi seemed to be behaving in much the same way towards her. It was as if he was trying, without being rude, to avoid all contact with Lucrezia. If her name were to arise in conversation, he would inevitably mumble something inaudible before asking about the latest weather forecast or a recent bike race or any other subject. Luca noted the way he barely looked at Lucrezia when they passed one another as they went about their daily business. Yes, Peppi would tip his cap and say hello as pleasantly as always, but that was all. It was as if the two of them were trying to pretend that they were complete strangers. Odder still, from what Luca could see, they each seemed quite content with this odd state of affairs.

One afternoon, after the factory had finally been closed down for the month of August, Luca decided that he had had enough of the strange situation. He had been looking out the kitchen window to the courtyard. Peppi was there, puttering around the flower beds and fussing with the grapevines. Behind Peppi, Luca could see Lucrezia through her office window. She was at her desk, looking over some papers. Her window was wide open, but never once did she look outside, nor did Peppi ever glance in. They seemed to be doing their best to ignore each other.

Luca slapped his hands down on the windowsill and turned to his wife, who was sitting at the table leafing through a magazine. "Filomena," he blurted out in exasperation, "what on earth is going on with those two?"

"Can't you guess?" his wife replied without looking up from her magazine.

"No, I can't."

Filomena sighed and laid the magazine down on the table. "You men never notice anything. It's been as plain as the nose on your face for weeks now."

"What has?"

Now it was Filomena's turn to be exasperated. "Your daughter and your best friend!" she exclaimed, slapping her hand on the table. "Don't you have eyes? Can't you see what's about to happen between them? She's a woman. He's a man. You do the math!"

Luca gazed at her pensively until the light of understanding suddenly flickered in his eyes. His jaw dropped and he turned back toward the window. "Are you trying to tell me that my daughter and Peppi are . . . that those two are falling in . . . do you mean to say that . . . what are you trying to tell me!"

Filomena broke out in a smile. She stood and hurried to her husband's side. "What I'm trying to tell you, *amore mio,*" she said, giving him a hug, "is that it's time for you and I to get out of the way and go back to Alba Adriatica. I'll explain it all while we're on the way."

Then she kissed her husband and went to the bedroom to pack their things.

CHAPTER THIRTY-EIGHT

It was late afternoon and the last few rays of sunlight were darting in and out of the dark clouds gathering over the mountaintops when Peppi heard the knock at the door. A hot, sticky breeze puffed through the window and the low murmur of thunder rumbled far off in the distance. A storm was brewing somewhere.

Peppi had been sitting at the table, looking over the flower vase he had purchased from Enrico just before Lucrezia's accident. A slice of the porcelain vase shaped like a small half-moon had cracked and broken off when it fell to the street from the basket on his bike. Only the layers of paper in which the vase had been wrapped prevented the whole thing from being smashed to bits. All things considered, the damage was minor. Never one to let anything go to waste, Peppi had glued the broken piece back in place and was pleased to see that it had dried to the point where the vase could once again be put to its intended use.

There came a second, more insistent knock. Actually, it sounded more as if someone were kicking the door. For a moment Peppi supposed that it must be Luca, but then he remembered that Luca and Filomena had already returned to Alba Adriatica. He had seen them off that morning just after breakfast. At the time, it had struck him as a bit odd that they should suddenly be so anxious to leave. Then again, there were only so many days of summer. Why waste them sweltering in the mountains when you could be lying on the beach enjoying the cool ocean breeze?

"Un attimo!" Peppi called to whoever it was at the door. "Just a moment!" He gently set the vase back down and pushed himself away from the table.

When he opened the door, Peppi was surprised to see Lucrezia standing there. In her arms she clutched two bags of groceries. A loaf of bread and the edges of a colorful bunch of flowers protruded from the top of one bag. A bottle of red wine peeked out from the other.

"Buona sera," said Peppi, not sure of what else to say.

"Out of the way," Lucrezia ordered. "These bags are heavy." She squeezed past him and went straight to the kitchen. "Go sit down," she said over her shoulder.

"Whatever you say," said Peppi, closing the door. "But what are you doing?"

"What does it look like I'm doing?" she answered as she started to lay the groceries out on the counter. "I've come to cook you dinner. You haven't eaten yet, have you?"

"No, I haven't," Peppi admitted.

"In that case sit down and just do whatever it was you were doing before I arrived."

"I was just fixing this," said Peppi, gesturing to the flower vase on the table.

"Can it hold water?" Lucrezia asked.

"Yes, of course."

"Good, then you can put these in it," she said, pulling the flowers from the grocery bag. She handed them to Peppi, turned back to the counter, and tied an apron over the simple cotton dress she wore. "They came from the gardens out back," she said of the flowers. "I picked them this afternoon."

"I hadn't noticed."

Peppi half-filled the vase with water and put in the flowers. It was, he saw, a nice little arrangement. He set it on the center of the table, pleased to note that the crack in the vase was barely visible. He turned away from the table and leaned over toward Lucrezia to get a peek at what she had brought. On the counter stood a bottle of extra-virgin olive oil, some garlic and fresh oregano and basil, two cans of tomatoes, a bag of rice, another of mushrooms, some sort of meat wrapped in white butcher's paper, lettuce, onions, a small pastry box, a package of ground coffee, a container of cream, some spices, and an assortment of other odds and ends.

"You brought so much food," he noted.

"I didn't know what you had, so I decided to just bring everything I needed," she replied. She turned to him and made a brief, unfavorable assessment of his appearance. "You could put on a clean shirt," she suggested before turning back to the business at hand.

Peppi looked down at his sweat-stained undershirt. Without a word he went into the bathroom. Once he had the door closed behind him, he filled the sink and splashed some water onto his face. Shaking off the droplets, he straightened up, took a deep breath, and looked into the mirror.

Time had chiseled some hard lines into Peppi's face, but his dark skin still had a healthy glow to it and his eyes were as clear and bright as ever. Peppi passed his hand through the thick head of black and silver hair that nature had allowed him to keep. He was certainly no youngster anymore. All the same, he knew that he was still fit and strong. Peppi seldom dwelt on these sorts of things, but for some reason, right at that moment he felt good about himself. He also felt very nervous as he looked squarely into his own eyes.

"Be careful, old man," he told himself. With that warning in mind, he reached for a comb and began to pull it through his hair.

The table was set and the pleasing aroma of sautéing garlic was already in the air by the time Peppi finished freshening up. Lucrezia, he saw, knew her way around a kitchen. With quiet efficiency, she worked away, slicing and chopping her ingredients as the frying pan sizzled and the steam rose off the pot on the back burner. All the while she seemed not to notice Peppi standing there watching with the towel draped around his neck. Not wanting to disturb her concentration, he turned away and slipped into the bedroom to find a fresh shirt and a clean pair of trousers.

"That's better," said Lucrezia when Peppi came back out looking more presentable. "Now go sit and read the paper. I brought *La Gazzetta dello Sport*. It's there on the table."

Peppi had already read that day's edition of *La Gazzetta*, but he decided not to say so. Lucrezia had obviously tried to think of everything and he did not want to disappoint her. Of course, why she had decided to go through all the bother of cooking him dinner that night was still something of a mystery to him. Certain that sooner or later she would get around to telling him, he sat down and began to peruse some of the articles that he hadn't bothered to read earlier.

Now and then, as he scanned the headlines, Peppi lowered the paper just enough to watch Lucrezia cooking. He was finding it very difficult to prevent his eyes from roaming up the sleek contours of her legs to the back of her apron. Tied tightly around her waist, the apron only served to further accentuate her figure. His gaze continued up until it reached the glistening skin of her bare shoulders where her luscious hair cascaded down like ruby-colored water tumbling over the falls. The parts, he couldn't help but see, were equally as beautiful as the whole. Peppi swallowed hard and tried his best not to stare.

"I hope you like pork," said Lucrezia, glancing over her shoulder. Suspecting that she could somehow feel him watching her, Peppi ducked back down behind the newspaper. "Even if you don't, you'll have to eat it," she added.

"Pork sounds fine," said Peppi.

He looked out the window. The sky had gone black and the first few heavy drops of rain were beginning to plop down against the dry earth outdoors. The breeze picked up noticeably, signalling that a storm was imminent, but the faint rumble of thunder suggested that it was still far off.

"Is there anything I can do to help?" Peppi asked.

"You could open that," she replied, nodding to the bottle of wine.

Peppi put the paper aside and went to the drawer beneath the kitchen counter. He began to rummage through it, puzzled as to why he could not find the corkscrew.

"What are you doing in that drawer?" said Lucrezia in a testy tone that suggested that he was somehow invading her own private property.

Peppi stopped and looked at her, unable to suppress a sheepish grin. "Um, I was just looking for the corkscrew," he replied meekly.

Lucrezia gave an exasperated sigh. "I already put it right there next to the bottle," she huffed. "Now close that drawer and stay out of my way while I'm cooking." Those orders were immediately followed by the hiss of the chopped onions as they slid from her cutting board into the frying pan.

Peppi obeyed and dutifully sat at the table, rereading *La Gazzetta dello Sport* until later when Lucrezia announced that dinner was finally ready to be served. By then the rain outside was coming down in earnest, but the thunder still sounded far off. The brunt of the storm, Peppi guessed, was passing them by.

"We'll have to serve ourselves from the pan," said Lucrezia, placing a pot holder on the table and resting the frying pan atop it. "One would think that by now you would have bought some decent serving dishes."

"It's been on my list," said Peppi with a shrug. "If I'd known that you were coming . . ."

Lucrezia ignored the remark and returned to the stove. "I was going to make a marinara to have over linguine, but I decided to make a nice risotto instead," she said, coming back to the table with another pan. She set it next to the frying pan and went back for the bread. Once all the food was put out and the wine glasses filled, she paused for a moment, looking over the table to make sure she had everything just the way she wanted before sitting down. With little fanfare, she reached over and removed the lid from the frying pan. Peppi's mouth instantly began to water. Inside were four perfectly cooked pork chops laid out on a bed of fried escarole. Like Lucrezia herself, it was a study in elegant simplicity. The whole thing looked like a picture out of a gourmet cookbook, and the aroma was indescribable.

"Give me your plate," she told him, pleased, it seemed, by the look of approval in Peppi's eyes.

"With pleasure," Peppi said.

Lucrezia selected for him the thickest of the pork chops and placed it on his plate along with some of the escarole and a helping of the risotto. Then she took a spoon and ladled out some of the juice and bits of garlic from the pan onto the meat before setting the plate back in front of him.

"Lucrezia, this looks wonderful," said Peppi, "but I wish you hadn't gone to all the trouble."

Lucrezia gave a little laugh, her demeanor softening a bit for the first time since she walked through the door. "What trouble?" she said as she began to make her own dish. "You're the man who saved my life. It seemed like the least I could do to say thank you."

"There was no need to thank me," said Peppi.

Lucrezia gave a half-smile and sat down. *"Buon appetito,"* she said, raising her wine glass to his.

They ate for a short time in silence before Lucrezia put down her fork. She winced and rolled her neck from side to side.

"What's the matter?" said Peppi.

"Nothing," she answered. "My neck is still a little sore, that's all." She glanced at Peppi and saw the look of concern in his eyes. "It's all your fault, by the way," she added testily. "You almost pulled my head off my shoulders the other day. You could have been a little more gentle."

"Well, at that particular moment I really didn't give it much thought," said Peppi. "We were, if you remember, a little pressed for time. I am sorry, though. Does it hurt very much?"

"It's getting better," said Lucrezia with a pout. She pushed a strand of dark red hair from her face and sighed. "And I'm the one who's sorry," she went on. "I know I really shouldn't complain about it. After all, putting up with a little sore neck is better than being burned alive."

"That's pretty much the decision I had come to," said Peppi, giving her a smile.

Outdoors, the clouds suddenly opened up and the rain began to come straight down in great torrents that pounded against the roof and ground so that it sounded like galloping horses. Peppi jumped up and went to the window to close the shutters to keep the rain from coming in. Before pulling them shut he took a look outside. Despite the intensity of the downpour there still came only a few flickers of lightning and a brief, faint rumble of thunder. It was a slow-moving storm, whichever direction it was heading. He considered the heavy rain and for a moment, worried that it might damage his tomato garden at the mulino. There was nothing to be done about it now, so he put it out of his mind and came back to the table.

"I think the sky's falling out there," he said, taking his seat.

"It certainly sounds like it," said Lucrezia.

"So, where were we?" Peppi asked.

"My neck," said Lucrezia. "And the accident."

"That's right, I almost forgot."

Lucrezia shifted uneasily in her chair. She looked down at her hands and fidgeted with the wedding ring on her finger.

"Actually, I've been trying to forget it myself," she said after a time. "Trouble is, I can't seem to stop thinking about it, no matter how hard I try."

"That's no surprise," said Peppi. "It was a traumatic event. It takes a while to deal with these things. Believe me, I know."

Lucrezia looked up at him with sad eyes. "It's just that when the car caught fire," she went on, suddenly letting the words pour out of her like the rain coming down outside, "and I thought I was going to burn, I don't know, something happened inside me. It was like that time after you were sick and you told me that you realized when you were going through it that you still wanted to live. The same thing happened to me. You see, ever since I lost my husband I've told myself that I didn't care if I lived or died. But in that moment, when the flames were breathing down my back, I realized that I was wrong, that a part of me still wanted to live more than anything else. For what, of course, I don't know. Somehow, though, I feel guilty about the whole thing."

Peppi smiled and for the first time let himself gaze at her without looking away.

"I'll tell you something," he said, looking into her eyes, "about that moment when the flames were coming and I thought that I wouldn't be able to get you out. Yes, I wanted to live too, but in my heart I was begging God to put me in the car, to let us trade places. I knew that wouldn't happen, so I made up my mind that if you were going to die in the fire, then I was going to die with you."

"Don't say that," said Lucrezia, her eyes filling with tears. "Why did you have to tell me that?"

"Because that's just what I felt," said Peppi.

The tears were streaming down Lucrezia's cheeks now. "Why did you have to tell me that?" she said again, bowing her head as if she were going to break down and sob.

To Peppi's astonishment, however, Lucrezia did not break down and sob. Instead she slammed her hand down on the table so hard that all the plates and silverware leapt off the tablecloth. Then she herself jumped up. In a fury far surpassing the weather outside, she reached out and grabbed the flower vase. Instinct told Peppi to duck, for he was certain that in another moment the vase would be whizzing past his ear. Instead, she slammed the vase down on the table, causing the piece of porcelain Peppi had just reglued to topple out.

"Lucrezia!" he exclaimed.

"What are you trying to do to me!" she screamed.

Peppi was too dumbfounded to reply.

"What are you trying to do!" she screamed again. Her voice, though, had taken on a more pleading tone. "Haven't I told you that my heart is dead inside me?" she cried, tearing at her dress. "Haven't I told you that my world fell apart when I lost my husband? Haven't I told you that I could never love another man?"

Lucrezia stopped at that point, panting from the outburst. She looked down in horror at what she had done to the vase. "Now look what you made me do," she cried.

She turned her eyes back to Peppi and stared at him with a look of torment and utter surrender. He gazed back, unable to take his eyes off her. Before he could open his mouth to speak, Lucrezia muttered something beneath her breath, rushed around the table, and flung herself into his arms. Peppi squeezed her tight and the two pressed their lips together.

As he cradled her on his lap and Lucrezia smothered his face in kisses, Peppi knew right away that he was powerless to resist what was happening between them. He was too overcome with emotion, the intoxicating scent of her hair, and the thrill of her body against his. Nonetheless, despite the overwhelming tide of passion he felt carrying him away, Peppi knew that they had to stop what they were doing at once or it would end in disaster for both of them. As difficult as it was, he tried to pull back from her.

"Lucrezia, stop," he told her.

"No," she sighed, taking his face in her hands and kissing him once more.

"Please," begged Peppi. He was trying desperately to control himself, but knew that he was losing the battle. "Please," he said once more, "we must stop."

Lucrezia responded by pulling open his shirt and running her hands across his chest and shoulders. Her lips moved along his cheeks and down the side of his neck. She was devouring him.

"I won't stop," she murmured.

"But we must," he insisted.

"I can't stop myself and I won't," she said. "I don't care if it's right or if it's wrong. I don't care about anything anymore. I won't stop!"

"But Lucrezia," Peppi pleaded, "you don't understand. We must stop this *now!*"

Finally, at hearing the urgency in his voice, Lucrezia relented for a moment and gazed at him in breathless confusion. "Why, Peppi," she gasped, "why must we stop? Are you saying you don't want me?"

Peppi shook his head. "No," he told her, "I'm not saying any such thing."

"Then what?" she asked, bewildered by the look of alarm in his eyes.

"It's this chair!" Peppi blurted out. "It's so old and rickety that I don't think it can hold the two of us for much longer. If we don't stop now it's going to collapse into pieces and we'll both end up on the floor!"

Lucrezia gave him a coy smile and pushed herself away from him. "In that case," she said, her eyes smoldering like embers, "why don't we end up someplace else where the two of us will be safe?" With that she turned from him and walked to the bedroom, letting the straps of her dress fall from her shoulders as she went.

Peppi rose from the chair and started across the floor. Just as he reached the bedroom, Lucrezia's dress came flying out the door. He caught it against his chest and stopped dead in his tracks.

"Do you think that old chair's strong enough to hold *that*?" he heard her say.

Peppi considered the question for a moment. Then he tossed the dress over his shoulder and hurried inside to join her.

CHAPTER THIRTY-NINE

The downpour had let up, but a steady rain was still coming down when Peppi opened his eyes. He thought that he had perhaps been asleep, that what had just transpired was merely part of a very beautiful dream. The warmth of Lucrezia's thigh resting against his and her arm draped lazily across his chest told him otherwise. She snuggled closer and laid her head on his shoulder. For a long while the two lay there in bed listening to the rain and the gentle rhythm of each other's breathing.

"Dio," Lucrezia finally sighed, running her fingers through the coarse hair on his chest, "I'd forgotten how that felt."

"I hadn't," said Peppi. He looked over at the picture of Anna on the table beside him and let out a nervous groan.

"What's the matter?" said Lucrezia.

"Oh, boy," he sighed, rubbing his face and eyes. "I'm going to have a lot of explaining to do someday."

Lucrezia lifted her hand and gazed at the ring on her finger. "We both will," she said thoughtfully. "Do you think they'll ever forgive us?"

"I don't know," said Peppi. "I'd like to think so. But what about us? Do you think we'll be able to forgive each other for letting this happen?"

"Hey, this wasn't my idea, you know," said Lucrezia, giving one of his chest hairs a painful twist. "I was perfectly content being alone and miserable for the rest of my life until you came along."

"Ow!" winced Peppi, rubbing his chest. "Well, don't blame it on me either. All I wanted to do was come home to my little *mulino* and die. Now look what's happened."

"Yes," said Lucrezia, arching up to kiss him on the cheek. "Isn't it amazing?"

"It's frightening," said Peppi.

"What on earth is there to be frightened of?"

"I'm not sure," he said, staring up at the ceiling. "I guess it's just that not too long ago everything in my life seemed so dark, like I was stumbling around in a cave, trying to find my way out. Now that I've made it back out into the light, I can't bear the thought of ever going back in there." He paused and caressed her cheek. "And I couldn't bear the thought of making someone else go back there," he added.

"I know what you mean," said Lucrezia after a time. "I've felt the same way. But what can we do?"

"I don't know," sighed Peppi. "Some things in life are just out of our control. There's no way of knowing what *Dio* has in mind, so I guess there's no point in worrying about it. If you do, you just end up with *agita* for the rest of your life." At that he let out a chuckle and shook his head. "I sound just like my cousin," he said.

"But can't you see that it's true?" said Lucrezia. "Can't you see that sometimes we just have to trust life instead of fighting it all the time?"

"That's easier said than done," said Peppi.

Lucrezia sat up and gazed out into the night where the flicker of lightning continued to light up the sky. "What's the alternative?" she said. "Would it be better for us to go through the rest of our lives wandering around alone, never letting ourselves find out if we could love someone again, or even just to feel love at all?" She paused and lay back down beside him. "But in any case, it's too late to worry about all that now, isn't it? What's done is done—and you did it rather well, if you don't mind my saying so."

"Experience counts for something, I guess," said Peppi, allowing himself a contented grin. "I feel bad, though, that we've let a perfectly good meal go to waste. Those pork chops really were delicious. I had no idea you were such a good cook."

"Hmm," grunted Lucrezia, "well, don't get used to it. I'm a busy woman, you know. I have better things to do than to tie myself to the oven just to keep a man happy."

"I don't mind doing the cooking," he replied. "I'm not so bad at it myself, you know."

"You *are* very self-sufficient," Lucrezia agreed. "I've noticed that about you. Most women, of course, hate that in a man, even if they don't say so."

"Do you hate it?"

Lucrezia propped herself up on an elbow. For a while she said nothing, but simply studied the features of his face while she ran her fingers across his cheeks and nose and lips.

"I don't hate anything about you," she finally said, barely above a whisper.

"You'll have to speak louder," said Peppi with a mischievous twinkle in his eye. "I'm an old man, you know."

"All right!" exclaimed Lucrezia, throwing her hands up. "I love you, old man! There, I've said it. It's out in the open. Now, does that make you happy?"

"Yes, more happy than I can tell you," said Peppi. "But *why* do you love me? That's what I want to know."

"Oh, God," groaned Lucrezia, collapsing back onto the pillow. "How can anyone explain these things? You can't pick the people you fall in love with any more than you can pick your father or mother. Life just sorts it all out for you whether you like it or not." She paused and rested her head once more on his shoulder. "But maybe," she said softly, "the answer is simply that you and I just need one another. Isn't that enough?"

Peppi smiled and ran his fingers through her hair. "It does put a different perspective on life," he said, nodding in agreement.

"And what about you?" she said, poking him in the side.

"Oh, I love you," he told her. "And quite honestly, it really doesn't matter to me why." With that he gently cupped her chin in his hand and brought his mouth to hers. Just as their lips met they were both startled by the crash of a tremendous clap of thunder outside.

"Wow," laughed Lucrezia as rain began to pound once more against the window. "You really know how to kiss!"

Then the smile on Lucrezia's face suddenly vanished and she pulled away from Peppi. She sat up on the bed and simply stared at him with a questioning look, as if she was trying to come to a decision about something. Finally, Lucrezia did something that took Peppi by surprise even more so than anything else that had taken place that night. Looking down at her hand, she slowly slipped her wedding ring from her finger, kissed it, and placed it on the table by the bed. She turned back to Peppi and gazed deep into his eyes.

"I'm yours now," she said, "if you truly want me."

Peppi nodded and raised his own hand, letting her slip from his finger the only ring he had ever worn. "And I'm yours," he said as she placed the ring beside hers on the table. "But how long can it last?" he added, unable to conceal the worry in his voice.

"That's not for us to decide," said Lucrezia. "But however long it lasts will be enough for me." She smiled and lowered herself onto him, letting her hair fall down over his face as they wrapped themselves around each other.

"You know, this doesn't change things," said Peppi.

"What?"

"You still owe me a vase."

He reached over and turned off the lamp just in time to let a brilliant flash of lightning illuminate the darkness.

CHAPTER FORTY

The news that Peppi and Lucrezia were to be married came as little surprise to those who lived in and around Villa San Giuseppe. By and large, the announcement was greeted with a shrug and a communal *"Come no?* Why not?" Everyone understood that no matter what the age, love has a way of blossoming wherever and whenever it pleases—and there's not much two people can do to stop it. Even Luca, who was at first unsettled by the notion of having his best friend as a son-in-law, finally decided that if Lucrezia and Peppi were happy, that was all anyone else needed to know.

On the opposite side of the Atlantic, however, the reaction to their engagement was not quite so muted. Carmine was out mowing the lawn the morning the letter from Italy found its way into their mailbox. It was a steamy August day and he was happy to take a break from his toils when he saw the mail truck pass by. He turned off the mower and went to see what of interest the mailman might have left them. Amidst the usual pile of bills and junk mail he spied the letter addressed to Angie. Pleased to have an excuse to go back into the air-conditioned house, he tucked the mail under his arm and headed straight inside.

"Let me see that before you sweat all over it," said Angie,

whipping the letter out of his hand the moment Carmine showed it to her. "It's about time he wrote," she added under her breath. "No one has heard from him in almost two months."

While his wife opened the letter, Carmine went to the refrigerator to pour himself a glass of lemonade. With his drink in hand, he sat at the table and began sifting through the rest of the mail. He was delighted to find a lingerie catalog hiding in the pile. Wasting no time, he opened it up and began to flip through the glossy pages.

"So, what does Peppi have to say for himself?" he asked his wife as he scrutinized one particularly appealing photograph.

When Angie didn't respond, he looked up and saw that his wife's face had gone white and her hand was trembling.

"Oh, my God," she said to herself.

"What, what is it?" said Carmine. "Did somebody die?"

"Oh, my God," said Angie aloud as she read on.

"Come on now," said Carmine. "You're starting to worry me here."

"Oh, My God!" his wife suddenly screamed, dropping the letter to the floor. She ran to the telephone and hastily dialed a number.

"What is it?" cried Carmine. "Come on, tell me!"

"Delores!" she yelled into the phone. "You're not going to believe this. He's getting married! What do you mean, who am I talking about? I'm talking about *Peppi!*"

Carmine's jaw dropped, but then he laughed to himself when he heard the squawk of incredulity coming from the other end of the line. He reached over and snatched the letter off the floor to read the happy news for himself.

"This should set tongues wagging," he chuckled as he

looked the letter over. Then he put it aside and settled back to enjoy his lemonade and the rest of the catalog while Angie and Delores carried on in fits of near-apoplexy.

Meantime, the postal service delivered a second letter from Italy that day to the barber shop. Despite the arthritis in his hip, Ralph felt like jumping up and doing a little dance around the shop when Tony read the part of Peppi's letter that told them of his plans to get married. He started to get up, but then decided that it wasn't worth the effort. Instead, he plopped back down on the chair, grinning nonetheless from ear to ear.

"Can you *believe it?*" laughed Gino. "You see, I told him that the best thing to do was to go out and find another woman!"

"*I* was the one who told him that," said Tony proudly. "*You* only agreed with me."

"Who cares who told him?" said Sal, waving his hand at the two of them. "I just want to know who she is and what she looks like."

"Hold on, let me keep reading," said Tony, turning his attention back to the letter. "Oh, my God!" he laughed. "You're not gonna believe this."

"Tell us, tell us!" cried Ralph.

"It's Luca's daughter!"

At that announcement the four of them burst into joyous laughter.

"Holy smoke!" roared Gino. "What is she, half his age?"

"She'll kill him!" laughed Sal. "I don't care how strong his heart is from all that cycling."

"What else does he say?" asked Gino.

Tony picked up the letter and skimmed it to find the spot

where he had left off. "Okay, where were we?" he began. "Here we are. He says at the end, 'I know that all of this sounds kind of sudden, guys, but this is Italy. Things happen fast over here when people fall in love.' " Tony looked up. "And that's all he wrote," he said with a shrug.

They were all quiet for a time.

"Well, isn't that just beautiful?" Sal finally snickered. He looked about at the others and rolled his eyes. "What is this, the Victorian age?" he groused. "I want some solid details here, not the PG version!"

They all laughed, except for Ralph. "Hey, wait a minute," he said, suddenly very serious. "Something just occurred to me that I hadn't thought of before. I mean, what's the big hurry? Why is Peppi suddenly getting married so fast? Hey, you don't think that maybe he *has* to get married?"

The other three gawked at him for a moment in silence as they mulled over the possibility.

"What are you, *nuts?*" they yelled in unison.

"Well, who knows?" said Ralph, throwing his hands up. "I was only asking."

Just then the door to the shop opened and a customer walked in. Tony dropped the letter onto his desk and ushered the gentleman over to the barber's chair while the others settled down to finish reading the newspaper.

"Peppi, getting married," mused Gino as he looked over the sports section. "Who would have thought it?"

"I'm not surprised," replied Sal, who was scanning the headlines of the business section. "These things happen all the time."

"I wonder if it will be a big wedding," wondered Ralph. He

looked at the others, expecting a reply, but by then no one else was listening. That being the case, he picked up a section of the newspaper for himself and perused the death notices to see if anyone he knew had departed this world. "Weddings and funerals," he muttered. "What else is there to life?"

CHAPTER FORTY-ONE

Peppi and Lucrezia exchanged wedding vows at La Chiesa di San Giuseppe one Friday evening in late August. The simple but joyful ceremony was attended by Luca, Filomena, Costanzo, his wife and children, and a few other relatives who lived in the area. Despite their efforts to keep it a quiet, private affair, a rousing cheer greeted the newlyweds when they stepped out onto the church steps. To Peppi and Lucrezia's surprise, dozens of townspeople had gathered in the piazza outside to wish them well.

Later, after a quiet celebration with the family at a local restaurant, the couple left to spend a long weekend on Capri. It was a short honeymoon, for both were anxious to return home to Villa San Giuseppe and start their lives over together.

Making a home of Peppi's apartment, however, would take a little while. For the time being, it was more than enough space for the two of them, but the Spartan decor did not suit Lucrezia at all. That being the case, the two of them stayed in the main house with Lucrezia's parents. Luca and Filomena were more than happy to have them while Lucrezia directed the long overdue redecoration efforts needed to rend Peppi's apartment more suitable for cohabitation.

One October night, a few weeks after Peppi and Lucrezia had finally settled back into the apartment, Luca showed up at the door. Both were very pleased to see him as it was his first official visit since the two had moved out of the house. Though all of them saw each other often enough during the day, Luca and Filomena had been wise enough to keep their distance after work hours; they wanted to give their daughter and her new husband time alone to devote exclusively to themselves.

"Ayyy, *finalmente,*" said Lucrezia when she opened the door for her father. She gave him a hug and a kiss and pulled him inside.

"I just felt like taking a little stroll," said Luca when he stepped into the room, "so I thought I'd stop by for a few minutes to see what you two have been up to."

"It took you long enough," said Lucrezia, giving Peppi a wink. "We thought you and Mama might be mad at us for moving out of the house."

"She's still upset about that," joked Luca. "She was just getting used to having the two of you around. But she'll get over it." He looked about the apartment and gave an approving nod at the new decor. "I like what you've done with the place," he said. "Nice and bright."

"Go sit at our new table with Peppi," Lucrezia told him.

"Very nice," said Luca, settling into a chair. "But what happened to all the old furniture? There was nothing wrong with it."

"Heh, gone with the wind," chuckled Peppi. "Your daughter is like a whirlwind. She tossed out all the old stuff the first day."

"Uff, *che brutt'!*" shuddered Lucrezia. "That bed and that rickety old table and chairs weren't fit for dogs to sit on."

"They weren't all that bad," offered Peppi.

"Oh, please," she replied, giving the two men a dismissive wave of the hand. "You're both the same."

Lucrezia went to the kitchen to make a plate of dry sausage

and olives for her father and Peppi to pick on while they talked.
"You'll note the new serving dishes," she announced when she
set them on the table along with a loaf of bread. "No more eating like barbarians."

"I hadn't realized I was so backward," said Peppi.

Luca popped an olive into his mouth and sliced off a piece
of dry sausage. While he chewed it, he looked about the apartment for a moment with a curious look on his face.

"Hey," he said. "I just noticed something. What happened
to your bicycles, Peppi?"

"Banished to the shed out back," said Peppi ruefully. "She
won't let me have them in the kitchen anymore."

"Lucrezia!" her father chided her. "What's wrong with you?"

"*Sta zita,* you!" she warned him, wagging her finger. "And
you too," she said, turning to her husband. "This is our home,
not a bicycle shop. I'm not going to have dirty wheels and bike
grease all over everything. I don't care what you two say."

In the face of such a hostile judiciary, Peppi and Luca knew
better than to argue the merits of their case. Instead they both
shrugged and resumed munching on the appetizers Lucrezia
had set out.

"Filomena and I have missed having you two up to the
house at night," Luca told Peppi. "What have you two been
doing with yourselves lately?"

"Eh," Peppi shrugged. "We've been keeping busy." He gave
his new wife a nod. "I put in some new plumbing fixtures this
week and Lucrezia was looking around for some new cabinets,
but we decided to put that project on hold."

"How come?" said Luca.

Peppi shrugged again. "We're not sure of what we want to
do yet," he said a bit evasively.

Lucrezia put a slab of cheese on the table before sitting down with them. She lopped off two good-sized slices and gave one each to Peppi and Luca. Her hand reached out for an olive, but then she changed her mind. Giving Peppi a sideways look, she settled back into her chair and let out a little sigh.

"What's the matter, Lucrezia?" said Luca. "Aren't you going to have something? These olives are good. Try some."

"Not right now," said his daughter, suddenly looking a bit pale. "Maybe later."

"Ooh, and I like this cheese," said Luca, taking a big bite.

"Please, Papa," said Lucrezia, putting her hand to her mouth. Suddenly she jumped up from the table, ran to the bathroom, and slammed the door behind her. A series of rather unpleasant guttural sounds ensued.

"Is she okay?" said Luca to Peppi, who seemed not at all nonplussed by the whole thing.

"Yes, she's fine," he said with a nod. "Don't worry. This just happens every so often lately. From what I've read it's nothing to be too concerned about."

Luca put down his cheese and bread, and stared at his friend. Peppi, for his part, was sitting there, looking very much like the cat who swallowed the canary.

"What's going on?" said Luca. "What aren't you telling me?"

Peppi shifted uncomfortably in his chair and fidgeted with the end of the tablecloth. He rubbed his chin nervously and opened his mouth to speak, but for some reason he couldn't quite make it form the words he wanted to say.

"Like I said," he finally managed to reply, "it's really nothing to worry about. Supposedly it will pass in a few weeks. This is just a phase a woman in her condition goes through."

"What do you mean, 'a woman in her condition'?" said Luca

sharply. Then he noted the sparkle in Peppi's eye. Understanding gradually dawned on him like the morning sun climbing over the mountains. Now it was Luca's turn to have trouble putting together an intelligible sentence. "Are you trying to tell me," he stammered, "that Lucrezia is . . . what I mean to say is that she's going to have a . . . that Filomena and I are going to have another . . ."

Peppi could only nod and smile in reply.

At that point Luca stopped and his face lit up in pure joy. With a great laugh he reached out and slapped Peppi on the shoulder. "Well, at least now I know what you two have been up to all these nights!" he cried. Then he paused for a moment and looked about the apartment.

"You two are going to need a bigger place pretty soon," he remarked.

"Yes, I know," said Peppi. "And I know just where to build it."

CHAPTER FORTY-TWO

After the baptism they all went back to the house. It was a sparkling June day and Lucrezia threw open the windows to let in the warm, pleasant breeze that tumbled down from the mountains. Before long the house was filled with people, some who had gone to the church and others who skipped the mass and came straight to the celebration. Despite the beautiful weather, everyone was milling about inside in little groups, talking and laughing. The women took turns holding the baby while the men wandered about, admiring the new home Peppi and Lucrezia had built. The food was put out and soon everyone was lining up at the buffet table.

Peppi walked in. He had been strolling around out back with Luca and Carmine. The three had been looking over the new flower beds and assessing the condition of the plants in the tomato garden. The grounds around the mulino had fallen into disarray from years of neglect, but little by little Peppi was bringing order back to things. One day, if all went well, he hoped to plant fig trees and apple trees and perhaps even some grapes, for those are the things a man plants for his son.

"There he is!" said someone when Peppi came through the back door to the kitchen. Everyone turned and smiled at the proud new father.

"Where's my baby boy?" said Peppi with a big grin. "Who's got my little Niccolo?"

"I do," cooed Angie, cradling the little bundle in her arms. "And don't ask me to give him to you. I flew all the way over here to see him, so I'm not letting him go—he's too adorable!"

"Okay," laughed Peppi, not wanting to ruin the fun, "but be careful, he's valuable property."

Peppi went into the living room and chatted with the men about how construction on the house was going. The house, parts of which were not quite yet finished, had been built on the site of the old mulino. Peppi had taken great pains to ensure that their new home, though much larger than the original, would still be of a style that evoked the memory of all the people who had lived there before him. While he had left the construction of the house to a local builder, the mill itself he reserved for himself. It would take a long time, but Peppi insisted on rebuilding the old mulino with his own hands, stone by stone, just as his father's father had done. The photograph of his parents, now restored to its proper place on the mantel, would always be there to inspire him.

"Hey, old man," he heard Lucrezia call. "Why don't you try paying a little attention to the mother of your child?"

Peppi was only too happy to oblige. He went straight to the buffet table, fixed his wife a plate of food, and poured a glass of wine. When he returned with the food and drink, he settled onto the couch next to her. By then Filomena had managed to snatch Niccolo from Angie's arms. She ambled about, showing off her new grandson until someone suggested that she hand him to Peppi and Lucrezia so that a photograph could be taken of the new family.

"Doesn't she look wonderful?" one of the women said of Lucrezia. "You'd never know she just had a baby."

"What about me?" joked Peppi as the cameras flashed. "Don't I look good too?"

"Why shouldn't you look good?" said Lucrezia, elbowing him in the ribs. *"I'm* the one who did all the work."

Peppi smiled and looked across the room to the window. A warm, gentle breeze caressed the trees off in the distance while the flowers and shrubs he had planted just outside the window basked in the brilliant sunshine. Everything outside was bursting with life and vitality. It all made Peppi feel young again.

Before long Filomena and Luca squeezed in to pose for a picture of themselves with little Niccolo. That's the way it went for much of the afternoon. Peppi and Lucrezia eventually were shoved off the couch so that all the relatives could take turns posing for photographs with the baby.

Afterwards, coffee and dessert were served outside so that everyone could get out and enjoy the gorgeous weather. One of the men had brought a guitar. He leaned against the edge of one of the old mulino walls and started to strum a soft, sweet melody while the other guests strolled about, soaking in the sunshine. Lucrezia set up the bassinet in the shade and put the baby down for a nap. Peppi and Luca sat on the grass nearby, sipping their wine as they surveyed the whole beautiful scene.

"You've come a long way since you came home, *amico mio,*" said Luca after a time. "Didn't I tell you there was still a lot of life left in this old place?"

"Yes, you did," said Peppi with a contented grin. "I thought my life's work was over, but now it looks like it's just beginning."

Luca nodded in agreement. "As long as there is life, there will always be work to be done," he said. Then he cast his gaze over to the mulino. "What do you think?" he asked Peppi. "Will *Dio* give you time enough to finish rebuilding it by yourself?"

Peppi gazed thoughtfully at the mulino. "It doesn't matter," he finally said with a shrug. "If I don't finish it, my son will." He turned a sly gaze to Luca. "And who knows," he added, "maybe he'll even do it with the help of a brother or two."

"Hah!" laughed Luca. "Now wouldn't *that* be something?"

Later, the sun was just beginning to drop behind the mountaintops when everyone began to leave. By the time the last of the guests had gone home it was almost dark. It had been a long, beautiful day. Now that it was over, Peppi felt tired, but very happy.

When he collapsed into bed and wrapped his arms around Lucrezia that night, Peppi lay awake for a time, listening to his wife's gentle breathing while he watched over Niccolo sleeping nearby in the basinet. A thousand plans for his wife and son were dancing in his head, dreams for a future that, just a short time ago, he would never have imagined possible. His life, he marvelled, had come full circle, like a wheel spinning around, always ending at the beginning, always beginning at the end. That, he saw, was just the way of things. Peppi tried to keep his eyes open for he did not want to miss a moment of it all. A blissful sense of exhaustion, however, finally overcame him and he soon drifted off into contented sleep.

HOME TO ITALY

PETER PEZZELLI

ABOUT THIS GUIDE

The suggested questions are included to
enhance your group's reading of Peter Pezzelli's
Home to Italy.

DISCUSSION QUESTIONS

1. The first and last chapters of the book are virtually mirror images of each other. What is the author trying to say about Peppi's life?

2. The story is set in Italy, but could it have worked as well for a character from a different culture?

3. How do you feel about the age difference between Peppi and Lucrezia? Why didn't the author make them closer in age?

4. What role does the preparation and sharing of meals play in bringing the characters together at different points in the story?

5. What is there for the reader to learn from Peppi's collapse after he returns to Villa San Giuseppe, and from his subsequent recovery?

6. What images of death and rebirth does the author show the reader?

7. Symbolically, what role does the *mulino* itself play in the story?

8. After all his years of living in America, is Peppi's decision to return to Italy too abrupt? Might someone in his circumstances have waited longer?

9. Is it ever too late to find love?

10. Luca does not seem bothered that his friend has fallen in love with his daughter. Is his reaction influenced by the Italian culture? Would an American father have reacted differently?

GREAT BOOKS, GREAT SAVINGS!

When You Visit Our Website:
www.kensingtonbooks.com
You Can Save Money Off The Retail Price
Of Any Book You Purchase!

- **All Your Favorite Kensington Authors**
- **New Releases & Timeless Classics**
- **Overnight Shipping Available**
- **eBooks Available For Many Titles**
- **All Major Credit Cards Accepted**

Visit Us Today To Start Saving!
www.kensingtonbooks.com

All Orders Are Subject To Availability.
Shipping and Handling Charges Apply.
Offers and Prices Subject To Change Without Notice